GW00543665

Bastard B

Daring New Literature

We sell radical new literature in paperback and e-book format, catching the authors in their most creative period; when their ideas are fresh and innovative.

If you're tired of reading wilting novels churned out by so-called famous authors or previously incoherent people famed for something else…
Welcome to **Bastard Books**.

For more stirring titles visit our on-line shop at:

bastardbooks.com

All our featured books have a brutally honest *Bastard Books* review and reader reviews are included as we receive them. We let you download the first chapter (sometimes more) of every book so you can see before you buy. You can either buy paperback copies of the novels via our secure server or, for a discounted price; they can be downloaded onto your PC, Pocket Computer or Rocketebook.

You are welcome to review any of the books and by optionally including your email address you can share your thoughts with other readers.

THE MEN WHO RAN AWAY

JOHN O`DOWD

Bastard Books

BASTARD BOOKS
(A division of Usualready Enterprises Ltd.)

Published in Great Britain by:
Bastard Books
85 Clifton Hill,
London, NW8 OJN.

A CIP catalogue record for this book is
available from the British Library

PUBLISHERS NOTE

This is a work of fiction. Names, characters places,
and incidents either are the product of the author's
imagination or are used fictitiously, and any
resemblance to actual persons, living or dead,
events, or locales is entirely coincidental.

ISBN 1-84346-018-1

John O'Dowd has lived, worked and scribbled on both sides of the Atlantic and has had several stories published in Ireland, Britain and on the Continent. His work has been short-listed for literary prizes including Listowel Writers Week and the Ian St James Awards. While living in London, John was an active member of Green Ink Writers and performed his work at stand-up events and on local radio.

When John's not writing, he provides engineering support for United Nations war-crime investigators in battle-torn regions, and he usually lives in Holland.

1. Nineteen Ninety Something.

It was not me who actually killed Scullivan. It was O'Hanagan walloping him with a shovel. But O'Hanagan was a simpleton, shy and frightened of the sheep. Even if they believed that he had done it, they would have assumed he had an accomplice. Worse still, they might have supposed that someone exploited O'Hanagan's bulk and stupidity to take revenge on an unctuous creature such as Scullivan.

Often, usually after a bellyful of beer, Scullivan was a pain. On that particular drunken night he emptied an ashtray into my drink for a laugh. I had to exercise great restraint for fear of a fight erupting in the bar and spilling out onto the street. Then the police would have realised that we were all in there drinking at that illegal hour of the night, almost morning. I suggested to Scullivan that he buy me a drink to show remorse and we could shake hands, and bury the hatchet, as they say. With that he became more offensive.

"Ah, Bart," he sang, in his long drawling tone, "twould be a sin to waste good money on the likes of you." Then he was flicking peanuts at me but I said no more. I just sat there and the peanuts were bouncing off my nose, and the place roaring with laughter. The landlord waved a shovel, ordering folk to stop. O'Hanagan, the poor simpleton with red wiry hair and a beaming pink face, only laughed because the others did. But his bellowing cry could pierce doors and walls and the ears of a policeman miles away. His shoulders were hopping with the laughter, dancing like the handles on a jackhammer. Eventually, the landlord had to give him a thump to make him stop and it knocked him through the toilet door.

It was a beautiful night outside and a fine time for a wander up the mountain road. But I had a temper simmering in my head, burning against the inside of my skull, and down my arms to my clenched fists. Scullivan was a little way in front, showing off to the girls. He was bouncing about, pretending to be a peanut. Then he was imitating O'Hanagan's bellowing laugh, and his fall through the toilet door. The girls howled to a painful pitch at his antics. They needed to wipe tears from their eyes to see their way home, off up the field and into their house. I caught up with Scullivan at the boreen and was mad enough to hit him so fast and furious that he would have thought he was surrounded by an angry mob. But Scullivan only scoffed at my stance, my imminent assault upon his head.

"Bart," he laughed. "Bart, Bart, O'Hanagan's cousin. Are you lost, up here at dis time of night?"

"I am not lost, not a bit of it. I'm here to batter you."

"Ah, Bart," he drawled, "you couldn't batter a fish."

"But I'll batter you, Scullivan. And I'll break you in half, and I will still fight the pair of yis."

But Scullivan was bigger and a dirty fighter. I'm ashamed to say that we had a scrap without either of us using fists like a gentleman. We were aiming our boots at each other's testicles and my only regret was that I was not wearing my steel toe-caps.

O'Hanagan stumbled from the dark. I forgot that he was with me. He had followed me the way he often did, like a sheep, but on this occasion he had a shovel. I caught a glimpse of the steel as it glittered, swinging through the night with such velocity that it was buried in Scullivan's skull before I could utter a sound.

It was a different night after that. My life was different. For the first few moments of it, I stared at a house down beyond the boreen. Rather that than look at Scullivan's corpse. They were still awake down there with light burning in a window. A dancing dot in the dark, a cottage full of life. Up beside me was a dead man sprawled and stiffening by the second. It was getting worse because O'Hanagan was gone with the faeries. He was talking nonsense as usual. This time about health insurance. He had heard that a patient could get a private room with a television in the best hospital if he had the right insurance policy.

"O'Hanagan," I called, wanting to yell with glass-shattering screams but I stifled myself. "O'Hanagan, yer fecking donkey, to get t'at he needs to be alive. The policyholder needs to be alive on arrival at hospital. Scullivan here is definitely dead." O'Hanagan was away in the dark digging a hole. "My advice to you, yer big bollocks, is to get out of Ireland." And then go east until you come to mountains, I thought, and I'll go south until I come upon the Mediterranean. But I said no more for fear of being heard.

No one but O'Hanagan knew I was up there on the Boreen High Road fighting with Scullivan. I had been seen in the pub, heard talking about going away to find work abroad. You won't do it, they said. I will, I said. You won't, they said. I will, I will. You'll go as far as the crossroads and be back like the dog with its tail between its legs. That night up on the mountain road I knew that I would do it. Go away and far away. I had to do it but O'Hanagan had another plan, to bury the shovel. He dropped it into a shallow grave. Then he had to take the shovel out to fill in the hole. It was obvious that I needed to get him out of the country quickly. So I drove him to Dublin in a stolen car. It's seldom that I would steal anything but I knew Scullivan would not be using it. I told O'Hanagan to take the ferry to Liverpool and then keep going, and to take the shovel with him.

"Don't let go of it until you get to Germany," I said. "Do you hear me?"

"I do of course, Bart, why wouldn't I hear you?"

By this time I had already done a penance for O'Hanagan's sins. Never before had I driven so far, or to a big city. It was purgatory with lights in my eyes and thorny thoughts in my head. Someone hooted a horn at me and I backfired, burped and nearly splattered the dashboard with vomit. Scullivan's car was a gem, an upholstered beauty cruising through the night but the driver was a wreck. O'Hanagan was in the passenger seat as cool as a corpse but with his beaming smile on his baby pink face. For him it was an outing, a rare occasion sitting in the front of a luxury car.

Strange are the thoughts that come to a troubled mind. Murder is a serious offence, I concluded at one point, while racing through the night. I could not remember if I had ever held another opinion, or if I had ever given the matter any thought. Then I decided that while Scullivan was setting stiff upon the Boreen High Road, I should not be thinking about fun and frolics at his wake. Sure, it would be good craic but a mortal sin had been committed and there would be no place in heaven or even purgatory for the assailants. It was a mistake though, I begged, and for the first time in my life I asked O'Hanagan for his opinion. This was a long time afterwards, in Dublin, many dreadful miles and hours later. O'Hanagan was wandering before me with hands deep in pockets. Off to Germany he was without a query in his head, looking up at tall houses.

"Do you hear me talking to you?" I called.

"I do of course, Bart. Why wouldn't I hear you talking to me?"

"So, O'Hanagan, what do you t'ink?"

"I t'ink houses in Dublin have awfully big windows. For sure, Bart, you wouldn't want to be a window cleaner in this town, sure you wouldn't, would you, Bart?"

There was no sense in talking to him, the eejit, and I was justified in having told him several times during our gallop to Dublin to shut up, although, to be fair to him, for the most part he didn't utter a word. Sat as dumb as the night. I drove through it, an agonising flight around hills and bog, following white lines and signposts illuminated by headlamps.

"Fine lamps on this car, sure t'ere are, aren't they, Bart?"

"Shut up, O'Hanagan, yer bollocks."

Eventually our route snaked its way out of the bumps and bog to flatland, straightened itself and opened up.

"Tis a grand road, so it tis, Bart, a grand road."

"O'Hanagan, shut up." I needed to concentrate, driving at a dangerous speed to get as far away in the shortest time, and keeping my eyes open for fear of a policeman. As we came to villages, I slowed, driving as if creeping home from a pub, as would be the local custom.

"Tis a fine night for a drive," he said.

O'Hanagan was right but I didn't answer him. I drove into the blackness with no consolation but to know that we were heading east where the sun would poke up at the end of the road. The end of a sleepless night, and how I love my bed. It was autumn though and the darkness would stretch into a late morning, my fatigue getting heavier and the thoughts in my head more troublesome. From Tipperary onwards, the thoughts were more vivid, a sharp edge to every image: the shovel, steel, the sound of the thump splitting Scullivan's skull. It would be a long wait for the sun, watching the horizon. Having an accelerator helped, a pedal to push down on as if I was pumping fuel to my brain to fight the thoughts.

"A grand road," O'Hanagan said again when I misjudged a bend and put sparks flying from the fender. "It tis, a grand road." As we got close to Dublin I was talking to myself, asking haven't we already been here? Maybe in and out and rambled about. My mind was gone. The road was wide and signposts were illuminated to direct me onto ring roads to whiz around towns and villages, towards the city. We were in Dublin before the sun, or at least into the suburbs where orange streetlights were scattered beneath the motorway, left and right and off to the distance like burning confetti. There was a glow in the sky and I was thinking it must be an awful big place.

"Grand houses, aren't t'ey, Bart?"

"O'Hanagan, yer bollocks, shut up."

I stopped at traffic lights and suddenly felt very tired, fearing that my mind and the car were going to stall, freeze upon the road as stiff as Scullivan. Stiffness; couldn't stop thinking about it. Lifeless limbs. It was the way he had landed after being walloped. His arms spread wide like a tree. Chopped down and they'll wither away like twigs. "Yer bollocks. Talking shite about big houses and look where you've got us. Well we won't be staying in one, not unless it has bars on the window. Where on sweet suffering Earth will we be this time tomorrow?" The lights turned green and I drove on, towards the city centre, peering at signposts. I wanted an escape route to England, a ferry to Liverpool. East I thought, yes, go to the sea. The docks would do and hop on a ferry. Swim. Anything. But it seemed as if we were spending as much time rambling

4

through Dublin as we spent getting there. O'Hanagan was quiet for a while but he must have been thinking of what I had said.

"You're right enough," he suddenly agreed, "it will be many a savage dog and a bad housewife we will meet before we come dis way again."

I supposed it was many a quiet dog that turned savage seeing O'Hanagan's bulk come its way. As for a bad housewife, she would need to be a saint to tolerate him. Any woman who had ever encountered clumsy O'Hanagan stepped away from him. To be fair to the girls' back in Ballybog, they usually pitied O'Hanagan and often told Scullivan not to ridicule the poor simpleton. Sometimes though, they couldn't halt a hurtful laugh at Scullivan's jokes. Their feminine giggles often fuelled his sadistic manner, but that was the way with youth. Scullivan was older though and should have known better. He could never resist the craic to impress the girls, and refused to stop when O'Hanagan's pink features turned disturbingly red.

The blackness was gone by the time we arrived in the city centre. It was a grey Sunday morning. People must have been going to mass because there were suddenly cars coming carelessly from side streets and driveways. Folk were stepping in front of me. Red lights. Green lights. I was stopping at anything amber rather than attract attention. A coat of sweat was on me, getting colder, freezing. I was iced, too stiff to steer the car but on it drove. My brain was hot, boiling, bubbling with the thoughts, millions of burning splinters embedded in my brain so that I couldn't think of a single thought.

"Ferryport," O'Hanagan said and pointed to a signpost.
I didn't know he could read. It was a big surprise, especially as I thought we were lost. My escape route to England was along a street of Georgian houses and railings.

"At home and in bed I should be." Traffic creeping into town and me with heavy eyes trying to guess where cars were going to hop from next. "Yer big bollocks, O'Hanagan, look at me, lost and ready to drop."
He was looking at chimneys, like a child. I would have enjoyed looking at some myself. There were some fine old buildings but I had enough labouring on my mind. I was thankful it was only a Sunday because I had heard about Monday morning traffic being the worst way to start a week.

"Come on, get out, you big lump, we'll leave the car here." There were plenty of signposts now showing the way to the Ferryport, and a walk would do me good. It did. A fine drizzle wet my face, a morning wipe. Along the quay on Sunday, almost lunchtime along the Liffy, following signs for Ferryport. My face was fresh but the fatigue was so heavy that it numbed me and put my worries into a slumber. It was then that I asked him that question, about what he thought of the situation. He stopped looking at the big houses momentarily and grinned at me. He liked being consulted.

"I t'ink houses in Dublin have awfully big windows. For sure, Bart, you wouldn't want to be a window cleaner in dis town, sure you wouldn't, would you, Bart?"

2 Today, I've had enough.

Itch Wool is the most irritating fabric in the world. It sheds its bits like a deadly dust of slivers with razor edges that shimmer in the air. Overalls, hats and gloves fail to halt the micro spikes penetrating clothes to embed themselves beneath my skin. I scratch and stab flesh with fingernails to kill the itch. Lagging, the filthiest job. Lengths of pipes, fat, thin, straight and bent, all waiting for poor men to take the job and lag them, wrap them from the cold. Valves and cylinders demand special effort and a man to wrestle with the lethal material, to take off gloves and use a knife to cut the fabric to make it fit. Awkward jobs down holes in sweltering heat and others up high where a freezing wind blows the bits into my face, through air vents on my mask and up my sleeves. But I needed money, so yes, I said, I'll take the job.

At least my palpitations have eased since getting rid of O'Hanagan. I was desperate for space, a nervous wreck every time I heard an Irish accent. Now I'm hopeful, albeit a lonely wanderer. And that's a lovely sky. It would make anyone stop work to loiter in an idle gaze. When I was back in drizzly old Ireland, stuck up in mountain mud, I would have given a limb for a sky like that. I enjoy limitless blueness.

"Work," shouts Hans, disturbing my pondering moments. His square head comes up at the end of the scaffold. He's heaving himself onto the platform. There's an eruption inside his skull because he sees me idling but I've finished my work. I'm waiting for new material. I've been told to wait but Hans is shouting, striding, pointing like a knight ready to lance me.

"I don't understand German," I reply. "Spreek U Nederlands?" Do you speak Dutch is what it means but he continues to hurl abuse in German, and ending with a bit of English. "... work, work."

"No, you work. I'm away fecking home."

O'Hanagan would have engaged Hans in conversation, asking, what work? Haven't we finished all the work? That's the way it was with O'Hanagan but I can't be bothered talking to the likes of Hans. I have no tolerance. To be honest, being a fugitive has bred a horrible animal in me. Some might say I'm a racist but whatever I am it's a great day for walking off the job, for telling the boss to stuff it up his arse. I go down ladders and trek across yellow mud. Their building sites, like most places in Germany, are clean. The debris is sorted into tidy piles; bricks over there and lumps of timber over here. I'll take a cup of their coffee before leaving. That's if the Turks will move out of my way. They upset me too.

They're normally a friendly bunch but I crossed swords with one and they clung together like a clan.

"Are you not doing any work today?" I shout, inching my way to the coffee dispenser. Credit to the Germans though, their catering department is top class on this site. Don't you foreigners be slagging off our hosts because this coffee here is for free. The Germans are generous but I have problems working with them. Anyone who howls orders at me antagonises me.

"Work," I shout at the Turks. "Work, go an' work," but they don't understand the craic. They probably don't understand English. I reach for my coffee. Lovely. One of the Turks is talking to me in a belligerent, seemingly angry manner. "Lovely coffee," I reply. "Cheers," raising my cup. That shuts him up.

What I understand from their argument with the Germans is that they want to be Europeans but are treated as aliens. I like them better as Asians. I have a problem with East Europeans, or at least a trait of theirs. A border guard mentality. I hate the way they stand over me, watching me work, but I've been told that hate is a very strong word. So is this coffee. A bit too strong today. That's how the Polish behave, domineering. Poles who have lived too long in Germany antagonise me. And the Croats. And labourers from Hamburg. Not all of them, just every labourer from Hamburg who has ever worked with me. And every Pole and Croat. With two working together, one has to be the boss, a big bollocks in boots blabbering orders. There is a definite pecking order on sites over here.

"Work," I shout again, "work for Jaysus sake."
They're responding in Turkish, tapping their watches, probably telling me it's time to go and fuck myself.

"We finish early on Friday," a long one says. "We go home now."

"Me too, finished for good."

Since the killing, I have worked only with foreigners. Recently though, since getting rid of O'Hanagan, I've started socialising with the rowdy Irish again. Fiona the feminist will tell me not to stereotype folk. Unless I'm saying something nice. It's only racist if it's derogatory. So I must be a racist because I went into an Irish pub and called them pissheads because they were all drunk. Me too. I was celebrating being back with my own kind because I spent a year hiding from them. I had to, for fear of meeting O'Hanagan in a pub, and hello there, he'd shout, and how's the craic, and do you remember that time we battered Scullivan to death? You with your boots and me with a shovel? And they're still talking about it back there. For sure, that was a good one, wasn't it, wasn't that good craic? And I'd be saying, shut up, O'Hanagan, you big bollocks, and he'd be saying, for sure, who cares here about an old Paddy from the bog?

So I avoided Irish pubs and communities. Even an English speaker on the street would unnerve me. The more foreign they were the safer I felt. Immigrants with language problems didn't ask questions. There was the odd word and laughter at gestures and a slap on the back, hand shake or tapping a nose with a finger to say mind your own business, or pointing to the head to suggest it's crazy. But here, in Germany, they ask me to do something, like get the tools. Then, next time, instead of asking me, they *tell* me to get the tools. Then they *order* me to get the tools, and ask why did it take so long. And hurry next time. Don't take all day. Work, man, work. Let's have progress. Time is money and them talking as if I'm lazy but I'm as good as the next man. The Pole who has lived too long in Germany has already had a word with the boss. It's none of his business but he has inspected my work, and needs to make a comment in the office. So I said to him, how would you like a smack in the face? A smack in the face if you don't feck off and mind your own business?

"Zo, my vriend," says the long Turk coming to join me at the door, "where you go?"

"I go home." I turn to see him, recognising him now. We were talking this morning, up on top. He thought I was one of themselves because of my curly black hair. The poor feller was wearing a helmet and safety glasses and a dust mask. He removed it to talk but I still didn't understand him.

"You finish?" he asks.

"No, I have argument with big bastard."

"Yes," he laughs, and wants to shake hands with me. "You go home now, to Ireland?"

"I'm going to the next nearest place, an Irish pub. To find a new job."

After one year on the run I'm homesick. The fear of being caught has faded. Yes, I decide, it's safe enough to go into an Irish pub in Germany and ask for work. Friday evening is the best time to catch coherent heads at the bar. An Irish pub is an information centre, currency bureaux, and an employment exchange. But I need to get there before the drunken stupor reaches their brains. The problem is transport. I hate these industrial estates in the far-flung corners of Berlin.

"My vriend," he shouts, pointing to rust on the top of his car. I think he wants me to sit in. "…I drive you."

"Well, that's very kind of you, sir." I open the flimsy door and slide onto the seat. If I had not seen the rust, I would have assumed this was a plastic car. It's good to leave early, at the front of the queue snaking out of the car park of shiny Mercedes and BMs and Volkswagens in new metallic colours. Refugees in their old cars, a few illegal immigrants, I reckon. They're leaving early because they start early. It's the same all over Europe, maybe the world: the peasants start work before the management. The lower your status, the earlier you start. It goes back to the industrial revolution when the workers had to be in early to stoke up the boilers and make the tea. Or coffee.

"Town?" asks my chauffeur.

"Drop me anywhere. A bus stop will do. Which way are you going?"

"I take you."

"T'anks," I shout. "But don't go out your way." I don't know why I shout at foreigners. I suppose the words come out better if I put a bit of puff behind them, blowing them out one by one, like bubbles to form a sentence. During the last year I've learnt that the most important language is currency because money talks. Anything else is small talk and I had no space in my pockets for small change. It was cold and I needed my pockets for my hands because I couldn't afford gloves.

It's not true that I've become a racist. Admittedly I stereotype a district by the colour of the faces and the clothes on their back. The cars that they drive. The job. Their shoes. Their jewellery. The poor who flaunt it, the rich who hide it. I've been doing it since I arrived in Dublin, and then in Liverpool, Birmingham, London and around the Continent. With the shattered state of my mind after the killing I saw everyone as a potential informer, a nosy-parker who wanted to know who I was. I judged books by their covers and folk by their style. We've been doing it all our lives up the mountain, weary of travellers coming to our door to sell a shirt, or a drunk in town stopping to say hello, and do you have any spare coins? he would ask. We shouldn't call them tinkers, Fiona the feminist said. Even O'Hanagan sized up the Dublin Jacks by the size of their windows. I don't dislike foreigners. I just react to traditions that needle me. This reaction might be a smack in the jaw if they become persistent, or a kick in the bollocks because actions speak louder than words. Fortunately, one word usually says it all with no need for further confrontation. Fuck off is the universal phrase. Had it myself, walked into a cafe and they assumed I was a refugee. My black hair was extra curly and long since a visit to the barbers became an extravagance. Could have been the state of my attire because my wardrobe has also become limited. My one and only leather jacket becomes threatening as it gets tatty. So they ignored me until I swore in English.

Driving into town at this time of day is better than sitting in that queue over there. It's a metallic snake inching the other way, exiting Berlin on Friday afternoon. O'Hanagan would be saying this is an awfully big road, and this is nice music. Near the end he started to listen to anything foreign as long as it was loud. Loud was cool. This car, this tin can might burst at the seams if my driver doesn't lower the volume.

My own kind is the worst. Back home years ago, driving to Limerick to do a day's work and I was fooled into bringing a few fellows to the job. Scullivan too. They were out to rob me. I took too long to learn that friends use fools. I was using my petrol to collect them each morning, an extra twenty minutes of my time. Sometimes someone was late and it'd be half an hour, then Scullivan needed to stop for cigarettes. Another twenty minutes coming home, the best part of an hour each day and they contributed nothing for the petrol. They saw me in the pub and they were gone for fear I'd expect a drink, something to show their appreciation. They were the meanest drunks in Europe, telling me that they'd settle up at the end of the week, and could I pick them up for work in the morning, and could I come around and knock on their door because their toolbox was heavy? Collect them and drive them to work because we were all friends when it suited them and I was just a fool.

This Turkish fellow is a good head despite his taste in music. He has a thin face with cheeks sucked in, moving with rhythm. But if he were working next to me everyday with this music there'd be some serious confrontation. Bigoted or not, I can't help but hate his music. It's the idealists who rouse me. Political correctness. How could we stop calling them tinkers when they called each other tinkers?

"You," I shout. I really must shout now to get above the pounding. "You."

He lowers the volume. He's smiling, nodding his head and almost laughing as he talks to me. I think he's asking do I like music; "… good? You like?"

"Good, man. You drink? I buy you drink. We have good time in Irish pub."

"No, my vriend," and he pats my shoulder before turning up the volume. He turns it down again to talk. "I take you to Irish pub. But I no drink."

"No, no need. Just drop me somewhere convenient for you."

"No problem. We may never meet again. This is my present to you. I bring you."

I'll leave him money for a drink, to show my appreciation. I'm not mean like Scullivan. Like Scullivan *was*. I'll leave enough for a pint of paint for his car, to stop the rust. This tin can says it all: dangerous vehicle driven by an illegal immigrant. He takes me through traffic, to the front door.

"Thanks," I'm shouting, "I really appreciate it," and I place the money on the dashboard while opening the flimsy door.

"No," he says, scooping the money.

"Yes, please."

"No," he insists.

"Please take it…"

"I am not a servant." He has bold warning eyes; an anger that could fight to the death. "You not give me tip. I do this for you, not for money," clenching the notes in his fist. He throws it at me.

"Sorry…"

3. Last Autumn in Liverpool, Birmingham and I don't know where.
.

There was no reason why Scullivan, or anyone else, should describe me as O'Hanagan's cousin or friend. Or expect me to go travelling around Europe with the simpleton. We were just distant relatives. Scullivan was closer to the O'Hanagans but was too arrogant to admit it. Most folk down the village avoided O'Hanagan because he was an embarrassment, a social strain. I too kept a distance, and as soon as I got to England I tried to slip away from him. His red wiry hair and beaming pink face disturbed me. O'Hanagan's rounded cheeks were alarm beacons on a hazardous being waiting for an accident. After the killing I needed space to recover, to think and forget. I could not relax while his face beamed near me.

My torn and worn nerves started to recuperate from the moment I landed in England, improving as I wandered alone. But I had only gone as far as a railway embankment when I met a policeman. The embankment was wet and slippy, and overgrown with briars that could cut into the bone but I had to get up and away. It was night time and I was looking behind because I feared O'Hanagan might be following in the dark. It had been like this for a whole day, my first day out of Ireland.

It started in Dublin after that awful reckless drive. We decided to go our separate ways and so goodbye, I said.
    "Goodbye," he replied and we shook hands several times.
A few minutes later we met again because we boarded the same ferry to Liverpool. O'Hanagan was on the stairs and on every deck, wherever I went. He was just there gawking at me, as if waiting for instructions.
    "Will you pretend that you don't know me, yer big bollocks."
    "I will, Bart, I will."
He wasn't following but always there before me. Just loitering. Looking at a fire extinguisher, he was, the way a child would study the knobs on it, touching it. Then he was in the cafeteria, not buying anything because he didn't know what to ask for but stood in the way. Sandwich, he said, but he didn't know what sort of sandwich, and when asked, he stayed silent. It was self-service but he was asking the cashier. He was standing at the front of the queue where people were trying to pay. What a big bollock's, I thought, and went to hide from him but even in the toilet I could hear him on the other side of the cubicle door. For an hour or more I stayed still, hoping he would go away but O'Hanagan splashed and spluttered until the floor was submerged and I had to lift my feet as water rippled in beneath the door.

"So, goodbye, and good luck," I said in Liverpool.

"Goodbye and good luck to you too." He liked shaking hands and I didn't want to be the first to let go, so we were shaking hands for a long time before we got off the ferry.

Merry old England. It didn't look so merry with tourists burdened with bags and shouting at children. It was a bit old, on the outside. Some old dock buildings in the distance for O'Hanagan to go and look at, and comment on the size of chimneys. We were moving along a walkway with a crowd, towards the arrivals lounge. There were brown tinted windows and O'Hanagan was peering through, probably thinking it was dark outside. Or England was the colour of chocolate. E.U. Citizens, said a sign. Everyone was going the same way, producing passports and cards as they passed a man in a uniform. Before I could panic, I was ushered past the barrier. Even O'Hanagan was through with nothing more than the papers he had in his pockets. His inside pocket was like a filing cabinet, everything from medical cards to letters from a priest.

"So, goodbye, and good luck," I said again.

"Goodbye and good luck to you too."

On the train, he was never more than a carriage away. Whenever I moved to another seat, O'Hanagan would take mine. I caught a glimpse of his awkward bulk following as I moved along the aisle. I avoided double seats so he wouldn't sit beside me, pretending he didn't know me, like I told him to. I moved again and again but was only keeping seats warm for him. It was like playing musical chairs. Soon I was in the front carriage with nowhere else to sit except up front with the driver. O'Hanagan was behind, his hair thick and uncombed, his jaw protruding.

There are lots of houses in England. More than in Ireland and I was looking out at them, wondering what sort of people lived there. Protestants. Thousands of them and not a drop of holy water in their homes or a saint upon a wall. There would be black people too. I saw a few on the train. We were flying through a housing estate and unmarried mothers came to mind. A lot of that in England, I had heard, worse than Dublin. Row after row of grey blocks, and houses mounted upon houses. Then I supposed there would also be homosexuals. Maybe folk from Ballybog from years ago who came to get lost in a concrete forest after things were said. Between the towns there were fine green fields, as good as the best in Ireland and without a hump or a rock. We were speeding through another city, houses and car parks, through a tunnel and stopped in Birmingham. I waited. Then, as the train was about to move, I hurried to the door without as much as a glance at O'Hanagan, and jumped. That's it, I thought, got rid of the big bollocks; then a sadness came over me. It was like a big cloud on a sunny day, suddenly dull, a bit chilly, maybe damp. A moment later O'Hanagan was beside me, pretending he didn't know me, the way I had told him to.

"So, this is it, O'Hanagan, our final goodbye."
"It tis. Goodbye and good luck." He started to shake hands again. We were lost in a concrete city centre and my hand sandwiched between his fat palms and he was throwing my arm up and down like it was a skipping rope. "God be good to you wherever you land, and goodbye t'en, and good luck."
"Enough, O'Hanagan." A bus stopped with its doors wide open and that was my cue to say goodbye for the last time and escape. I had to pull my hand loose, and him trying to squeeze it tighter. The bus went without him. I turned to see a sorrowful sight; O'Hanagan, dumb and pale on a grey concrete ramp. Neon light from shops illuminated his jaw. I had to go though. It was best if we went our separate ways.

It was not the first time that I had left O'Hanagan at a bus stop. Years ago, I would avoid the school bus if he was on it. Even as an adult he was an embarrassment. If he saw me in the town he would follow me around shops, asking what time were we going back to the village. I would tell him that there was no room for him on the bus, and that he would have to wait for the next one.
"But, Bart," he would cry, "t'ere are seats galore, empty ones at that."
"But there's a big crowd getting on before we get back to Ballybog."
"But sure, I can stand, can't I ?"
"You can't, O'Hanagan. It's much too dangerous, especially going around corners for someone as big as you. And it's against the law and you'd only be getting the driver into trouble if a policeman saw you." I would often feel bad for failing to defend him when others were using him for fun. In Birmingham though, I was feeling so guilty about leaving him lost in a busy concrete city, that I was contemplating on confession. While the bus crept along a congested pedestrian mall, I tackled one of the thoughts, about why I really ran away from Ballybog. I supposed it was because I could not bare to explain to the authorities how O'Hanagan had killed Scullivan. I would have had to say some awful things about him to convince a jury, because locals would not believe that O'Hanagan would do such a thing. He could not do it, even if he wanted to, they would say, because O'Hanagan was too clumsy and not able to hit a nail with a hammer. For sure, they would say, it was no harm to give Scullivan a

wallop, he had it coming to him, but it's wrong to blame a simpleton. While I was imagining the faces on them back there in Ballybog, the bus moved a little further along the pedestrian mall, stopping for traffic and shoppers and trolleys.

The centre of Birmingham was a precinct cluttered with customers and delivery vans and lampposts and illuminated kiosks, a frustrating place for a man on a bus, a man on the run. It crept along and I had never spent so much time on a bus and travelled so little. Walking would have been quicker, even inching along in the adjacent queue to buy a newspaper. I tried to read the headlines with my face to the vibrating window. We did eventually reach the next bus stop. The doors flung open and O'Hanagan stepped on, asking how much for one adult and a shovel.

"Will you get lost, ye fecking bollocks yer." It was evening and lampposts were everywhere, an impossible place for hiding. I wanted to get out of the light, to go to the country where I could fade into the dark. It would be better behind the houses where I could slip down an embankment and scurry like a rat along railway tracks and out of town. I thought about it while eating a curry. Birmingham was a great place for foreign food and it was no wonder that so many Asians were attracted to the place. While O'Hanagan was asking for spuds and boiled bacon, I stole out through the back, and jogged down to the end of a garden. It was a junkyard littered with lengths of corrugated iron and tyres piled at the end. I scrambled up, wrestling with them as they rolled and tumbled and bounced, eventually hooking a hand on the top of the fence. Being skinny, I was able to worm myself over the top, something O'Hanagan couldn't do. On the other side I was sliding down a slippery slope till I was splattered with curry and rice beside the railway.

It was a beautiful night and I must have walked a long way because I was in the country, a very English place with dew on fine fields. It was different from Ballybog yet I felt an empathy with the place. It was not like other, more hostile parts of Britain where it's advised to stay near main roads and then be wary of traffic. This place had a freshness in the breeze, a wetness in the layers of leaves beneath my feet. For the first time since the slaying of Scullivan, an easiness came over me. It was comforting to know that I was unlikely to meet people here and be coaxed into conversation. I was in no mood for it. In any case, for the short time I had been in England, there was little desire in anyone to pass a greeting. This was no big surprise to me for I had often heard it said that folk in cities seldom struck up conversation with their neighbours, let alone a stranger.

So it came as a surprise while scrambling up the wet embankment overgrown with briars that could cut into my bone, that I met a man with a dog. The dog and himself were watching me as my knees pounded up and down like engine pistons. I was scrambling away from a train, an intercity express heading south. They probably heard me shouting at O'Hanagan. Although I had been trying to get away from him, I was howling warnings just in case he had followed me.

"Some stupid people come over from Ireland," said the man.

"You're right," I replied, "The clever ones stay where t'ey are." I was suddenly in an argumentative mood and so, to see how clever *he* was, I quizzed him with a riddle. "Let's say," I said, "t'at a man got up in the morning and walked ten miles east, then walked ten miles south and shot a bear. Then he walked another ten miles and came back to where he started. What colour was the bear ?"

There was not a murmur from the man. The dog showed some interest but the man had no idea of what I was talking about. Then I realised that he had very shiny buttons and he was taking out a notebook and licking a pencil.

"Now, let's start again," said the policeman. With that I ran away, down the embankment and across the track, not stopping for the intercity express train coming back from wherever. And it not stopping for me. The poor dog, God love it, didn't know what hit it.

4   Tonight, I'm to the pub to find a job.

.

It would have been a good wake, Scullivan's farewell. A funeral in Ireland is often as good as a wedding. Better, because you don't need to bring a present.

What a day I've had. Lost my job, threw it away during a moment of temper and then I angered a Turk who was generous enough to drive me to here. This Irish pub is a thatched cottage set beneath a concrete tower in Berlin. Pubs should be called The Mortgage, or The Endowment Insurance Policy, or The Inheritance, named after whatever financial function gave birth to them. This one's called the Thatched Cottage. I'm in a cynical mood today, causing one confrontation after another. This morning I snapped at the bus driver when he almost passed my stop. Reared up in English and it was probably my fault. If truth were told, they irritate me, foreigners and natives alike. It's not their fault, it's mine. It will get better though. Getting back to my own sort of people and drinking in Irish pubs will be a tonic. I have finished the first year of my sentence, my time as a fugitive, a loner with only O'Hanagan and foreigners. Until now, a cold sweat would burst from me if I heard a murmur of an Irish accent. There was an awful fear that they would ask questions: and from where in the old country do you come from? Ballybog? I know it well, and were you there for the murder?

Beer mats are submerged in slops of beer, and smokers' debris swamps an ashtray. It looks like the morning after but it's early evening with time to buy a pint and ask about a job. There are only tourists at tables rather than boozers along the bar, so I suppose I'm early. All the more space for me while I wait for the influx of workers.

Paranoia is an awful ailment. It happened outside a travel shop that offered flights to Ireland. The big hand of the law came out one day to drag me in and fly me back to Ballybog. It was only a customer waving, at the door shouting out to a traffic warden to say they won't be a minute, just collecting a ticket for Cork.

Irish pubs are an institution across Europe. They are magnets for foreigners whether they are tourists or immigrants, or the new guest workers and tax dodgers, the loners, drifters, backpackers. Drunks. There are wagon wheels upon walls in here and signposts pointing the way to Dublin and Killarney Lakes and to the toilets and this way to kiss the

Blarney Stone. It's a grand place for finding a job. Of course, having earned a wage, a pub's a fine place for spending it too. Some heads cash their cheques here, or exchange currency, turning money into drink over the counter. I'll be sensible though, making small talk, a few drinks and then away home to bed before the drunken stupor seeps along the bar. Post offices too. This pub is my postbox. Many contractors drifting across borders use pubs for collecting mail. A postal address for fugitives. Service is not good this evening though because Rita is attending to the tourists. Americans, wouldn't you know? They want to listen to a traditional ballad and she's down under the counter fiddling with the sound system. No hurry. I'm really here to find a job. Collect my post. And yes, a little drink after a hard day's work. Rita's a blonde Scandinavian who speaks English with an Irish accent. The Americans think she's a sweet colleen despite the height of her. Hurry up, Rita, and get along here before closing time. I need to ask if a letter has come for me.

When I came to Germany a few weeks ago, after I abandoned O'Hanagan, peace came upon me. I acquired a sense of security in knowing that I was further from Ireland and the scene of the crime. If anyone asked where I was from, I said Holland because that's where I'd just come from. When they asked if I could speak German, I boasted that I knew some Dutch and would that help? I was there for ages, long before Scullivan's murder. That stopped folk asking if I had just arrived from Ireland, and was I there for the Ballybog killing? But no one asks anything. As long as I pay my way no one cares if I'm from Ireland or England or Holland or Turkey. I don't think anyone knows about the Ballybog killing because it is by now a dot in history, gone like Scullivan.

I should get a letter from home because I sent a postcard to Mom last week to test this pub as my postbox. It was the first time since the killing that I wrote to anyone, a few lines to ask if she received my other letters. Of course, she will tell me that she did not and not even a phonecall and that I missed a grand wake. There's no doubt that Scullivan had enough money for a fine funeral, flaunting it all the way to his grave and a big Celtic cross as bold as his head. The wealthiest box of bones in Ballybog's churchyard.

"Rita," I shout to the end of the bar, "any drink for the workers?" She's down talking to tourists, turning to dance attendance on me. It's no wonder with the kind of money us contractors splash out in these bars. "And is t'ere any post for me?" I say. "It won't be a postcard. A letter, Rita, look for a letter." I'm counting on my fingers the number of days it would take for a letter to get to Ireland and then the same for one to return. I've even allowed a day for my mother to write her reply although, I'm sure, that after receiving my casually written postcard, she would do nothing else until she had finished scribbling and sent all her love to me.

"No, darling, no one loves you."

There's thin Terry, the English eejit and here I go again slagging them off but he really does annoy me. On my first day in Germany I bumped into him. Heard my accent, he did, and how's the craic? he sang in a mimic accent and told a joke about stupid Belgians. As if I had not heard it before, the Irish version about a stupid Paddy from the bog. Why are Irish jokes so simple? I replied. So the fecking English can understand them.

"Pint of stout," says Rita, placing it on the counter.

"T'anks. And a packet of crisps." When I'm lonely and irritable a taste from home is a comfort.

I wrote the postcard on Tuesday when I realised that I had recovered from the killing. Not well enough to phone home yet because fear could still grab me in conversation and have me stuttering in a panic. However, my palpitations did fade when O'Hanagan was gone. I was suddenly raring to write, went into a café to scribble a postcard to Mom. I'm in Berlin to make my fortune, is what I wrote, and how's the craic since my last letter? And I heard the awful news. What awful news? they would wonder. Scullivan's death. Dead the day after I left. And buried before I heard the news.

I sip my stout, a cushion for my belly. Pubs and continental cafes are dark on the inside, like sitting deep in your head looking out at the world passing by windows of frosted glass. Someone comes in from the outside world, peering in to see if it's okay. An American seeking adventure but terrified of strangers. Come in, you big bollocks, we're not drunk so early in the evening. I'm an expert now, walking in on strangers and natives alike, up to the bar and climb upon a stool like it's a throne and I own the place and I can't even speak their language. But who cares so long as I'm spending money? That's the international language, money, money, money and so I need a job. What a fugitive needs is a job on the black which means no tax and no questions and no forms to fill in.

It's at times like this, while sipping stout, that simple things mentioned by my mother come to mind. Don't let people know your business, she would say. It's true enough. The Irish were great people for keeping secrets. Cute whores they would call each other. There was no talking in front of friends for fear that they would tell the taxman. Unless it was to do with tax evasion in England, which was okay. I had often heard my uncles say, on their return from London, that it was a good craic working there and screwing the state for all the wrongs committed by Cromwell and the Black an' Tans. Tax avoidance is as much a part of Irish culture as the music and the myth. Something from my Celtic heritage tells me that if the taxman cannot find me, then a policeman, detective or Scullivan's mother will not find me.

Although I'm able to sleep at night now, I have dreadful dreams. Itch Wool at work. Last night I was catapulted into balls of itchy insulation. Another night I was thrown into a lake of it; new improved liquid itch, it said on the packet. Of course, O'Hanagan followed me into my dreams, making them nightmares. He had a large unshaven jaw. Nicki was stroking it. Then she was sucking it. Her cherry red lips were pressed against O'Hanagan's enormous jaw. She was wet with lipstick, slurping it on his animated chin. It was a cartoon cut-out and she so close. Her lips were swelling to the size of his jaw. A glossy inflatable kiss. All she was, was an enormous pair of cherry lips bouncing on his stubble, red rubbery on bristles and then bang like a balloon

They're coming in now, the workers. They knock off early on Fridays and I had better get another drink while there's space at the bar. A pint of stout if you please, something creamy for my belly and I look around to see who's in.

I don't understand why Nicki chose O'Hanagan and not me. I wouldn't consider myself handsome or stylish but next to O'Hanagan I'm the best of men. He was a lump, a brick. Beside him I was an average looking clothes-peg with a mop of black hair. Maybe she didn't like my leather jacket, my one and only coat because I had to leave Ballybog in a hurry and never earned enough to start a new wardrobe. Anyway, forget about them and think about the letter that will come tomorrow at the latest.

"Rita, a pint of stout before the herd comes in."

Last Tuesday I sipped coffee in that café while I wrote home. I pondered about the first sentence. There was another coffee on the table before I wrote a word. Then I did it: *Dear Mom.* I was a long time scratching and thinking before scribbling the rest of it. I eventually decided not to mention Scullivan after I got a perverse but subtle shaking of the hand. *Dear Mom, did you not get my letters? I have not heard a word from anyone back home, saint nor sinner, but then again, I've been*

21

gallivanting an awful lot. And I heard in a pub here that someone back there was murdered. They didn't know the name but it happened only a day or two after I'd left.

"Tim," calls a head. He climbs upon the stool beside me, labouring, drunk I suspect.

"The name's Bart".

"Aey," squinting to see me. "Fuck." He slides off the stool and is away before I have the chance to ask where's the work and what's the score and how's the craic?

"Pint of stout."

"T'anks Rita."

At the time I was glad to get rid of O'Hanagan. I only wanted foreigners. O'Hanagan would say things like, mind the tram. If that tram went over your toes, he'd say, you'd know about it, for sure, you would, wouldn't you, Bart? He wouldn't shut up about it for hours. Wake up at night and ask me what did I think of the trams and he'd already asked me several times during the day.

"How's the craic?" asks thin Terry, the skinny English eejit come to annoy me.

"How's work?"

"Don't ask."

Well, bollocks to you, Terry Thin, because you're too mean to give out information.

Friday evening is the beginning of the weekend and I've nearly finished my second pint. I am talking to anyone who listens. My paranoia is dwindling and I could talk of home, skilfully avoiding any mention of Ballybog. They talk about work and football and I move in amongst them. Inching between pints of booze, elbows and waving arms…

"Sorry," bumping a shoulder. "How's the craic? Christ, it's suddenly a full house here tonight. Aey?" But no reply.

"Same again, a pint of stout," shouting to the bar, pushing bodies and saying sorry. "I'm a plumber."

"Feck a plumber. More money going up high. Piece of piss," turning away.

"Depends."

"Na, the money's on the high jobs." The stranger turns back to lecture me. "Tell ya, work the weekends an' retire. Do ya self a favour."

"Okay, so I'm a high-up plumber, worked in England during the boom."

"Where in England?" asks a fat man. "I woz plumbing back home. Doncaster. But doing concrete shit here. Brickying, chippy, bit of shuttering, pipework...." His English accent shouts at me, listing towns and trades and the price of tools.

"The man at the top," argues the other, "slotting in girders." He's slurring his words with the same accent. Can't quite catch it as it swirls around our circled group, a harsh sound on the wall of drunks, around it goes. "... Unemployment? Krauts want white- collar jobs. That's their pissin problem..."

"Plumbing though..." interrupts the fat man.

"Plumbing, don't make me laugh..." saying it with saliva on his lips.

An arm snakes between heads, trying to give me my pint of stout.

"... So fuck plumbing. Terry's job is up high. Phone that fucking number, mate, an you'll get his job. Terry's from Leicester but he's okay. That pisshead over there."

"Who? That skinny..." I nearly said it, that skinny English eejit who annoys me. Terry Thin. But if I have nothing good to say I'll say nothing and be thankful for what I get.

"They wan 'im to start this new job but his back's fucked. Beautiful bird he has. Candy. A beautiful bitch."

"A devious bitch," interrupts the fat man.

"Fuck off. Anyway," turning back to me, "Terry's got problems. Were expecting him on the new job. But he's fucked, so they're looking for a man." He burps. "Just the job for you, mate, cash in hand."

It sounds like the job for me and so I'll add it to my numbers.

"Who say's he has cancer?" asks a head. "Just a bad back."

"Still say, I'd rather be doing plumbing."

"Fuck off you fat fucker..." but a punch lands on his nose and shuts him up.

I didn't actually see it happen because I was looking at my telephone numbers. Apparently, I already have the number for the high-up job. I got it in another pub. Suddenly I'm somewhere else, been drinking all evening in and out of bars and cafes and I'm here in a drunken brawl. Time goes so fast and he has a bloodied face. I can't remember coming here or how many places. Drink has the better of me and I've not eaten since midday. Hands are pushing the fat man. Palms in his face and now a fist. There's a German too with a mighty swing. Little men spitting snot and blood are willing to match him with head butts and a smack in the jaw. I walk around it to get another drink and there's the door. If I keep walking, I'll

23

be away from it all. Go home to bed now and save some money and avoid a fight and be up early in the morning to phone for a new job.

5. Last autumn, in custody.

.

If the poor policeman wanted to catch me it would have been easy but he was down looking at his dead dog, what was left of it. There were two streaks of matted blood along the rails. The rest of it would have been tattooed to the buffers, arriving in Birmingham's New Street Station at platform four.

I was trying to escape, tearing at grass and nettles. No doubt, I was a nervous wreck, having just missed the biggest wallop of my life from a speeding train. The embankment was so wet and slimy that I must have been trampling and sliding on the slope for several minutes. Suddenly I found a footing and was up and away. I could still escape in the dark but I bumped into O'Hanagan's shovel. It caught me across the forehead causing me to lose my balance and I fell back down the embankment.

Fair does to O'Hanagan, simple as he was, he didn't say a word about the murder. Only that he might have, or might not have buried a body. It was a straight answer to a question. O'Hanagan was too stupid to know that the policeman was only making fun of him when he asked the first time. When he was asked the second time, O'Hanagan began to stutter, insisting that he did not bury a body but had only intended to bury the shovel.

In another country and without full identification, we would have been treated as illegal aliens and would have been locked up. However, the English have a tolerant nature despite their tone and even the British police have their pleasant moments. They were everywhere, looking at bits of the dog, the shovel, peeping in our pockets, and asking for more identification. Then they asked if we were fighting. That was my cue.

"Yes, officer, we had a terrible row and it was all my fault," and I apologised to O'Hanagan. I shook hands with him to make it seem sincere, hoping that the police would leave it at that and tell us to go home now and behave. But O'Hanagan said, no, we were not fighting.

"Ah, but, Bart, what would we be fighting for? And in any case, for wasn't it my fault if we were fighting?" Then he wanted to shake hands with me and nearly pulled my arm from my shoulder.

It wasn't my fault that the dog leapt in front of the train. At the police station, the sergeant accepted my story about a fear of Alsatians from an early age.

"A hound with a head on it t'at would frighten a bishop, and teeth in its jaws the size of a shark's." I was speaking the truth, for I had been bitten one day while coming home from school. It was easy to recall the time when Murphy's mad mongrel leaped up and nearly took the head from me. I didn't need to make up a bit of it to convince them that, even as an adult, I would bolt like a horse from the bark of a dog.

O'Hanagan was in another room, refusing to let go of the shovel, I heard. One by one they would go in to interrogate him about why he was following me in the middle of the night along railway tracks. One by one they came back to my room shaking their heads, throwing eyes to the ceiling and then one of them needed a cigarette.

"We're only asking simple questions," said the bewildered sergeant. "Just doing our job."

"He follows me everywhere, officer. And I promised his mother, an aunt, that I would look after him in England. And he's a handful."

There were three of them, nodding their heads in agreement. It was true enough, a Protestant country where a young simple Catholic boy isn't safe to walk the streets.

"I must confess, officer, t'at sometimes I have an urge to lose him."

"Yep," agreed the sergeant without a hint of friendliness. "And stick a plaster on that head," he said to a constable. "I'll try again to get some sense from the baboon."

The constable applied first aid to my blooded head, dabbing it with cotton wool while I sat stiff and upright. I could barely hear O'Hanagan in the other room, his heavy bog brogue bellowing through the wall. He seemed to be insisting that there was no blood on the shovel, that he was only digging holes and that they could ask me if they didn't believe him.

"Your cousin is a turnip," said the constable snapping a plastic lid onto the first aid box.

"Ah, well, he's a distant cousin."

"Yeh, the more distance the better."

Then a cup of tea and a digestive biscuit arrived for me. I was left alone and O'Hanagan was still insisting in the next room. When the sergeant came out he didn't even try to hide the words following him out through the door; O'Hanagan was confessing that he had dug a grave.

"We have to look for a grave early in the morning," said the sergeant. "Just in case there is something rational coming out of him."

"Ah, now, officer, it's the effect of his first day in England. He'll be looking for a job, a grave-digger. But he's confused and thinks he's in an interview for the job."

"If you'll come this way, sir."

They showed me to a cell. As I passed the room I could hear O'Hanagan insisting it was just a shallow grave to bury a shovel but never a body and that the spade only cracked the skull.

It was the first bed to touch my back since the killing, yet I couldn't sleep. Sheer luxury but thoughts filled my head, uneasy like indigestion. Trespassing was a serious offence but I knew it was only a holding charge. Held at Her Majesty's Pleasure. I wondered. If so, I was in good company for so were many of Ireland's heroes. Prison decor probably hadn't changed since the times of Wolf Tone or Oscar Wilde. The walls were a pale putrid blue, cold in colour and to touch, bare, in need of curtains or a picture, maybe a portrait of the Queen. The light went out and I rolled over, wrapping myself in the blanket. We must have looked an odd couple armed with a shovel, and O'Hanagan stuttering about skulls and shovels for a shallow grave. It was no wonder we were spending our first night in England under lock and key. Throughout the night my insides were bubbling with palpitations while I calculated our chances. It was still good, with no mention of Ballybog or Scullivan. But why should the police have serious suspicions? I was obviously paranoid. Maybe I looked like someone in England, a wanted man, a robber, terrorist, a murderer in need of a shave. There was little chance that O'Hanagan would be mistaken for someone else because no one else had a head like his, a jaw the size of a housebrick. It was like this all night, possibilities still passing through my head when morning crept in through a high up window.

It was pouring with rain out there, bouncing on the tarmac. The police had had enough of us. They were up early looking for a grave or buried bombs or some damaged skull along the railway tracks, from one end of England to the other by the look of them. As they returned, the sergeant gave them tea and was collecting shovels and telling them to kick off their rubber boots. There were towels and newspapers and chunks of mud from the front door to the back. Their poor faces, I could see, had been pelted by the weather.

O'Hanagan was laughing.

"They didn't ask if the grave was in England or in Ireland, and I was clever enough not to answer a question until it was asked."

"O'Hanagan, shut the feck up until we're out of here." I needed to get him further from the scene of the crime, to where they don't speak English. "Berlin is a great place for earning money, O'Hanagan. We'll go straight to a Euroline ticket office and make a reservation, the moment they let us go. If they ever do."

"That would be a good one, Bart, it would."

They were eager to get rid of us. Keep away from railway tracks, they said, because it's dangerous and against the law. On the way out O'Hanagan told a policeman that he was off to Berlin. The officer was sitting in the corridor, sipping tea. He had two hands wrapped around his mug to feel the warmth and bring his fingers back to life.

"That's a good idea," he replied, "but why stop there, what about Siberia?"

"It tis," continued O'Hanagan, "tis a grand idea." He liked it when strangers spoke back to him. "Tis a grand place for earning money, Bart told me."

"Did he?"

"He did. For digging trenches. And have you done much digging yourself?"

Then the policeman stood up and poured tea onto O'Hanagan's big head. I took O'Hanagan by the arm and guided him away because there are times when a bit of police brutality is justified.

6. This morning, I'm out to get that job.

I did it. Last night I walked around that heap of brawling boozing bodies and straight out through the door. I remember a fist flying into a fat man's face, and he returned a forearm smash that buffed some teeth. It was a swamp in there and I was drowning but I hung onto a beer mat, like it was a rubber ring. There was a phone number on it that could save my life.

Despite my heavy head this morning I'm enjoying this walk to find a phone. Out of bed I was to make a call. This corner seems immersed in coffee aroma. It's seeping out through café walls. Maybe the door and woodwork is marinated in it. Birds are singing and, *guten morgen*, I say to strangers, a trickle of strollers and striders heading for their Saturday shops. I'll phone from a kiosk. Could have called from my lodgings but I'm too clever now to pour coins into those private phones. Automated legalised robbery. The number is written on a beer mat and there's something scribbled next to it: Terry has a fucked-up back. I vaguely remember him being mentioned and it's his job that I'm chasing. Terry Thin was paid cash for a proper job.

"Hello, can I speak to Connor, please."

"What about?"

"About a job. Terry's job."

"Do you know the job?"

"I do, of course. I was just leaving town but heard you were desperate for a man to work up top."

"Were you talking to Terry?"

"I was," I lie, "last night." I think Terry was the one person I didn't speak to after I was fired up with booze. But this is not the time for actualities down the phone.

"We need a good man to start on Monday morning."

"Well, I'm your man."

"And are you afraid of heights?"

"I am not, not a bit," I reply. I'm only afraid of falling.

"Where are you? Maybe we can meet..."

So that's it, a meeting arranged. Work for Monday morning with cash in the hand and no questions asked. That's the place to meet with the taste of coffee seeping out through cracks in mortar and under the front door. It opens and out comes the waitress. The winter's coming too but still warm enough to sit out here. It's a great day, free from work and that irritating Itch Wool. Connor's on his way to give me a proper job for Monday morning.

"Coffee," I say to the waitress standing tall in her stripy dress, apron, whatever it is; she looks like a tube of toothpaste. "Danke."

Paying tax annoys me now. It was okay at the beginning but now I'm feeling used. I'm annoyed to see deductions, my contribution for others to learn the language. I'm not a racist but too mean to support schemes for foreigners. I'm one myself who enjoys the company of strangers but I'm not paying for their free lessons. It's a dog eat dog world while English speakers are not foreign enough to join the class. I'm peeved, begrudging those claiming benefits while I must work. Dirty jobs are all I get, like the others who fail some bureaucratic test. A job for cash is what we need to keep our names off computer files. But no more dirty jobs. No more Itch Wool and what I get goes in my pocket.

"A grand day," he says, disturbing my morning mood. "A grand day," holding out a hand. "Connor McHaul."

"It is," getting up to shake hands with him, a middle-aged hefty fellow with a belly that strains the buttons on his shirt.

"So," he says, sitting at the table, "we have a brave volunteer, ready to get in there for Monday morning?"

"The best day for starting work."

"Jaysus, it is. And what's your name again?"

"Bart."

"Well, Bart, you know the job, I suppose?"

"I do, of course."

"Ah, that's the man. It's short notice for us, to be left like this without a man at the top. Terry's back's gone all of a sudden. But I hear he was in pain for a long time. A serious ailment but kept it quiet. And tell me, you know the job?"

"Well, I wouldn't be wasting your time if I didn't. And tell me, tis all cash?"

"Ah, now, wait a moment," holding a palm to me. He leans back to call the stripy waitress. "Missus, kann ich a pot of tea haben when you're ready? Danke."

She places my coffee on the table.

"You see, Connor, I was heading out east for a job. But I heard you were stuck for a man. T'at you were able to pay cash…"

"Agh, but those days are gone." He says it softly, with sadness.

"Almost," I agree. "I don't like the tax…"

"Jaysus, you're right."

"But I'll tell you this, I'm your man to do the job. A fair day's work for a fair day's wage." I'm in a buoyant morning mood, surprising myself with my confidence. "But ask no questions and you'll get told no lies."

"But do you know the job?"

"I do, of course, why wouldn't I?"

I sip my coffee, feeling the richness on my tongue and up against the roof of my mouth. For a poor man without work or benefits or a legal home, this is extravagance. I have only worked one week here, for a pittance, virtually penniless after running from Holland. The occasional drink at night was medicinal, to keep me sane and to hold my palpitations at bay, to stop me bursting out in bouts of paranoia.

And O'Hanagan, the cause of it all was as cool as a cat. No, he was cold like a corpse, oblivious to my nervous disposition. Then we were working with the Itch Wool, exploited because we didn't speak the language. Yet we were not considered foreign enough to get help. O'Hanagan was put lifting heavy boxes and I was stuck down a dump to lag a pipe. I had lengths of it to wrap in Itch Wool, in and out of holes persuading the lethal fabric into place without breaking it. I had to wrestle with it, so of course bits broke off, crumbled at the corners, shedding millions of irritating micro slithers into my breathing space. The dirty dust penetrated my mask, up my nose to clog my nostrils. More came in when I removed the mask. I had to take it off to let out the snot. I was sneezing and coughing up phlegm. It was on my clothes, around my cuffs and collar, creeping closer to my skin to cause a fiery rash about my wrists and neck. Then it was inside my goggles, carried by the sweat of my brow and I felt micro slithers perched upon my eyelashes. I wiped my brow and felt a million pins pierce my skin. No, I did not like that job.

"I'll be honest with you Connor, I'm a wanted man."

"You are? And for what?"

"I have the taxman after me."

"Ah, for Jaysus sake, that's no great sin at all. If that's the only crime on your books, you'll be by-passing purgatory." He looks around to see if his tea is coming.

"Well, Connor, I'd rather stay off computers…"

"Well, I'll tell you what we do now. We pay you a small salary and big expenses. Tax your wage and your expenses go cash in the hand…"

That's what I wanted to hear. Connor turns to see his pot of tea coming on a tray. A middle-aged woman in a coat too long is waiting for the waitress to go away. She's holding cardboard with a message scrawled in German. Obviously begging and as she comes to our table a child appears at her side. Like the tinkers back home, and Fiona the feminist said we shouldn't call them that anymore. They're travelling people. Me too. Was but now I'm going to find a better home and send the bill to Connor. The woman with the cardboard is staring at Connor, obviously a wealthier looking man.

"Jaysus," he roars, "can I not have my breakfast in peace?"

My feelings too. Nothing worse than beggars disturbing your meal but I'm a hero for a moment, giving her coins. Some are foreign and useless but I have cleared out my pocket and my conscience. Wouldn't I have spent more if I'd used that private phone back at the lodgings?

"Christ, Connor, we'd earn it in a few minutes."

"That's what the last Good Samaritan said and encouraged her to come here."

"You're right I suppose."

"Missus," he suddenly calls, and reaches out to give the child money, notes if I'm not mistaken. "Now they'll be hunting around tables."

"And the child," I say, "isn't it a fine lesson he's seen today, the rewards for begging?"

"And did you know Terry?" asks Connor.

"Did I? You mean, do I?"

"Sorry," roars Connor, "Jaysus, sorry. It's a terrible sin to talk as if the poor man was already dead! And his woman, works in a strip club or some joint."

"Is that so?"

"So I heard now. But a nice bit of talent from what I saw of her." He pours hot water on his tea bag.

I remember her being mentioned in the pub last night. Candy. I dislike Terry in the same way as I loathed Scullivan. There was something flaunting about him, the way he wore jewellery outside his clothes. Gold is conspicuous against a faded T-shirt with a frayed collar. Wealth but no style.

"I know Terry, and I know his job. And let me tell you t'at I wouldn't be after his job, I don't need it, but it was him that said you were desperate." Connor lifts his hand to indicate that I need say no more. "Well, the job's yours. Any friend of Terry is a friend of the firm. Anyway, Bart, what part of the old country are you from? Obviously the wild west."

"But I haven't been there for many years."

"Is that so? And you've still got the brogue. Like you've just come off the boat from, let me guess…"

"Well, it's difficult these days to get away from the Irish wherever we ramble."

"Well now, I bet I could pinpoint where you're from with that brogue."

"Is that the time?" I cry, getting to my feet before he asks if I'm from Ballybog. "Connor, you'd better write down the address there and I'll see you bright and early on Monday morning. I have an important appointment to keep. Saturday is such a busy day for me…"

"For sure you'll come around the house one night. And which part did you say you were from?"

"I will for sure. And where's the waitress?"

Sometimes the palpitations return with a vengeance, Scullivan taking revenge. My face is on fire with a simmering beneath my skin. Connor didn't even utter Ballybog but Bally something was about to bubble out of his mouth. It seemed as if he was about to pinpoint where I was on the night of the killing as easy as he'd finger my house. I stride towards town because it helps to dissipate energy if I walk with long steps. A nice clean street this. No cow shit on the roads like back home or rubbish at the corners like in London. The beggar and her child turn to see me, holding out a hand as I pass. I've already given.

That was hypocrisy, donating a pittance to impress Connor with my charitable manner. Throwing coins to the poor and I might be one myself by the end of the week. Kicked off the job for being a donkey without a clue what to do. I expect she's from Romania. The beggar. Or Slovakia. Fiona the feminist said I shouldn't stereotype folk but I can't help it. It's anticipation, knowing where that person is coming from before they tell me, where in the head. Experience tells me that no one approaches me in the street to give. They are all on the take. Experience also tells me that politically correct folk react harsher towards those asking for crumbs than those who take our time.

I wonder what Mom's been thinking all this time. She must have been going out of her mind with worry but I really was unable to write. I had the shakes and gone with the faeries. Mom must have thought I'd eloped with Fiona, - The Goat, she called her. She wasn't so bad but her personality would evoke the worst parental traits in any mother. Fiona said that Germans hung their duvets from windows. She shouldn't stereotype them because folk don't do it on this street. Maybe Berlin traffic fumes would contaminate the duck down stuffing.

I need a drink. Better to have it in a place with strangers where no one pinpoints where I'm from. That would suit me fine, a café with a table circled with empty chairs. Just me and a jug of beer and drink myself silly on Saturday morning. But I must collect my mail so I'm back to the Irish pub, the Thatched Cottage beneath a concrete shell. I'm still in my cynical mood, wanting to call it The Mortgage, The Inheritance, The Liquidised Bank Account. How clean it is, swept and cleansed of stupor. The wooden floor is still tacky with booze though, clinging to the soles of my shoes.

"Rita, any post for me?"

"A letter from Ireland. May I have the stamp?"

"You may, of course. And a pint of stout." A few heads in this morning, almost noon. Couples sipping coffee over at the tables and three lads lined up along the bar. A dead head at the end, the awful state of him so early in the day.

"There you are, now," and she hands me the envelope minus the stamp. It will be a sad day for collectors when the European Union adopts a common postage stamp.

I rip open the envelope for the first bit of news in a year. My mother has been in an awful state and is so happy to hear from me. No, she did not receive my earlier letters, isn't the post office in a bad way these days? she writes. *And do you not have telephones over there or what sort of a backward place are you living in? And do you know the whereabouts of poor Kevin O'Hanagan? He's gone missing too, and the police looking everywhere for him, but of course, he'd be too simple to go off to foreign lands like you. Aren't you clever enough, and what a notion you took? But you always were off gallivanting without ever a plan in your head or a penny in your pocket. But did O'Hanagan follow you? and maybe got lost somewhere, and I hope he wasn't murdered, and who told you about a murder? Aren't there murders now every month in Ireland, soon it will be as bad as New York with one murder every three minutes. Things are getting very bad here, even Mrs Meehan had her bicycle stolen in broad daylight. And poor Scullivan, your friend from up at the boreen, dead and buried since before Christmas and you missed a wonderful funeral. But sad the way he went and we're still not sure how it happened because they're too sly to admit to anything. No doubt there was drink involved, been drinking all night but sure isn't there a place for all of us in heaven, God bless you. And there's been people looking for you too, business people by the looks of them and they say it's important. So I gave them your address.*

"What?"

"Pardon?"

"N- n- nothing, Rita. Just reading aloud. Gossip from back home." She gave them my address, business people by the looks of them and they say it's important. *So I gave them your address. They asked were you living there, in a thatched cottage in Berlin?* Who? I look around in case detectives are stalking this pub. No one's looking at me.

"Pint of stout" says Rita, placing it on the counter. "You look terrible. Is it bad news?"

"It's not. Not at all." But bad enough to force me away from here and all the Irish pubs. Detectives have my address, albeit a Berlin bar. A thatched cottage. Business people, she says. Plain clothes detectives. "Rita, Rita, I need a drink, a whiskey."

"Looks like you need a big one. Are you sure it's not bad news?"

"No. Yes. Not really. Just the taxman. But he has this address."

"Taxman," frowns the drunk at the end of the bar. "You might be dead tomorrow. Don't worry about it."

"Terry," shouts Rita, "shut up if you can't stop talking about dying."

I look at him; it is! It's Terry Thin, looking worse than before. The whiskey burns my throat. I go back to my letter. *They must be business people. First you were gone and then O'Hanagan was gone. We thought you were taken by the faeries. They were wondering did you leave together, and asking questions.*

"What's wrong with talking about dying?" continues Terry.

"Terry," says Rita, "just shut up and drink your drink."

"I don't mind having an illness," he persists, "but can't even talk 'bout it, like I got a disease. It's not contagious yer know."

I turn to see Terry. He has an illness and I have his job. His skin is withered and red with booze. The wrinkled face seems deflated, a slow puncture as his head, his skull sinks inside, slipping down his neck. It's a flabby neck, the only part of him with fat on it. The rest is skinny, definitely dying. I can't imagine him on a construction site last week, climbing scaffold and walking beams or lifting loads. I can't imagine him out in public, in a wind or near the traffic where he could get blown away. He lifts his glass and sips beer, now a smaller glass, an easier one to lift. A whiskey chaser. It's bad manners to stare at people, especially while they're dying and so I turn away.

"Rita, if anyone comes into this pub looking for me, anyone, tell them nothing. Nothing. The taxman might come snooping about."

Maybe it's not the illness, maybe it's the booze. Terry has probably been drinking all night. I'm not much better so I'll make this my last drink. Get out to the street to see what Germany looks like in the daylight, have a walk while I'm a free man.

"Rita, auf wiedersehen."

"Bye, bye."

"Aey, mate," shouts Terry, "one for the road." He comes towards me, holding stools to support himself.

"I won't, but cheers."

It's a lovely day out here. Great to be free but maybe I should go back to Terry. He's drunk, too delicate to be left alone with gold draped around his neck and his washed-out T-shirt. I'll suggest a drink and escort him to another bar, and then see him safely home. It's the least I can do because I'm going to interrogate him about his job. I have to, because I don't have a clue what I'm suppose to be doing on Monday morning.

7.   Last autumn, on a bus and getting off the bus and getting back on the bus.

.

London was bigger and more congested than I ever imagined a city to be. I didn't mind it being unfriendly because the less I had to talk, the less I had to lie. Look what happened the last time I spoke to a stranger in England, a policeman. It was better to be like the others and keep our distance. To be fair to them, they were not hostile but just busy, hurrying for buses as if there would never be another, and in and out of shops without as much as a hello to another shopper, or time to take in the state of the sky. I looked up and saw that clouds were gathering over London, the same as they would above Ballybog. It was like a glimpse of back home. On the street there was chaos, bumper to bumper traffic with engines throbbing and then revving to inch forward to take a space. There was a yellow cement mixer with a barrel rolling around on its back, reversing while pedestrians were walking in its way. As stubborn as pigs and the driver kept creeping back, bold to the last millimetre and then a woman hurrying for her life.

"Tis an awful busy place, tisn't it, Bart?"

"It is, O'Hanagan. Now, in here for the bus to Berlin, change in Cologne." That was a far away place. I watched him get on it. He was going on sideways, telling me that he would change buses in Germany, and would get on one for Berlin.

"Good man," I replied.

The shovel was pointing up to the roof and the spade was wrapped in a plastic bag from Marks & Spencer's. Like myself he had bought new clothes, a change of jocks and socks. He had them stuffed in his pockets with packaged sandwiches.

"Can I change in Cologne for a bus to Berlin?" he asked the driver. The driver was busy with a big bag, coming backwards, struggling with the most awkward lump that could wedge onto the aisle of a bus. He was trying to get it off the bus. O'Hanagan was asking again. He wanted to be sure that he could change buses in Cologne. So he tapped the driver on the shoulder. It was for my benefit, to give me peace of mind, to be sure that he would be in Germany, like I said he should be. But the big bag seemed to be getting bigger, or at least heavier. The driver was labouring with it to lift it over his head to clear the seats. The head-rests were too high and causing an obstruction. So was O'Hanagan, getting under the bag, asking again.

"I can, can 't I?" he was asking. The driver was saying excuse me in a very polite manner. O'Hanagan was saying, "Tell Bart that I can change buses in Cologne." I was telling him that it didn't matter anymore, just get on the bus and feck off. But first, get off the bus to give the driver space. Get out of the way. The bag was wedged against the ceiling, with one end pressed against the driver's head and the other end being stabbed by the shovel. "I can change buses in Cologne, I can, can I not?" O'Hanagan wanted an answer. He got it, the bag full butt in the face. O'Hanagan, the shovel and the luggage came flying out of the bus.

"And get lost, you big bollocks," said the driver. He had a temper.

It turned into a beautiful day. Grey sky with bits of blooming blue opening up and then the sun itself shining through. The traffic moved slow enough for me to check that O'Hanagan was still on the bus. I went with it on a hired bicycle, out of Victoria station and down the Old Kent Road with crawling traffic. There were places where I had to wait for it to catch up with me, but sure enough, O'Hanagan was still sitting with the shovel near the window at the back. It was a sad, dumb face, staring through the glass, at traffic and buildings. His lower lip protruded and curled, and his eyes were round and watery, ready to burst. Like a child, he clenched the shovel as if it was a comfort blanket. But it was no time for emotions, he had to go. I knew that once the bus was on the motorway, there was little chance of him getting off. I watched the back of it, in the middle lane, motoring towards the coast.

That was the first time that I got rid of him. Guilt grew inside me, like a rising damp, a fungus. I was wondering day and night what would become of O'Hanagan, wandering aimlessly in foreign fields. Then I was agonising but at least the guilt swamped the murderous memories, quenched the fiery thoughts of the actual killing. I needed that, space to sleep and let O'Hanagan look after himself.

8. Today, I need Terry but Nicki's dancing on my mind, bouncy bouncy on my mind.   .

The week started okay but now I'm worried, concerned by the way the job is working by itself. There's momentum, automation without my participation, a clockwork mechanism all around, which is strange because I'm supposed to be the boss. I didn't know that Terry was a foreman, or gangerman, or some sort of working supervisor spearheading the building towards the sky. I'm disturbed by the confidence others have in me, as if my reputation has come before me. Everyone else is at ease because of me, Bart the Top Man, the construction expert. They are all waiting for me to guide the metal lengths into place. Even the crane driver came over to shake hands with me, speaking in English to say welcome and asking about Terry. Fine, I said, he's just fine, although the last time I saw Terry he was vomiting into an ashtray, overflowing and a rope of phlegm upon the table. Nothing to do with his illness, but the booze. We went to a few bars and talked about work. I listened while he boasted about all the skyscrapers that exist in this world because of him. Then, when he was really drunk, I asked him, what was the job, what exactly do you do, Terry? Because I've got your job on Monday morning and not a clue about what to do.

Today started good too, like every other day, until Gunter reared up on me. He's stumpy, short for a German but I suppose I shouldn't stereotype them all as having to be tall and loud. But he is loud, a fierce voice that carries across the site. I went down the ladders and tried to talk to him but couldn't get near for the barrage of words. He pointed to the yellow cabin office. I had to scramble over heaps of mud and before I reached the door Connor came out to bombard me with more words.

"Bart, are you not lining up the holes?"

"I am, of course," I lied. I didn't know what he was talking about. Suddenly, I remembered something that one of the Turks had said about hammering in wedges so holes would line up and bolts would drop into place.

"Well, Jaysus, Gunter's saying none of the holes are in line and not a bolt in place."

"Now, now, Connor, don't worry a moment more. The holes are lined up, and I'll have all the bolts in place while they're deciding what to do next. He's an awful man for exaggerating. And he won't speak English, but barking orders like a dog."

"Ah, he's a bit of a bastard, alright. But get up there now and fix the bolts for feck sake. Don't give the pig's bollocks anymore to say."

"Connor, it's as good as done." And it was. I have all the bolts in place now and tightened. I'm mastering the job bit by bit but the young lads working under me are beginning to suspect that I don't know my arse from my elbow.

I can't walk down a city street now without gazing up at buildings, along walls knowing that beneath that concrete there are vertical lengths of metal, braced with links and bolted at the ends. I understand it now but I can't afford more mistakes if I want to be with the building to the top. I'll meet Terry and ask him about banging in wedges, tightroping along a beam and doing the hand signals. He's not such a bad head. After my ordeal with O'Hanagan I should be able to handle the likes of Terry.

There's a crowd of lads in the Thatched Cottage. When the pub is hopping like this so early in the evening you'd think there must be plenty of work in town. These are not tourists but workers, contractors. Guest workers is how the Continentals call us. We're not immigrants or economic refugees because we're not bothered what the natives call us.

"Missionaries," Terry said. "On a mission, and yer cheeky bastards try to tax me." That was the last he said before dropping his head into a puddle of vomit. I was drunk myself, embarrassed and didn't want to be seen with him. I'll squeeze through this untidy mob now to see if I can find him.

Every moment though, I'm checking nosy faces and listening for voices fishing for information. This is a perfect jungle for a detective to creep up on me. The crowd is due to a sudden bout of unemployment. If these lads are not working then they're in here looking for a new job or a booze-up. Always, one for the road. There's a lot of able-bodied men who would have taken Terry's job if I was not so quick last weekend. There he is, holding the bar. I'll squeeze through the crowd and ask about the job before he dies.

"Terry, my man, you survived?"

"What's that, pal?"

"I was saying, you survived the other night."

"Who wants to know?"

"Christ, I was just asking, concerned like. You were in an awful state."

"Aey, yer no fucking oil painting yerself, like does some cunt wanna make an issue 'bout it?"

"For feck sake, you lanky streak of piss, I was just making conversation," leaving him swaying with his drink.

He was a bit like that the other night too, so I left him to fend for himself. There were times I felt like giving him what I gave Scullivan. Although, I never actually killed Scullivan. It was O'Hanagan with the shovel but I did have a temper that night. It was building for years, naturally because of the close proximity with an arrogant neighbour. But now I walk away from them. I don't need those people. Yes I do. I need to know about Terry's job or I'll be relegated to the poor refugees' class. I'll be worse because fugitives can't use the system but are down with illegal immigrants. Begging is the only option for beings on the street. But illegal foxes like Terry are above it all with offshore bank accounts and exploiting his German-speaking girlfriend. In his drunken stupor he revealed it all, not just the job but the maverick's lifestyle.

"Rita," I say, "has anyone been in looking for me."

"Like who?"

"Like the taxman?"

"No one's asked. A pint of stout?"

"Not today, Rita. I have to leave. And if anyone asks, say you don't know me."

"A postcard."

"Oh, that's grand." I take it, a postcard from Amsterdam. It's from O'Hanagan.

"Sorry, mate," interrupts Terry. "Didn't recognise yer back there in the dark. Wanna a drink?"

"I have to leave, Terry. In a hurry."

I want to get out of here before a heavy hand lands on my shoulder. Mr Rabbit? Bart Rabbit from Ballybog? Could we have a few words with you? About a friend of yours found dead on the Boreen High Road. Anyway, I want to read my post. What a surprise, a card from O'Hanagan and he writes quite well.

"Na, na, one for the road," insists Terry, following me to the door. "Just a misunderstanding."

"Well, how about one in another place? I can't stay here, there's a man from the tax coming to get me."

"Say no more, Squire, know the score," winking, and he almost keeled. Just caught the doorframe before he fell out onto the street.

It's an outing for him, to go to another bar because folk in there are tired of listening to his moaning monologues. He doesn't actually talk about his illness but boasts about his past, what a great innings he has had, and still has, and could go a few rounds with any man in the bar. He staggers sideways, turning to wait for me. "That one there, Squire, worked on it to the top, bitch of a building..." boasting along the street, the highest and fastest and the most complicated contractions. "... Couldn't get blokes back then to run jobs an' bits o' work. Came in an' sub-contracted we did, like. Woz na afraid to gerra hands dirty. We'd do der shuttering work az well, double up an' shovel concrete. Fucking Krauts never seen nowt like uz. We were fucking brilliant. Never seen nowt like uz. Then the metalwork..." Lifting arms to explain like a puppet on a string.

"Here," I suggest. "In here." Before you fall over. It's a safe café stuffed with bodies. There's space for standing at the bar and he's still talking. I'm trying to read my post, O'Hanagan's scrawl, while Terry reveals the secrets about slotting girders into place. The hand signals are common sense but he's going to show me the markings.

"Excuse me," he slurs, towards a woman at the bar. "Got a pen? Danke." He explains it on beer mats. Work will be easy after this if I could just concentrate but I'm reading O'Hanagan's scribble. It's all over the place like flying off the postcard to knock a drink. And now he does it, Terry knocks a drink, trying to write and explain in his stupor and he wallops a cocktail.

"Sorry, love. Listen, no problem. What yer drinking?"

While Terry looks for a cloth or buys them drinks, I'll read my post. O'Hanagan's writing is a gas. He is still living in a butterfly hotel, near a butterfly canal in Amsterdam. And everything is butterfly. The other words are block letters but butterfly is scrawled like a doctor's signature. I expect he scribbled it on purpose to hide the fact that he can't spell it. But it's still amazing that someone as stupid as O'Hanagan could even think of that.

"... I said, you wanna beer?"

"Sorry," looking up. "Sorry, Terry. Sure. Just a small one."

I go back to O'Hanagan's postcard. I suppose he means a beautiful hotel near a beautiful canal. Everything is beautiful. He goes on to say that he has a new job taking Nicki to the casino and making sure no one steals her money. He writes casino in the same style that I remember seeing it on a neon sign in Amsterdam.

His employer is chic, expensive, never cheap. Nicki likes her gentlemen friends to wine and dine her and she seldom says thank you. The privilege is ours to show our appreciation. On a leash, she led us to exclusive shops, to spend that money I earned lagging pipes. Then it was the best hotel.

"A double room, sir?" the receptionist asked.

"The penthouse," Nicki said. "And a single room for the gentleman." She made a scene when I disagreed. "Yes, you're quiet right, darling."

Kissed my cheek and stroked my nose with her teasing finger. "Cancel the penthouse suite," she told the receptionist, "And order a cab. I'm going home."

If I stayed, it was here, in the hotel that the lucky gentleman might get his wicked way. It was seldom, I expect. She would let us touch, just enough for arousal to make us pant. "Naughty boy," running fingers behind my ears and around my neck to tug my hair. She could hold her man by his hair, sometimes by his ears, and plant a kiss upon his lips while he trembled on his knees. Suddenly, she called room service to order wine.

"Wine? More wine?" her gentleman cried, getting to his feet.

"Yes, darling, more wine. I don't like that wine, I want another wine, new wine."

Heavy breathing is all she wanted, to make me jealous. It was fun to call friends and invite them to her penthouse home. Come and have a party at his expense, and maybe *you* can make him laugh. "Oh, jealous baby, darling please, just a few friends to help us drink the wine." Friends, male or female, acquaintances would do, to make her gentleman jealous and sometimes fly into a rage.

"Room service."

"Oh, thank you, you've brought the wine, and while you're here, would you show this gentleman back to his room." His single room. Kevin, she calls him, Kevin O'Hanagan at her bidding, the Ballybog bouncer on duty outside her bedroom door, "In here and escort this man back to his single room."

"… Do yer fucking want this or not?"

"Pardon, oh, sorry, Terry…"

"Fuck. Yer ask me to come for a drink an' then ignore me."

"Sorry, Terry. Good man, cheers. Go on now, what were you saying about the job. That's the difficult part, the metal plates?"

"Is for some people. Piece o' piss…"

I slip O'Hanagan's postcard into my pocket and forget about Nicki, watching Terry's demonstration. I'm safe. No detective will come to arrest me here. It's night school, listening to my drunken tutor. Beer dribbles down his bony knuckles as he sways, constructing the carcass, the metal ribs of the structure. We're getting drunk again, Terry and myself in a café assembling a skeleton and in the morning I'm really going to be the man at the top.

9. Last autumn, got myself a bed in a box.

.

In my lifetime Ireland had known backwardness, and folk emigrated to any place that would take them. Then the country became a prosperous part of Europe with tourists swarming in and up the hills. Pubs became nightclubs and drinks became small and expensive with miniature umbrellas on toothpicks. Foreigners bought bits of souvenir bog and got photographed with donkeys. They seldom came up to the bog though, where time, place and people stayed backward. That is, slow and simple compared with the flat part, down where Scullivan inherited the farm. No doubt he would have had cocktails. I know that Fiona, who often scorned his sexist antics, went to his party. Back there, they would have supposed O'Hanagan was working up the mountain, miles from a telephone. If he found one, he wouldn't know how to use it. They knew that. After inserting coins he'd spend ages listening to the dial tone, and if he heard pips, he'd stand back to watch for them to appear. As for writing, I don't expect anyone knew he could. I didn't.

Depression rather than relief came over me after putting O'Hanagan on the bus to Germany. I got some comfort in assuming that O'Hanagan would find an Irish pub somewhere and meet English speakers. Maybe he would learn the local language because he enjoyed saying strange sounds, repeating like a parrot. Hard work was no problem for O'Hanagan so he could at least make money. Anyway, he had to go. I had nightmares about meeting him in some pub in England or on a building site. Just imagining his stupidity brought on palpitations. Hello there, he would shout through the crowd, do you remember the time when we battered Scullivan? We stood up to him that night, didn't we, Bart? Shut-up, I'd be saying, and he'd be telling people it didn't matter now because we killed him. Didn't we, Bart, didn't we kill him? And people listening and palpitations driving perspiration out through my forehead with the fear. Maybe he wasn't *that* stupid but I never took risks. I avoided Irish pubs in London.

There was not enough money to take me to Spain so I decided to stay a while in England, to earn a few bob. London was bigger than all the other cities I had ever been to put together. I had been to three in that hectic week: Dublin, Liverpool and Birmingham. But London was a sprawling metropolis with suburbs and then another city centre and then more suburbs and back to another cluttered downtown. I was on a train en route to answer an advert for accommodation. I was near the window looking down at congested streets and into back gardens littered with children's tricycles and deflated paddling pools. It was in the evening newspaper, the advert. It said a studio on the edge of London for a working gentleman. But I wasn't so green and naive to think it would be anymore than a room with a bed, floor and maybe a television. Only a bedsit but it would be away from any Irish neighbours. The train was hurtling through tunnels, alongside junk yards and rows of Victorian houses, and in the distance, tens of tower blocks standing like giant chess pieces. Between the lumps of concrete and slabs of tarmac, greenery was sprouting out. Bushy backyards, weeds in yellow brickwork cracks and wild embankments sloping up and then down to the back gardens. We came to villages nicer than you'd see in Ireland, quaint but sandwiched between grey industrial sites instead of greenery.

A girl beside me was eating a sandwich. Maybe she was a woman, I couldn't see but had an awful urge to turn and look. The sandwich came from Marks & Spencer, out of a packet, like the one O'Hanagan bought and stuffed in his pocket with jocks and socks. People didn't talk in London, not so much. They sat upright, as stiff as Scullivan, as we sped over roads and roofs. We were flying over more junkyards, redundant double-decker buses and cars piled onto cars like they were biscuit tins. It was a great place for bargains and I had a new bag of plumbing tools.

"A fine town for bargains," I eventually said to her, just to get a conversation going. She didn't reply for a while but glanced and then nodded an agreement.

"Ah, but it's not the best time. The January sales are the best time. And have you been here long?"

Christ, as Irish as myself and asking questions.

"No, no, n – not at all," I stuttered. "But yes I mean, years and years here. Up in Liverpool, born and bred, was only ever back t'ere for a weekend, years ago. No, I haven't been t'ere in years." I almost said I wasn't there when it happened, I know nothing and I murdered no one. She didn't accuse me of anything but I couldn't stop denying that I had ever been west of Dublin. "... Lovely place, I hear, but never been t'ere." I sweated and stuttered nonsense about having always been in England. She got off.

I eventually arrived at the edge of London, Essex, where the English countryside rolled up from railway embankments, wove between semi-detached houses and stretched out to rumbling motorways. The bedsit was a box. A bed in a box. More space in Scullivan's coffin. It was my first time inside a Protestant house and as I had heard, there was not a crucifix or a picture of a saint upon any wall. I was not a great one for religion but with the thoughts in my head and palpitations between my ribs, it might have been nice to have something to pray to. In school we were taught that they were a focal point in any room: portraits of the Virgin Mary Mother of God, the Sacred Heart of Jesus, St. Jude of the Hopeless, St. Bridget of the Biddies Ball, and the rest of them. Long before ceasing to pray at night, I had harboured heretical thoughts and challenged this view. I felt that, for me, the focal point of any room was the fireplace. It's a great comfort in troubled times to stare into flickering flames and ponder about possibilities. But Fires of Hell, I suddenly thought, a thorny thought, a sign for the future. Palpitations nearly choked me and I took a deep breath looking around my new home, a room in England to settle into and take it easy. Take it easy, I was saying, or stay cool, the way Americans would talk in films, in a thriller with a man on the run. I kept looking around my room. There was no fireplace, only a skinny radiator looking as cold as a fridge door in a morgue. There was no television. A sponge for a pillow. Then I saw a Bible beside the bed.

I went to pubs to watch the news and for a bit of warmth. Not a mention of the murder, and people coming in and out without as much as a row, just sipping drinks and quiet conversation. Very civilised and a lovely carpet.

"Alright, mate?"

"Alright," I'd reply, and lift my glass. I was calmer now. Yes, I was right to get rid of O'Hanagan. Could not have done this with him around, I decided, talking shite about graves and skulls. I'd lean on the bar and sip their Suffolk ale. Not a bad pint and I got to like it. No women on their own. One or two with men, powder puffed and their heads permed.

"Working around here?" someone asked.

"Was, but I'm finished, contract finished. Plumber..."

"Plumber? Yer need to talk to that ol' fucker in the corner."

That's how I got my first big break in plumbing, a barn conversion for an eccentric Englishman with more money than sense. He had his own design business but no knowledge of practicalities or building regulations. There was little need for anything I installed to be in working order but it had to look good. Pipes should never be vertical or horizontal, and every bend should be unique and coming loose from the wall to be a decorative feature. He loved my work, leaking or not, and recommended me to clients. I only worked for the rich. I got paid to install it, and paid more to remove it. It was always their own fault and they were so sorry to be wasting my time, ordering me to do crazy things with copper pipes. I grew to like the English. There was no need to be stuck with an Irish mob on a building site. The chances of ever meeting O'Hanagan again were, at this time, very slim.

My box room got smaller. The same putrid blue as in the cell at the police station. Going to bed had not changed much since my first night in England. The bed was a thin wafer and the walls seemed to close in when I put things on the floor. It took up space but I had to make a pile because the wardrobe was too small, like a coffin on its end. Not tall enough to fit a corpse as long as Scullivan. I was thinking like this a lot but there was little fear that he would come and haunt me while I was in Essex. I would be more afraid back in Ballybog where banshees came down from purple peaks, crying in the mist. No, I thought, noise and pollution were a repellent for ghosts, Scullivan's howling. I was more likely to be haunted by a car alarm or a throbbing diesel engine in the early hours.

"What on earth are you doing in your studio?" asked the landlady. She was looking at the pile on the floor. Studio, she called it. It was a large living room sliced into three with plasterboard walls. "What on earth is it?" She was shocked to see that I was collecting copper pipes.

"Ah, now, it's just for a while," I said. "It's all away on Saturday. To the junkyard." But she walked out.

Between bouts of plumbing, the murder would come to mind. Going to work was an escape from the thorny thoughts. Bending pipes and tightening valves dispersed the fragments from my head. Then it would come again like the blade of the shovel through my skull. The killing, I called it, because it was hardly intentional homicide, just a wallop on a drunken night that took the head off Scullivan. Or at least a chunk of it. Anyone who knew Scullivan's sarcastic and cynical nature would not blame another man for giving him a thump or a swipe with a shovel. But O'Hanagan didn't know his own strength, the way he couldn't spell his own name. Scullivan was dead and we had run away before there was time to think. Now a new thought was in my head, a thorn of a thing. While not feeling guilty for Scullivan's death, it was a bad deed to send a simpleton off to the other side of Europe. But I argued that it might do O'Hanagan good, like a kick up the arse instead of him moping up the mountain with only the goats and the yellow bog. The drive to Dublin had confirmed it, all the way in a car, and him sitting in the front. It was an adventure for him. He was used to rambling on his lonesome, and when in company he was better with strangers than with his own kind. Sure, it would be a powerful dose of an adventure for him. A better man he'd be for it.

"Na, sorry mate, it's for living in, not a poxy junkyard."

The landlord looked under the bed to see if there was any more. "Na, yer 'ave to move it." He didn't stay either, walked out before I had the chance to say that I'd take it away on Saturday. Then he was raring up on the wife downstairs, fucking tinkers in the house, he was saying. It's true what they said back home, that the streets were paved with gold in England. It wasn't exactly gold but copper scrap had its price and the English were terrible people for throwing out good rubbish. I stepped over the pile of pipes and onto the bed to give the wardrobe a push, to straighten it up, to stop it collapsing on my head in the night. That would be an awful nightmare, dreaming of Scullivan coming back to hammer me. There was only a coat in there and some valves yet the wardrobe was coming apart at the corners. The price of them in the shops, copper valves, and they as good as new except for a bit of wear and tear. The bed, now that was worn; an old foam mattress with the life gone from it long ago. There'd be more bounce in a doormat.

Anyway, I said out loud one day, why should I have to be the one to take him by the hand and be his keeper? There were problems enough in my own life without O'Hanagan. I needed to call upon all my wits to survive, steer clear of the authorities, slip through the fingers of administrators and away from the law. It became difficult because the boss sent me to a big job, an empty building to rip out the pipes. There was no cash on Friday night but a miserly cheque, and a wage slip explaining massive deductions; tax and contributions backdated. On Monday morning a gang of men invaded the job. I was given a drill, told to make holes along a wall and someone followed me, fixing brackets. Two others followed them, fitting pipes and I was on a conveyer belt snaking through the building.

"Are we working on the black?" I eventually asked. We were sitting around a table, one for pasting paper but we were using it for our lunch break.

"No one on this firm works on the black, Paddy."

"My name's not Paddy."

"Where you work before?"

"Manchester."

"And didn't they give you something when you left, something official with yer name on it?"

But I said no more.

Work was suddenly slack after I queried my wages. I had time to clear out my room, my studio. As promised, I removed the pipes and valves, the wardrobe too. What I earned for hoarding copper lengths of rubbish was enough for a treat, a few pints of Suffolk ale. The Kings Arms, a quaint English pub with a polished wooden floor and velvet papered walls was a cosy place for a read. It had a low ceiling with wooden beams that were hundreds of years old. There was a rocking chair near the fireplace. Few customers came early in the day so I had the place and the chair for myself. I enjoyed stretching my legs towards the hearth while reading, rocking the chair to and fro. I was browsing through my Irish newspaper while waiting for new work. Then I had the shock. I saw my name in the personal column. Bartholomew Rabbit and his cousin, Kevin O'Hanagan, both from Ballybog in the West of Ireland and believed to be working in England. There was an address of a solicitor in London who could help. Help? Scullivan's solicitor? Maybe Scullivan's mother's solicitor? Some solicitor specialising in tax avoidance, being paid to find a fugitive for a private prosecution, looking in places where no policeman or taxman would normally look. Maybe I was paranoid but there was no pondering because I was up and out of the chair, leaving it rocking behind me like an abandoned boat.

10. Today, I could be plucking nails from timber. If I was a chippy.

.

The crossbeams are ready for assembly now, to put a roof on the hole to make a basement. They'll be the supports for the ground floor, the first of many, but there are problems. I understand some German, the swearing; scheibe (means shit). The engineers are shouting it a lot. For the sake of looking busy, I told the labourers in my gang to clean up the site. That's important for safety but my helpers are a pair of sarcastic teenagers from London who, I suspect, know more than myself about this job. Then Connor sent them to another site so I'm on my own, wondering what to do, struggling to look busy.

Out of sight out of mind, so I sneaked off site this morning. Since getting another postcard from O'Hanagan, Nicki has been on my mind. While I had the time, I read it again, trying to decipher O'Hanagan's scribble. He's coming to Berlin on business with Miss Nicki but the rest of the message was barely intelligible. I couldn't even read the phone number except the code for Amsterdam, and the name of the hotel in Berlin. Hilton was written, or sketched, in the same style as I remember seeing it on neon signs. It was cold this morning with a driving rain and I'm still too poor to buy winter clothes. Shivering, wondering about Nicki, worrying about O'Hanagan, and not an engineer in sight. Nothing was happening so I walked off the job.

The Hilton hotel was of course warmly plush with wall to wall carpets, like a prairie field and matching upholstery. Having just walked off a construction site, I felt uncomfortable, intimidated by porters and chic guests speaking French. My boots looked enormous, and I noticed my muddy trail from the door. I retreated outside to kick my toe-caps against a wall, knocking off yellow chunks. I tried again. The reception was a long polished counter where young women in immaculate blouses and pencilled eyeliner attended to men in suits. They were switching from English to French and back again to tell them to have a nice day. O'Hanagan here? I was trying to imagine it when a receptionist spoke to me.
　　"I'd like to leave a message," I replied. "For a guest arriving this week"
　　"Certainly, sir."
I left a message for Mr. O'Hanagan, telling him to meet me in a cosy little cafe around the corner, away from the posh people. I need a place to meet, where I can relax and talk. Serious talk.

When it rains in Berlin, it can be as dismal as in Ireland. Worse because concrete is a picture of greyness, the essence of depression. The next item on my shopping list is socks and thermal vests to keep me warm. My wages this week were so small they resembled nothing like what Connor promised. My payslip was littered with deductions and explanations in German, extra tax until I fill in forms. And where's my expenses? I'll say to Connor, you conniving snake.

"What the feck are you standing about for?" he suddenly shouts.

"I was told to stand here." It's the first thing to come into my head. When in doubt, blame someone else.

"Who?"

"Some German engineer."

"Well, look busy for feck sake. And where the feck were you this morning?"

"I was down cleaning the basement. The nuts and bolts were all over the place..."

"Connor," calls an engineer. That's fortunate because I'm lying through my teeth. I need time to think of a more convincing tale.

If I was a bricklayer I could carry bricks, humping them up and down ladders to look busy while waiting for engineers to decide what I'm supposed to do next. If I was a carpenter I could pluck nails from scraps of wood but there is nothing for the likes of me to do. I don't even know what my trade is; a journeyman of some sort, a fitter I suppose, working with steel lengths at enormous heights. But I haven't got off the ground yet. In reality, I'm a chancer on a wage. Connor is returning with a stride, shouting, pointing to ladders.

"Will, you get the feck up there, and be ready for them. Then they won't be saying that we're standing around."

That's good enough for me. At least I know where to stand. That's important on a construction site, being in the right place at the right time. I climb the ladder and stand on a plank waiting for a crane to lower a steel beam onto the tops of concrete columns. There's confusion and engineers are shouting. I'm waving hands, like Terry said.

"Scheiber," roars Gunter coming up the ladders, swearing, "scheiber." His stumpy stride shakes the platform, shouting at labourers and into his radio. The crane swings the steel beam into its seat. Perfect.

11. Last autumn, I got off at the first town where the bus stopped.

It may seem easy to keep a good distance between oneself and a murderer, because Europe is big enough for two people to travel in without either of them meeting the other. After all, I did put O'Hanagan on a bus to Germany and few weeks later I was heading south to Spain. However, the extensive network criss-crosses in several places, which allows folk to change buses and meet in stations. After the shock of seeing my name in the newspaper, I fled the country. I hurried to London's Victoria station where I boarded the next bus to the Continent. It travelled down the motorway and crossed the channel on the night ferry. It was a beautiful autumn night, like the one back home when Scullivan met his awful end. As the sun like a big balloon rose out from flat fields of foreign crop, we were motoring through France to Belgium. The girl beside me was not interested in plumbing, road-signs or anything I mentioned. I was tired but unable to sleep and needed to walk and scratch myself. So I got off at the first town where the bus stopped. It was Antwerp. It didn't occur to me that O'Hanagan would have done the same.

An enormous cathedral adorned with Ruben's work spiked the morning sky with its steeple. The cobbled alleyways with holy statues perched on ledges were great for pondering. It seemed a very holy town and I took to wandering along the narrow streets lined with cafes. People were out to clean their steps and sweep the street. There was a smell of disinfectant. My mind was wandering too, and I felt that maybe O'Hanagan should have gone to confession before leaving Ireland. Murder is a serious sin but it was not too late. Here, in this holy town of Antwerp I came upon a cafe filled with statues, next to the cathedral. Saints were along the walls and up the stairs, in the toilets and even sitting at the bar. I had a drink with one, or rather a little prayer, an act of contrition on behalf of O'Hanagan. To be safe, I said one for myself although it wasn't me who killed Scullivan. But a prayer in lieu was no harm because soon an awful sinful urge came upon me as I rambled into the red light area. Shameless women in windows. Exhibitionists and provocative posing and even here, amongst decadence and debauchery, there were saints upon window sills blessing sinners in the street. Loitering they were, me as well. I wanted to stand and watch women in windows. Ankles and elbows and stilettos and stockings. Shyness had me, taught at an early age not to stare. So on I went, almost creeping, just a glance to catch a glimpse. Whatever I did they were better at staring back with brazen eyes. As I passed I could hear them tapping the glass with a coin or a key. If I looked they would beckon and I was flattered until I realised they did it to older, fatter and uglier men. It was morning and they closed while I rambled around thinking of what to say. Their night had finished. It was time for breakfast.

English is usually the second best language to have in Belgium. That's because it's not the other official language. With that I was able to get breakfast but I wasn't so successful at starting conversation. The guttural sounds come from the back of the throat, like coughing up phlegm into your mouth. Pronouncing goedemorgen for good morning could catapult a spit onto the person you're greeting. So I kept my mouth closed and winked as I talked.

"You have a tooth ache, darling?"

"I haven't," I replied, "not a bit of one."

"A speech impediment. You poor thing. It's always more noticeable when you try a new language." She was not wearing make-up like window women and not a string of bleached hair. A tall business woman in a trouser suit, the length of a tree, in here for a bite of breakfast.

"Ontbite," she said.

"Pardon?"

"Ontbite. That's Flemish for breakfast. Let's start with easy words. I'm Diva, a speech therapist. How long have you been in Antwerp?"

"Not long but I'm from England, not Ireland. Never been t'ere."

"Didn't ask where you were from, my little nervous friend. It's where you're going. Let me introduce you to the throat technique. We need to develop your sounds." Her long fingers collared my neck. "In Antwerp we harmonise with our inner voice, and you my English nervous wreck must do the same. Let go of inhibitions."

"Now you're talking." It was just what I needed, a friend to help me speak the language and touch me with her finger nails. We tried a few sentences, simple phrases for tourists, like ordering drinks. Nobody understood me except the barman who was placing drinks on the counter as fast as I said them.

"Alstublieft," I was saying, then "no, I mean no, ney, no, ney, cancel t'at last order. We have enough, sweet suffering saints..."

"It's obviously tied vocal cords, my poor darling, a common medical condition."

"It is?"

"Certainly, but I specialise in it. Come."

And she did, a proper professional with a clinic around the corner. Appropriate looking equipment was upon walls, and the white tiles as squeaky clean as a morgue. My eyes were squinting against the shine and brightness. Lights suddenly dimmed, the whiteness switched to just one red bulb. It illuminated a framed certificate on the wall and surgical appliances with straps and locks.

"Now the fee," she said, "so very small this time of day."

"And how much would t'at be?" as if I knew the going rate.

"Oh, this will cover all," taking notes from my wallet. "Now put it away, an inside pocket where it's safe. That's it, and don't be frightened." Diva could put a man's mind at ease. She coaxed me back into a dentist's chair. Her long fingers walked up my neck, my chin and prised apart my lips.

"Just to help you growl some guttural sounds," she purred, rolling the R and ran her fingers down my throat, and down my chest. She had to undo my shirt and said that there would be an extra charge for this. At this point, I suspected something was wrong but again she eased my mind.

"You don't have to get up and pay immediately," and she nibbled my ears, and behind my ears and down my neck. It seems that she had already taken the money from my wallet. She had me sandwiched. Her fingernails clawing my chest sent ripples through my skin to tickle bones and nerves. It was unbearable pleasure while her other hand unfastened my trousers. She grabbed me in a frightening but gentle manner, holding me in her palm to make my sounds come out soft.

"That's much better," she said, and took off her blouse. When she was pressing herself into my face, she said, this will cost extra, and it's worth every cent, don't you agree? Of course, being the meanest man from Ballybog I was not prepared to pay a penny more. But she could see from my posture that I'd pay a million francs, pounds or euros, whatever she wanted to go to eternity. Yes, I had the full treatment to evoke my inner voice and I was howling, hooting and huffing all kinds of guttural sounds.

It was an expensive lesson but I was feeling like a new man, although my energy had been sucked from me. My wallet had also been sucked dry and I had no money for the fare to Spain. It was still morning with time to find a job. So, I went looking for an Irish pub to enquire about work. I knew that in these times virtually every city in Europe had an Irish pub, like America and Australia. The centre of Antwerp seemed more of a big town than a city, quaint for tourists and easy to walk around. That's what I did until I saw a sign advertising Irish stout. It was hanging above a door like you would see in any village back home, or in London. Still, I wasn't convinced that it was a real Irish pub, home from home, a place to enquire about work, lodgings and to have the craic. It wasn't called Kelly's or Murphy's. It did not have a theme name either, like the Shamrock or the Harp but something foreign. I was in no mood to decipher it but I was no sooner through the door when I knew it was the real McCoy. A tricolour in green, white and gold draped a wall and Gaelic road signs were posted about the perimeter, pulled up from their roots it seemed and brought to Belgium. These in themselves didn't persuade me that it was anything more than a theme pub. It was the English tabloid newspapers strewn about tables that suggested that fellows were in looking for jobs. There was more than one brand of stout on sale, always a sign that discerning clients visit the bar. And whiskey was not spelt the Scottish way, and Londonderry not the British way. Yes, it was a real pub.

It was the barman who started talking to me, asking what did I drink? He didn't ask if I could pay for it, and like O'Hanagan, I wasn't going to answer a question until it was asked. It was a beautiful pint of stout that he was pouring, its body blackening and its head turning to a creamy white. It was early, and only him and me in the bar although I could hear the laughs from last night lingering in stale air. They were ghosts, choking in ashtrays. Beer mats and wooden walls were soaked in sweat. The barman was wiping it all away with a cloth dosed in Detol. I could smell it poisoning the voices. He came around to sweep the floor, out towards the door, swinging it open to the crispy morning. The sun came in and zapped what was left of the night-time.

"And where are you from?" he asked as he came back from the door. He left it open and a beam of autumn sunshine was like a furnace about him, a halo. My accent had already betrayed me so I admitted that I was from the west, near the sea but up the mountains. I didn't want to be linked with Ballybog but he detected more of my brogue than I expected. He topped up the stout for me. It was a perfect pint.

"You're not from Ballybog, are you now?" he enquired.

"Agh," I gulped, drowning on a mouth of stout.

"Only," he continued, "we had a fellow in here not two minutes ago from Ballybog. A tone like yours but a head on him like a bullock and him carrying a shovel like it was a murder weapon."

I knew it could only be O'Hanagan. "Make t'at a whiskey."

The man could see that I was alarmed and so he made it a big one. "Is he after you for wages?"

"No, no," I was saying, and I grabbed the whiskey.

"I just thought I'd ask. We get a lot of t'at around here. Looking for a bus to Berlin he was and by the talk of him, you'd swear he thought he was already in Germany. Been living rough in the bus station, so I hear."

It was O'Hanagan right enough. After only a few hours on the bus the fool thought he had landed in Germany, and so got off at the first stop, in

Antwerp. It was just as well that I had no money to pay because that was my excuse to run out.

So, as in London, I had to stay out of Irish pubs, lost with the language and too poor to pay for my therapist.

12. Last autumn, winter came suddenly.

.

There was a heap of Irish in Antwerp, I could tell by the heads on them. Sometimes I would think it was O'Hanagan's beaming pink face in the crowd, and his fiery red hair leaping like flames. To avoid him I'd veer into a shop, as if I had money. From there, I'd wait to watch him pass. The square jaw on him and the size of it. Occasionally the assistant would ask if I needed help.

"Goedmorgen," I'd say, practising Flemish. Then I'd be looking out at the commuters to see if he was amongst them.

"Good morning," she would reply in perfect English, "and are you on holiday from England?" I would watch him walk by the shop and realise that it was not O'Hanagan but someone else from the bog. There were many with similar but smaller heads who came over for the work, around the harbour or on petro-chemical plants north of the border in Holland. They had red faces because they had been working up high in the wind and wet, or they drank too much. But no one had a head as animated as O'Hanagan's and I'd question my imagination.

"Excuse," the shop assistant would say, "is there anything wrong?"

"There isn't," and I'd assemble a few Flemish words to make a sentence of a sort, often one without a verb but good enough to make them laugh. A conversation would usually follow in English. We'd mention scandals at the European Commission or the weather, and what about the Eurovision song contest? That was always a good one but eventually she would ask what did I want?

"Ah, but I'm just practising, tot ziens en goed luck."

I practised the language in the street, around a square where men would meet. It seemed more difficult in the open air, as if daylight induced poetic energy into words. It was a rhythm that came with the breeze and stirred the men into a frenzy. They would rise to argumentative fervour, waving hands as they speedily spoke, and then break into a merry mood. Never the stern style I had heard in shops. I'd reply, a sentence without a verb, then another stuffed with verbs. All sorts of combinations were good for a laugh but I was not communicating with gargled words that hurt my throat. Then I was asked if I spoke Portuguese. They were here for the work and were as baffled as myself with Flemish. Like the Irish and the Brits, they were chasing the short contracts and tax-free expenses. I didn't know it at the time but it was them and not us who were the most efficient and least expensive gang in town.

"Rotterdam's good for work," said a skinny man with greasy black hair. He pushed it back from his eyes, up over his forehead so he could see me. "An Irishman, Jim Kelly is driving there next week to get his things from the police station."

"Why the police station?"

"Don't know. You know him? The contact man in your Irish pub. Maybe you arrange some travel for us. Yes? And a telephone number."

"Yes," I replied, "maybe I could." But I had no intention of introducing myself to any Irishman, let alone travelling with one. I could imagine the conversation we would have: From where back home do you come? Ballybog? And did you hear about the murder on the mountain road, smashed a man's skull with a shovel? Murder is a fine subject for killing time while in a car. I was going my own way, away from anyone Irish. I was staying away from the bus station too, for fear of meeting O'Hanagan. He'd still be there with his shovel, holding it because I told him not to let go of it until he got to Germany. The buses would come and go and he'd stalk them, approaching strangers and stunning them with his smile, asking the same question: Is this the bus for Berlin?

It was easy enough to get on the train without paying. Easier than getting food. I was starving.

"They steal cars in Rotterdam, dinnae they?" I looked around to see who was asking such a stupid question because cars are stolen in every city. He had a loud mouth, speaking English with a hard Scottish accent. They were all Scottish. I had to sit amongst them, just for a while because I was desperate with hunger and so lacking energy. A pain in my belly. Someone was telling a story about a junkie who broke into a van.

"Wis going ta work we were, fuckin freezing in the morning, driving. Yer ken? Ah looks in the mirror and sees this junkie fast asleep in yer back o' the fuckin van, man." Everyone laughed as he told the story about driving out of Rotterdam on a cold morning at half past six. "It wis fuckin freezing," he said again, and everyone laughed more. "Wisn't it?"

"Fuckin freezing," agreed his friend, "fuckin freezing, man."

"En we had this fuckin junkie kipping in the back o' the van. Jist fucked the lock in the night en gits in, the bastard. So we drives oot to Europort."

"Fuckin freezing," his friend said again.

"I mean we drives to nowhere. Yer ken? Somewhere between here and there, no even a bastard fuckin tree, jist railway tracks, then we fucked him off oot intae the snow, man." Everyone laughed. "He hits the snow and wakes up. Hits the snow and shits himsel," and everyone laughed more.

I thought the story was a bit funny, and was laughing enough for them to think I was one of them. After all, the junkie did break into a car and damaged someone's lock. A lock for a car door is expensive so I supposed it served him right. Anyone would think the same if they were driving to work one morning, looked in the mirror, and saw a stranger sleeping in the back. But I was hungry and hadn't paid my fare and I took to thinking about being kicked off the train in some isolated place. The hunger hurt more when I thought about walking along railway tracks, inching towards Rotterdam in snow. Thankfully the winter had not arrived, yet.

As soon as the hunger pains subsided I was en route to another carriage before anyone asked a question. And from where in Ireland do you come? Far from Ballybog? And did you hear about the murder back there? And they reckon they headed over here on the run. Paranoid. If I had some food it would have been easier to handle. Weak with hunger and when I heard a mere murmur of English my heart pounded pain to my bones. I had to labour on though, to another carriage. Foreigners were what I wanted, folk who wouldn't want English conversation. The other end of the train seemed to be miles away. I just kept walking past seats and baggage. I had to squeeze past young women, the type that tour Europe and spend nights in luxury hotels. They had American accents and designer hiking pants and hand-knitted sweaters. Everything about them was expensive; their baggage and headbands, one had earmuffs around her neck in case the winter came without warning and another wore sunglasses. As I was squeezing past I felt the hunger twist my guts. They were eating continental delights. An urge came upon me with crippling pain to devour their food.

"Sorry," I said as I fell amongst them, correcting myself and moving off her lap. There was a diary on her knee, a pencil in one hand and a rolled pastry stuffed with delicacies in the other. She was probably recording her departure from Antwerp and saw the hunger in my eyes. A murderous glare it would have seemed. Sorry, I said again, retreating to the aisle. It was hard to go without a bite but I couldn't bear to be there while they scribbled, nibbled and giggled and then licked the taste from their manicured fingers.

It was a long walk and I could have expected to arrive at a border checkpoint. I continued northbound through carriages. Then someone shouted, 'Bart!' I ducked. The Portuguese gang were in the last carriage, looking as rowdy as the Scottish mob in the other. They welcomed me. Yes, they were my friends, and someone gave me a sandwich and then a banana. I told them straight, I was starving and couldn't claim unemployment benefit. I hadn't paid my tax, I said. For that, I was rewarded with another banana and they assured me that I'd be working in the morning and getting paid in two weeks.

"Cash, my friend."

"Cash in the hand?" I asked.

"Cash in the hand, my friend." The skinny fellow with a greasy black fringe shook hands with me. "Migael's my name."

"Bart," I replied."

"Yes, my friend, cash in the hand."

13. Today, I'm much better but I'm stuck in a queue, in a bank, in Berlin.

Normally I hate standing in a queue but it's a consolation to know that I'm waiting for money. For cash, albeit not immediately. I'm confident about turning this paycheque into cash without having to pour too much personal history onto forms. The trick is to open an account and make little fuss about restrictions on withdrawals. Just deposit the cheque and wait a week.

The most immediate problem is the queue. Like Belgians, Germans stand beside rather than behind me when they join the line. Of course, I shouldn't stereotype folk but this mob of well-dressed customers really is inching into my space. I can handle it though. I had to endure it in Belgium while I was sick with my nervous disposition. During my paranoid phase I was petrified of being spoken to for fear of being questioned, interrogated. So I stayed silent when they jumped the queue. I was so meek that I did not need to remind myself that some bad manners are acceptable on the Continent. Now though, I have to restrain myself, remember that they are host citizens with more right than myself to be in this country. But if this German thief steals another millimetre of my space I'll kill him. I move forward, pretending to gaze around the bank. I step into his path. It's like playing chess, predicting his next move and now a woman advances on the left side.

Historically, the Irish aided people who did this, conquering bits of land, inching over borders and provoking the British. A traditional rebel's principle was that my enemy's enemy is my friend. It was a response to years of British rule. Whereas it was acceptable to fight conquerors, it was obligatory to abide foreigners who had purchased the land rather than stole it. Scullivan sold acres for the building of holiday homes. For the sake of the local economy we were pleasant to the Continentals who came to invest and walked to the front of a queue. Here again I am quiet in a line, holding my tongue. At times like this, when a temper simmers inside my head, I give credit to the British for waiting their turn. Even in a city as hectic as London, the English had very fine manners.

The woman has her collar turned up as if to keep warm her ears. I catch a glimpse of her pointed nose as she casually wanders forward with her hands sunk in big pockets. My move. I step sideways to gaze up at walls and to block the businessman on my right. He holds a leather case bulging, I fear, with statements and bankbooks, a time-consuming cargo.

Stop him at any cost. This really is an elegant building, I suddenly realise. It has plants in pots around the perimeter, and pillars that stretch to heaven. Of course, they can afford to have such space and pay to keep it warm. Someone has left the door open. A cold breeze with razor edges is streaming in. No one else seems to feel it. Why would they, wrapped in their cashmere and duckdown and designer knitwear? The chill snakes along the disfigured queue and cuts the legs from beneath me. There's no such thing in Germany as cold weather, only the wrong clothing. New socks are what I need. Connor, you bollocks, paying me with a cheque and condemning me to this. Cash, we agreed, and my toes are cold. My one and only leather jacket serves me well but fails my feet. They won't budge so I leave the queue to close the door. Now I'm a doorman, holding it for a nice lady who takes her time while a man with long legs strides past us. The queue swells like a balloon.

14. Last year, it was suddenly Monday morning in Rotterdam, with a job to do and lies to tell.

Rotterdam was nothing like the postcards I had seen of Amsterdam. But this was Rotterdam, where tourists could believe that they had landed in an American city. There were no cobble-stoned streets with hump-back bridges. The canals had been filled in years ago with the rubble left after the bombs. There were shoebox skyscrapers standing on end, and miles of pedestrian walkways that took us past street sculpture and up and down ramps. Bicycles were everywhere. We stopped to talk at City Hall. This had survived the bombs and planners but even here, someone erected an American hamburger cabin in the forecourt.

I was hungry again but had no money and detected something derogatory in Migael's voice. The way he frowned and turned away was enough for me. So I made a scene with them, insisting that I would not take a penny from them although no one offered. During the journey it had become obvious that I was penniless and my new friends became wary of my hints about a bed for the night and a bite to eat. Migael wanted to know why I wasn't mixing with the Irish.

"They're Scottish," I said, and told him that we didn't mix.

"So why you no ride with Irishman, with a car, Jim Kelly?"

Yes, I was a man with no money or friends, and they were beginning to show contempt. Hence I took to telling lies at City Hall, about meeting old friends near the harbour and collecting money and getting a meal. Migael detected lies and frowned again and walked away. It was obvious that I knew no one in this town and if I did it would be me who owed them money.

The city became sleazy as I strolled alone and wide-eyed past coffee shops and over a canal with ducks. A woman in red stilettos said hello and walked beside, then behind me. A glimpse of messy mascara deterred me from looking again. It seemed as if she followed me for miles. I came upon a bigger canal with ships, looked behind and saw that she was gone. On the other side was Delfs Haven, the oldest part of Rotterdam. Quaint, complete with windmill and boats moored along a quay. It was not far from this postcard setting that I stole a banana. I had meandered into a Turkish market, feeling the produce like others and suddenly the banana was in my pocket. I hurried away, hunching shoulders against the cold and my body aching with hunger, trying to curl into a cosy ball. I pressed my belly against a metal rail across a bridge. While looking into water I bit the banana, sucked out the inside while squeezing it like a tube of toothpaste. Like a tourist, I circled the windmill. Then I returned to the market to steal a tomato.

There was no need to take risks by stealing because soon there was food galore. As they cleared the market, slamming shut the legs of foldaway tables, I joined the birds picking scraps. I washed it down with milk. Thankfully, the cold weather had kept it fresh. I had come a long way down the social ladder since my heyday of designer plumbing, working for English eccentrics. My new trade was going to be in the petro-chemical industry and I had to pretend to be a fitter, and pray that no one asked me to weld. The job was somewhere between Rotterdam and Europoort, an isolated refinery near railway tracks, I supposed. It was important that I was in the right place in the morning to get a lift with the Portuguese. So I went in the evening to find them, or at least to see where they lodged.

Dutch cafes have big windows. People sit on high stools along the bar and others just inside the window looking out at me. I passed a less elegant cafe with posters advertising cheap food, beer and rooms above. There I saw them, a merry mob around the bar. Even Migael was overtly friendly and came to the door to invite me for another drink. His hands were on my shoulders and he rested his forehead against mine so that our noses touched. He was trying to say don't worry about the money but he had tears in his eyes. As he collapsed into hysterics another arm pulled me over him and up to the bar. He gave me a beer, and good luck to you I shouted as I raised my glass. Cheers, he said. Jolly good, imitating an English accent and swung around to dance. Some legal substance was being passed about and soon I was inhaling it myself. I took big sucks to fill my lungs and drug my mind so I could be as mad as they. It became a wonderful evening for a while. We were drunk and drugged, dancing whenever we recovered from crippling hysterics.

At times I found the good time overwhelming me, and I was shouting that I was having a bad trip. Whenever I stopped dancing my brain would keep galloping with madness. Then it was waltzing with awful thoughts of the murder: Scullivan's mother, my mother, O'Hanagan's mother, the poor simpleton in a bus shelter. Why were you not at the funeral if you didn't kill him? Didn't even send flowers. And what was the reason for taking poor Hanagan away to foreign lands if it was not to kill him too, the only witness? To lose him. I was outside to slow down, to let the cool breeze take the thoughts away. There was a drink in each hand and I was taking alternate gulps to get drunk. I needed to get beer to my brain to make it slow down, like quenching a fire. Had to drown the drug with alcohol.

In this doped and drunken state, two men attacked me. More of a trick than an actual attack. One of them tapped my shoulder and as I turned to see him the other had a hand in my pocket. I staggered into a fighting position but they continued to go through my pockets. They hit me. Not hard but just out of frustration because my pockets were empty.

"Here, try dis one," I laughed, "I'm sure there's something here." They walked away but I followed, calling them arseholes. They must have figured I was a junky, a lunatic, someone best left alone. I was following and pushing my hands into their pockets and I think I left an empty bottle in there. Then there was singing. I remember singing and I bit an ear for a laugh and I got a fist in my face. Although I was on the floor, I was in great form for a fight and so got up to finish it but my opponents were gone. Running with a stamping stride, I was, to stop myself falling. Sideways and longways and my feet like flippers smacking the floor. I was searching for the bar, to be back with my Portuguese friends before I crashed to the ground. Blood was in my mouth, swirling with saliva. I washed it down with the other beer and my brain was slowing. It stalled. My body was suddenly delicate and the weather cold, threatening to snow and I wanted to sleep in a cosy car. My words came out wrong when I asked for directions. Even English words sounded distorted. I was saying sentences without a verb again, falling asleep while I leaned against a van. I was only asking for Migael, to say thanks for the drink and the smoke. I wanted to show my appreciation but it was taking ages to explain. Then it occurred to me that nobody was listening except the wheel of this van. I was talking to a tyre, wishing for a bed, blankets and I would love the hubcap to be a pillow. I had to get up for work early in the morning and the hubcap was cold.

While in this abyss, I had a dream. It was about words attacking me but worst of all, it was one of those dreams that starts in a morning, so you're fooled into thinking that you have finished your sleep and done your dreaming and now it's time to go to work.

I woke up that morning and was pleasantly surprised to find I wasn't alone. There was a sentence in my bed. Of course it wasn't just a string of words, that would be silly because they would be caught amongst the sheets with verbs and vowels between my toes. And as I hate bits in the bed, I can't imagine anything worse than dots and commas against my skin.

No, this was a sensible sentence stuck to a page that held it together. I kicked off the covers to have a look and saw it naked without a verb. Shameless sounds and miss-spelt words, a rather disabled piece of verse. But I had never slept with a sentence before and fell in love with this crazy line of words. I asked it downstairs for breakfast, as if it could hear as well as talk. At the table I read it aloud and from its tone I knew it came from a dream and I could never let it go again. It was a long winding sentence with a foreign air, sort of talking dirty in double Dutch. It stretched across the page, turned around like a worm and came backwards along the next line. Strange and daring but it was certainly a sentence, starting with a capital letter and it finished with a full-stop, maybe two or three to keep it from flying off the page. And here and there it had a comma as if to make it decent.

I was so obsessed that I took it with me when I went to work. In the factory I spoke to no one in case I uttered words without a verb. I was having an affair with the sentence in the toilet, taking out the crumpled paper, mumbling like a monk, and wondering was it really just a sentence. It seemed to be a paragraph, sprawled across the paper, several lines thick, leaving hardly any space to dot an I or cross a T. Then while hiding in the toilet, the sentence multiplied into another paragraph. It was a cancer growth, a bulging nonsense, soaking through the page until words came at me from two sides of wrinkled paper. Paragraphs grew political, preaching propaganda that threatened my promotion. I rushed from the toilet and across the factory floor. Scullivan, the foreman, shouted but I had to reach for Yellow Pages and call a poet.

The poet told me it was a hopeless case, and what I had was a psycho sentence. Back in the toilet I had to cry, especially when I flushed the crazy words away. I was relieved when Scullivan banged on the door, telling me to do some work. I laboured at my bench to forget about the words without a verb, which seduced me in my bed and tried to lure me from the factory floor. I began to speak again and have tea with the men. We laughed, talked about unimportant things and played a game of cards. I went to the toilet like a normal man, to hide from the foreman and read graffiti on the back of the door. Then I saw the sentence and I nearly had a shit.

It had risen from the sewer and was scrawled across the paintwork. I took away the sentence to kill it beneath a train. Scullivan and his dog chased me across the factory floor as I hurried with the toilet door beneath my arm. I went down steps to platform four where express trains come on the hour, and threw the words onto the track. The train came rushing into the station, like a long cruel sentence, never stopping or even slowing for a comma or colon. Each carriage was like a deadly word without meaning or purpose, just an endless cutting-remark passing through, en-route to some distant full stop.

I looked down on the track to see Scullivan, his dog and the toilet door cut to bits. But the sentence wasn't there. It was spread in spray paint across the wall on platform three. It had a new delinquent style, defacing posters and preaching to passengers. After distorting every advert, it reached across the ceiling with its disturbing words and came down ceramic walls to spread its dirty propaganda on platform four. I ran away, but like a snake, the sentence without a verb followed me up the stairs, trying to have me, eat me. I could feel the full stops coming up my trouser leg when the men in white coats arrived. They stabbed it with a syringe to inject a verb. With enormous pliers they extracted vowels to correct the spelling and tried to form some endearing words. But it wriggled and spoke the awful truth with spit and spite and splattered my face with sarcastic venom. So I chopped it with a shovel, walloping it from skull to tail to make it stop, stop, stop, chop, chop, chop...

Monday morning was bitterly cold. It seemed as if I had been thrown from a vehicle and had landed on a hard surface. It was still dark. I felt the floor with my palms, trying to guess the place. It wasn't snow, grass or concrete, but it wasn't a bed either. Not even a mattress. My trouser leg seemed to be stiff with frost. I felt again. Kitchen tiles! I was curled up near the fridge with its door left open. Someone must have been gulping water during the night and let it spill and soak my leg. A radio switched on blaring music. There were other bodies in the room, an arm trying to swot the radio, hitting the snooze button. Another radio switched on and then an alarm clock went mad.

No one said anything about bringing me home. And I didn't ask. It wasn't because I didn't appreciate it but because I would not have been able to complete a sentence. If I had, no one would have had the energy to listen. Some brown light was coming in from the landing, through a filthy window above the door. Bodies struggled onto delicate legs and farted in the dark. It was a long room with beds, cushions and a kitchen sink.

Fingers were feeling walls to find a switch. I stood on an ashtray. When I fell into a pile of clothes I went back to sleep for a moment or more. My nose was buried in clean laundry and it was a dream to escape the stench of feet. When the light came on, one fellow was asleep at the kitchen end. We stepped over him but when someone stood on his fingers he awoke, swearing, seemingly in Turkish. Men were making coffee and gulping mugs of water. The toilet was along the landing and stinking. Someone had missed the bowl and dropped his load on a pretty pink mat. Migael was emptying bleach on it while another brought some back to the room, between his toes. The Turk had gone back to sleep on the kitchen tiles but smelt it. It was by his nose and he awoke with more swearing, bolted upright and hit his head on a cupboard door.

The oil refineries seldom stop working. If they do, for an overhaul, it must be for the shortest time. A shut-down is a job with an enormous workforce, men like us to work overtime. We were still intoxicated, crammed into a mini bus en route to an oil refinery. It was a massive operation and hundreds were heading towards Europort. The motorway ran parallel with the Maas River and in the distance was the metal mish-mash of pipes, cylinders and scaffold. Another mini bus overtook us, and like ours it was filled with tradesmen, or maybe chancers like me. More important than qualifications was a greed to work twelve hours a day, seven days a week. It didn't attract family men or those with a hobby. The Dutch tax system penalised the locals and so it was no surprise to see vehicles from Belgium and Germany. The next mini bus to overtake us was stuffed with the Scottish mob. When we arrived at the gate, I saw faces from Antwerp. The barman from the Irish pub was there, pretending to be an electrician. I could see that his tools were brand-new and his overalls straight from the packaging. He was talking to me before I remembered him. He'd obviously forgotten that I owed him for a pint of stout.

"This will be a good one," he was saying. "A few weeks and a nice earner if you stay the distance. And not too much paperwork," he winked.
I winked back, assuming that he was talking about tax avoidance. Just what a fugitive needed; the fewer questions the better. I wanted to ask if he'd seen that simpleton, the one with the shovel but stopped myself. The less said on both sides, the better.

Kitty from Liverpool was selling bacon sandwiches at ten o'clock every morning. It wasn't just us and the Brits, but everyone seemed to be eating them including the Muslims. The smell of sizzling bacon against a crispy cold air was great for my nose. On that first morning, still suffering, I was lured to the wagon. I sunk my teeth into the bread before she had the chance to ask for money.

"And don't we pay at the end of the week like everywhere else?" I said. I wasn't the first to ask and she had already made arrangements to deduct money from our tax-free expense account. Every morning I was like a bird swooping down from the highest beam to get my feed. Then I would scurry up again with my coffee and bacon sandwich. While down there I spoke to no one for fear of hearing that O'Hanagan had joined the Antwerp gang. A friend of yours? they might ask, or would he be a cousin now? nice but not quite right in the head, carrying a shovel and he's supposed to be a fitter. Said he was on the run, murder and for sure, he couldn't fight a mouse, as big as he is. Unless he had an accomplice, and are you his friend from Ballybog, the one that ran away with him?

I was away from them all, near the top. Volunteered on the first morning. I was climbing and looking busy before the foreman could send me on another job. From high beams, I could see ships cruise up the Maas, feel the wind and smell salty air and laugh with Migael. Like me, he was able to enjoy the height and work in a wind. From up there, I could see them better than they could see me. I scanned the heads in helmets, catching glimpses of a jaw, a nose and listening to the accents. There was a hefty body of Scots on site. I'd tightrope along a beam and spy down a tube. There was a gang from Antwerp, Irish, English, Scottish and an American. There was no sign of O'Hanagan and after a week I was satisfied that he did not get a lift up with the Irish mob, nor did he wander up along the railway tracks. I asked the American had he seen the likes of him around Antwerp.

"There's no one as simple as that," he said, "or with a head like that in Antwerp town."

It became a good life and I was happy that I had left Ireland. Holland was a great place and I hoped that O'Hanagan was having as good a time in Germany, or wherever he landed. I was only bothered once by the Dutch foreman. Fortunately for me, he assumed his English was so bad that I couldn't carry out his instructions. He sent the English-speaking chargehand up to see me.

"And are you a fitter or what kind of a dumpling are you?" He would have thrown me off the job but they were desperate for men. So he put me drilling holes on metal beams. For as long as I looked busy and kept to the safety rules no one would question my existence. I just fitted in with the rest of the men. We were issued with helmets, which we had to wear at all times. That was safety rule number two. We had to wear goggles to protect our eyes when drilling. That was rule number three. Protective footwear was number four and number five was concerned with loitering on fire exits. It was as easy as the Ten Commandments but I was heeding the safety rules.

For now, I was safe as I climbed up the steelwork, back to wind and wet. With our yellow helmets and goggles, we were issued with rainwear.

"The Dutch are the best dressed workers in Europe."

"They are," I agreed. "No truer word said, Migael." We had bright yellow jackets to match our hats, feathered inside to keep out the cold. If a stranger, policeman or taxman, looked up at the steelwork, he would have thought a flock of canaries had landed on the job. We were perched upon the beams, fixing bolts and drilling holes in every weather. The coats were too good for wearing to work, and had folk been given such clothes back in Ballybog, they would have taken them home for their wardrobe. That made Migael laugh. We were like models at a fashion show, walking along catwalks, the highest and thinnest beams. I was willing to work late and able to carry a load to the top and along the most awkward beam. Migael's humour complimented his generosity and he started saying words like Jaysus. Jaysus, you're better than a crane. Jaysus, you'll do them out of a job. Twelve hours a day I worked, dark when I started and dark when I finished. They fed us for free if we stayed after eight but I stayed all night, sleeping in the locker room on a pile of overalls, and toilet rolls for a pillow.

No one in Ballybog would find me now, I was thinking one day. Then the Dutch foreman called my name and caused my heart to stop. He wanted us to follow him. Migael and myself left our job and scrambled down ladders. The hefty foreman walked with a hasty pace, leading us into a brick building without windows. I thought it was concerned with the security department but was relieved to see it was a control room.

"Have you dressed cables before?" he asked, opening a metal door.

"We have, of course," I lied.

"No problem," added Migael, as big a fibber as myself. We were looking into a metal cabinet containing circuit boards and fuses, switches and other contraptions, the likes of which I'd never seen before.

"You," said the foreman, "onder." So Migael went under the floor, down steps to a crawl space beneath the metal cabinet. "And you," pointing to me, "here pull cables."

It was an easy job with Migael down there pushing cables up through a hole and into the cabinet. I took the ends and pulled them out. We still needed to think though because the cables had to be bundled in neat parallel lengths. It was best to do the thin ones first because they tangled. Then the big ones.

"Warm job," commented Migael.

"It tis," I agreed, "a nice job in here while it's cold out t'ere."

"We'll put these here, and those there and make a neat job."

"Fair play to you, Migael, we make a fine pair. They'd t'ink we're electricians." We were doing a professional job, keeping the cables straight to avoid a pile of spaghetti. "What do you say, Migael, a job for life in here where it's warm?"

"Another man to help you," interrupted the foreman. He went away, leaving the new member of our team looking into the cabinet.

"Fuck," said the new recruit. I was thinking the same myself because I had seen and heard him before, on the train from Antwerp. He looked Scottish too, with a head of red Celtic hair and a face that had been battered by wind and rain, probably on North Sea oilrigs. "Fucking bollocks, aey?"

"Aey," I agreed. I don't know why. He just looked at me. Was still looking at me and I couldn't help but stare at bulging purple veins on his nose.

"Where you from?" he asked.

"Agh, spent most of my time down London."

He wasn't really listening because his attention drifted towards the cabinet. "Fuck sake. For fuck sake."

The Scot had a different way of doing it, dragging lengths out through the door to drop about the floor.

"Let's keep the big ones to the back," shouted Migael. His black mop of hair was popping up and down through the hole as he worked with the cables. The Scot winked at me, pulled another hefty cable up to get his shoulder under it and dragged it out across the floor. A spaghetti mess piled up, spilling from the cabinet.

"They're knotting down here," complained Migael. "Let's start at the back."

"Let's you awey an' fuck yerself," replied the Scot. He dragged a cable up and out and dropped it. Then he winked again. "That cunt doown t hole want's up here giving orders."

"No, no, Migael's okay…"

"Aey, they're okey in their place."

"Let's start at the back?" said Migael.

"Let's you fuck off where you come from, Pal." Scot turned to me to have a private word. "This job's ney problem." He winked again before shouting down the hole. "Aey, I've done this job before, Pal. What you normally do yersel for a living?" He reached for another cable to pull it from the cabinet, feeding it to me. Before I knew what was happening I was working with the Scot, and Migael was down his hole. "Aey, greasy fucking refugees come over here an' the nex week telling every cunt how tey do his job. Aey, he cen awey en fuck himsel." He dropped the cable and went back to grab another. "Call yer sel a cable man? Fuck sake. Some cunt's bundled the power an' control cables together. For fuck sake. Aey, you doown there, away an' find yer sel a job in a kitchen. I hear Kitty's lookin fir a man at the sandwich truck, te butter the bread. For fuck sake."

15. This afternoon, I'm still in a bank, in Berlin, in a better mood because I'm at the front of the queue. At last.

Connor, you bollocks. When we meet again I'm going to demand that my expenses be paid in cash. This ordeal in the queue exhausts me, and now I must lie through my teeth at the counter. And my teeth hurt because I chewed my plastic bankcard. There are other ways of defacing a card but it's important to create the impression that a dog mauled it. It also helps to have a payslip from a local employer and to use the same bank. It creates a sense of family, and the bank treats me as a guest-worker rather than an immigrant. They are pleased to know that Connor recommended them and they're so sorry that I've experienced problems transferring money from my Irish bank account.

"It was a fierce dog," I say, "with teeth on it like a shark and made bits of my wallet."

"Yes, you have half your account number lost," he says, examining my card. "But yes, we open an account now. It is not true that you wait for every small detail to come from Ireland. That rumour is not total correct. We are happy to help you fast."

"Lovely people here, despite our little problem about waiting in the queue."

"A misunderstanding."

"Twas. I hope I didn't sound too aggressive."

"No," he replies, lifting palms to me and shrugging his square shoulders. "And have you written your other details?"

"I have," a fictitious address for home and another for the branch of my bank. There's no better way to track a fugitive than through accounts and international cash dispensers. By the time they've discovered that I can't confirm my bank details I will have withdrawn my wages from the account. That's fair, I'm asking for nothing else.

"And how's Connor?" asks the teller.

"He's fine. Have you known him long?"

"We have had Connor as a customer since his first contract in Berlin."

"Is t'at so?"

"We look after all his business, and his employees. If you wish to stay long time in Berlin, you might request extra banking facilities, yes?"

"Well now, I'm sure I would. You're very kind. Lovely people in this town."

16. Last winter, in Rotterdam, a job at the top without a coat. Or a goat.

A man from management stopped me just after lunch to say that he knew I was Irish. He stunned me with his Dublin accent.

"… It's obvious. Jaysus, you can't be anything else with a brogue like that. But, for Christ sake, we need your passport. You're here because we vouched for you, taken responsibility but we still need the paperwork complete. So, for Jaysus sake, get your arse over to administration now and see what they want. They'll give you a clearance to take to your man in security. Your electronic pass is cancelled till then."

As I walked across the site the cold froze my face and palpitations erupted inside me. I knew that my application was littered with lies, false addresses and numbers that fell out of my head. I tried to recall what I had written. There was an address of a squat in England and a fictitious telephone number with a London code. My correct name from a driving license was the only item to connect me with Ireland. Outside the administration office I gave my boots a kick against the wall and tried again to remember what I wrote.

"Mr Bartholomew Rabbit," she said as I came through the door. She was a tall, attractive middle-aged woman wearing glasses that sat low on her nose. There was a grin on her face, as if she had been eagerly waiting to see me. "Mr Rabbit," she continued in perfect English, "we must all pay some tax."

"We must of course."

"And we, in this office, must deduct some money from your wages."

"You must of course."

"For tax, insurance, pension and zickerfund."

"Yes, of course." I got the impression that she had already assumed a lot about me.

"This National Insurance number, is it an Irish number?"

"It's British."

"And are you British or Irish?"

"British," I said, sounding like an Ulsterman.

"Well, it's unlike any number on any list in any E.U. state. Are you sure?"

"I am."

"Well, we must deduct maximum money from your wages until further notice."

"I see."

"And if the number is wrong, the money will go to Limbo. To Limbo van de Nederland."

"It will of course."

"Nothing to a pension fund for you," she said, shaking her head slowly as if she was talking to a naughty boy. "Nothing to unemployment insurance, nothing to zickerfund for when you are sick. No hospital. No dentist. Absolutely nothing for Mr Run-Rabbit-Run except what is left of your wages..." She was still shaking her head at me when I interrupted.

"And the tax-free expenses."

"Yes," nodding up and down, "you get the tax-free expenses. Now, here is a new form for you to fill in when you like, Mr Rabbit. If you like. Now, bring this to the security office."

If I would like some more money is what it amounted to but I was still earning more than I would get in Ireland. I was laughing as I left the office, imagining the type of number O'Hanagan would write if he were asked. He once tried to write a telephone number, scribbling each figure but omitted all the zeros. I asked why did he leave out all the zeros. But Bart, he answered, they're naughts, they're nothing. They were indeed nothing, and the number that she had on my paperwork and on her computer was nothing, just what a fugitive needed. She was a kind woman who had already forgiven me for my little sins. Tax avoidance was a socially acceptable sin anywhere in Europe. In any case, I was doing my penance, paying the price with maximum deductions to keep the taxman away and no hope for a Mr Run-Rabbit-Run to ever claim benefits.

There is a marked difference between guest-workers and immigrants. This occurred to me suddenly while looking at the clutter of men in the security office. I pushed open the glass door and walked into the foyer and joined the queue, a mob that crowded the reception counter. The confident Euro workers were impatient tradesmen who objected to questions and told the uniformed staff, in English, to hurry up, for fuck sake. Security officers were stamping papers and issuing plastic cards to get rid of them. For once the British were pushing to the front of the queue. The tradesmen passed through an electronic gate to get back to work. The remaining men were suspect-immigrants from the East or from Africa, reluctant to go forward. They were obediently holding papers with explanations for failing to produce documentation. Excuses, and I would be amongst them. But no, I followed the English speakers who shuffled towards the electronic gate.

"For fuck sake," said an Englishman, "there's work to be done." He was sliding his pass under the officer's nose, urging him to stamp it, and hurry up about it. I was confident that I too would be rushed through if I barked in English.

Then I stalled. A stiffness took hold of me, as cold as Scullivan's corpse sprawled on the road. My eyes were focussed on O'Hanagan's oblong head with red wiry hair. Of course, a net had been thrown across the site to weed out illegal immigrants and caught him too. I panicked, retreated and stepped through the gateway. An alarm sounded, not loud but an irritating beep that caused heads to turn. It got worse because O'Hanagan followed me.

"Bart, Bart," he was shouting, and like me, his electronic pass had been cancelled so the alarm beeped at him too. A security officer called me. I kept walking, even when a woman in a blue uniform appeared from a doorway and held out her arm. I just walked towards the control room, to my job with Migael. He'd be waiting for me and I didn't want to leave him there labouring with an antagonistic Scot. I was walking fast to dissipate energy. Palpitations. A red light signalled me to stop but I walked towards the metal mish-mash of pipes where I could hide. It was a place to get lost in while they forgot my face. Then I'd go back later to say that I have just been told to report to the security office. I'd deny that it was me who bolted like a horse at the sight of O'Hanagan. I broke into a trot but he was behind me, telling the woman he was with Bart. Then a car came beside me and a puzzled face stared out. It was useless.

"Fecking bureaucracy in this country," I complained. "There's work to be done."

"Please, go back to the office."

"Bart, Bart," cried O'Hanagan, "tisn't it great how we've met?" His face was beaming as bright as the flashing light, a giant of a man, even next to the tall Dutch woman who held his sleeve. We stood looking at each other. Scabs on his lips. We had no helmets or safety goggles.

"Safety rules two and three," said the woman.

We were not brought back to the security foyer but ushered into a back office with a long table. They seemed to except that we were European citizens and entitled to work legally. They didn't question us about that or ask to see identification but phoned the recruitment agent. Jim Kelly, I heard him say. O'Hanagan's face was still beaming with delight while I was numb.

"Please, your pockets."

Mine were virtually empty but O'Hanagan's pockets were like Magpies nests. The contents spilled onto the table. There was a spoon there and a collection of spent phonecards and tickets, items picked from the street, I suppose. Then he took out a cigarette lighter. That contravened safety rule number one.

"Crazy Englishman," one of them said. Why did you have a cigarette lighter on a petro-chemical plant? It wasn't actually said. Nothing was said, nothing asked. Nothing. They just showed us where the door was.

It didn't occur to me that someone would have been working on a higher beam than myself. While I was spying on the men below, O'Hanagan was above. Yes, there were higher beams and O'Hanagan went up there the way he went up the mountain back home. He was in a bad state with the scabs around his mouth turning green. The hunger did it. He was owed money for clocking into work each day but he didn't get it. He was waiting for Jim Kelly to explain the procedure because Jim Kelly drove him from Antwerp and arranged the job and had to deduct his fee. O'Hanagan didn't even have a proper yellow feathered jacket. He was still wearing his brown coat from Ballybog.

"Anyway," he said, "it was a lonely old job up t'ere with not as much as a blade of grass nor a goat."

17. This morning, I'm driving Terry to the clinic.

I don't understand why I need to make hand signals for the crane driver if someone else is shouting instructions to him through a radio. It's plenty that I don't understand. I'm wandering childlike, as aimless and as innocent as O'Hanagan would. Of course I'm learning but I need to learn faster to keep my job. And nothing in life is free, least of all education. It's going to cost me half a day's wage to get a lesson from Terry, a miser of knowledge. I've virtually admitted to him now, that I'm a chancer on the job. And he hasn't wasted time pricing his lectures. He asked me to take the morning off work so that he could explain in detail what his job entails. So come around to the classroom for a lesson, he suggested, to his kitchen. But first I must pay my way and drive him to the doctor.

"Alright, mate," he says, opening his door wide to see me.

"I am, of course," you mean bollocks yer, getting me around here when I should be at work. Any decent man would settle for a pint in the pub.

"Come in, come in," standing aside to let me through. He pushes the door closed and steps back to rest against the banister. He seems exhausted but sober.

"Have you just got up?"

"What?" he cries. "Me? I've bin up ages. Up every morning. It must 'ave bin seven when I got out o bed, which is late for me. Candy was awake with me. She's never bin up so early in all the time I've known 'er. That's 'cause she bin working nights."

I can hear her walking up there. The stairs twist up beneath a hanging jungle of coats and frocks, to where, it seems, Candy fumbles from the bedroom to the bathroom. Her dancing shoes are stacked on steps. A dangerous place for storing things.

"Yeh, it's Candy's first morning out o bed. She normally works nights but quit. A dancer. Come on, Squire, 'ave some coffee."

"You need a hand?"

"No, no, just a bit of stiffness in the morning. Nothing serious. It's because I'm used to being up climbing for a couple of hours by this time." He shows me to the kitchen, stepping laboriously over more dancing shoes and thigh-high boots in brazen red leather. Something shiny for her late-night sleaze routine, I reckon. There's sequin dresses hanging from the door. Candy has them on hangers with feathered frills. "So, you reckon they might be kicking yer arse off the job?"

"Christ, Terry, nothing like t'at. I'm ahead of schedule. Connor even gave me the morning off work an' all. No, it's not a problem but there's a personality clash with the Germans. Couldn't be arsed asking them."

"Hi," says Candy, drowsy, holding the doorframe to step over shoes. "This is Bart."

"Hello," I say, retreating from her path.

"You expecting breakfast too?" Her bleached face under stringy blond hair doesn't look at me.

"No, no, not atall. I've eaten…"

"It's okay, she speaks to all my mates like that, don't yer, Pet?" wrapping an arm around her waist to scoop her close. That's a sleepy head she has. "She promised me faithfully, didn't yer, Pet? That one morning y' would be up to cook breakfast for me. Didn't yer? Years ago. I reminded her last night an' she said it'd be no problem, now that she's quit the club. Aey, ain't that right?"

Terry wants to say something encouraging, to congratulate Candy for dragging herself out of bed so early but it's obvious that she's not in a merry morning mood. The pain in his back makes him let go of her, otherwise, despite her drowsiness she could have dragged his lanky body to the cooker. One's as skinny as the other.

"Is it painful this morning?" she asks, bringing her feet in floppy slippers.

"Getting better." He watches her bending to see into the fridge. "Ye're alive then?"

"I'll make you breakfast but I won't join you. I couldn't eat so early."

"It's really nice to see yer up in the morning. Yer'll get used to it, yer'll see."

"I know."

"Yer'll love it. The best time o the day…"

"So you keep telling me."

"Yer could have continued with the nights for a while if yer wanted to. I didn't wanna put pressure on ya."

"You didn't."

He winks at me! She puts rashers of bacon in a frying pan and cracks an egg. Candy's cooking an English breakfast for him.

"Sometimes, at six in the morning she'd cook me breakfast, singing and sometimes, full of energy, yu'd do a little dance, wouldn't ya, Pet? Dancing Candy. Isn't that right?"

"I'd be slightly drunk and just home from work," she explains, lifting eyelids to see me, or to scare me from the floor; I'm in her way again. "Why don't you sit down?"

"Sorry," retreating to a seat at the table with Terry.

"I'd be leaving for work at six," he continues, "trying to tell her it's different when yer awake. Everything is better in the morning. Even now with this illness, I can cope because I'm a morning person…"

I can see that she doesn't care to be a lark but wants her right to have her sleep. In her morning misery, Candy is struggling to focus on the frying pan. I'm wondering why she's doing it, labouring painfully for her man. They catch each other watching.

"Yer a good-looking woman in the morning," laughs Terry.

"I know."

She toasts his bread and makes his tea the English way; the milk in first and then pouring it from a pot.

"You can still go dancing." He stirs his tea. "Evenings. Like I used to go to the gym. Look at this body, in perfect shape despite this problem now." She's not listening so Terry turns to lecture me. "But yer can weather an illness if the bodywork's in fine shape. Before doing the damage on my back I was working out in the gym after a day's graft." He fails to convince me, using hands to adjust himself, one on the table and another clasping the chair. He eases himself back and I can see why he needs a chauffeur. He might need an ambulance. "If yer went dancing, Pet, yu'd meet people just like yer meet people in that nightclub…"

"Schie…" she cynically sighs, in her guttural German tone. "I quit because I wanted to quit. I'm not telling you lies."

"Lies? Candy, slow down, woman. Who's calling you a…"

"Listen," she snaps, "I decide for myself to quit nightclubs and I was always honest about having children. And I do want children. I have always wanted children and to move to a bigger house."

"So what's the problem?"

"The problem is that I don't like this early morning lark. So eat your breakfast and shut up." She lands the plate upon the table with a thump and walks away.

"Women in the morning," he says, winking at me. Terry picks up his knife and fork and tears apart a streak of bacon.

For a person who hates mornings, she spends a lot of effort sorting through paperwork. Candy has taken a mobile filing cabinet from somewhere. She's going through it, labouring and it's almost as painful to watch her sleepy head struggling to read as to witness Terry's demise.

"You have to bring these to the clinic." There's anger in her voice but she spent her energy getting out of bed. Candy has papers in her hand. "Your health insurance documents. Do you know what all this is about? Of course not, you can't read German. Ten years in the country and not a word in your mouth. Ten years you slagged me for dancing in nightclubs. Boasting about how brilliant you were in the morning, persistent about how I missed the best part of the day. Hints, like your mother, about me being a dancing girl, a good-time girl and not fit to be a mother."

"Candy, Christ sake…"

"But in the afternoon I am looking after this house and the official letters that come through the door. Insurance, tax, bank statements. You could not fill in a simple raffle ticket. Don't you think it's time to be responsible? You need to think about health, life insurance. You want children, well they would want a father. If you fell off one of those buildings, what then, Mr Danger Man?"

"Candy, I have finished." He tries to spit out streaky bacon, letting it drop onto the plate so he can talk. "No more Danger Man. I start my new job soon, on the ground floor. Safe and sound, so why all this now?"

"Scheibe," she swears, and drops the papers onto his bacon. Candy turns away, tall in a long gown and her hair tossed with tufty bits pointing to the ceiling. He glances at me and down to his plate. A patch of bacon grease is seeping from the corner of the paper. Terry lifts it and runs a finger through ketchup to takes a taste.

"Well, now that yer finished with the nightclub we can try for a family."

Couples that argue drive me away. I leave the table, their silent kitchen, and walk into the hall gloved in theatrical costumes. I glance back at them. Terry's eating his breakfast and Candy stares out at the suburbs. She's awake now. I steal a few more moments to see the side of her face. She's taking it all in, the blue sky and the sun glittering on upper windows across the way.

"I just want you to know that I was always honest," she starts. I walk further from the door, to save myself from embarrassment. I can still hear her though. "…I never wanted you for your money. But now that you have a bad back you'll want me to be a nurse…."

"But Candy, I 'ave finished with heavy work. I start night school to learn the language. We're both starting…"

"Okay," saying it softly, "shut up and finish your breakfast. Not with your finger." I can see her through sequinned folds and feathered frills, touching his lips to shut him up. "Eat your sausage." She bends to kiss his head and hugs him tightly around his neck.

"Okay, ye're choking me." He's poking toast into his mouth as I return to the kitchen. "I'll never understand yer," he's saying, "one moment yer crying, next yer kissing and squeezing me. But yes, I believe ya. We both wanna family and that's what matters."

"What matters is you know where you go this morning. It's the pink building," turning to tell me, the chauffeur. "Where the bus turns..."

"We know, we know," he interrupts. "I virtually built the place on my own. And those skyscrapers opposite."

She's awake now, and yes, she's a good-looking woman. Candy glares at me, instructing me where to go while Terry talks of buildings he has built to the sky. I expect she's heard it all before but lets him talk, probably feeling sad to see him in such an awful state. She's a woman who knows about men at night, in bars and drunken blether. Despite her unaccommodating tone, Candy has a mothering trait, folding papers for us.

"That's a map for you. Terry doesn't believe in them."

"I don't need a…" he starts.

"Shut up and finish your breakfast. I'm putting your documents in your pocket. So you don't forget."

"Nice meeting you," I say but she seems to love him again, too busy kissing Terry's head.

My studio flat is not as warm as this. Terry has a cosy home, a ground floor apartment littered with feminine attire. My room has pale green walls that swallows warmth, like an ocean beside my bed. Even with extra money I would fail to find a home like this, a permanent place with my own front door. When I tried, they wanted to see documentation, my history and passport and a couple of references and to know my bank. I open Terry's front door and step out amongst shrubs. He's still saying goodbye in the kitchen. She obviously doesn't like mornings. Despite her good looks I detected a strain in her face, something inscribed deeper than sleepiness. Maybe, like Terry, she's getting too old for the life that she had. They're a peculiar couple but I feel a tinge of romanticism. It's my first time inside a Continental home, and although Terry's a tight-fisted boaster I want a happy ending for him and Candy. I need to witness joy to rekindle my faith in life. I really hope things work out for them, the doctor's report and things like that.

"Ready, Squire?"

"I am, Terry."

Terry has never seen so many commuters except from where he worked so high up. At this time of the morning he'd normally be on the end of a beam where most wouldn't dare to tread. Terry would have the world to himself. He was above the rat race and even beyond the rules that insisted that he wore a helmet. Only birds were above his head. He would look down and see them like ants rushing for their offices an hour and more after he had started his day. Now he's down here amongst them.

"Could 'ave travelled in on the bus," he says. "But na, I reckoned yu'd fancy a drive of this. Ever driven a Jag before?"

"I haven't, Terry, not a bit of one." This is better than Scullivan's car. The suburbs cruise by, a conveyor of homes behind shrubs and bushes.

"Worked on that block there," he says. "Done a bit of brickwork. Ever done brickying?"

"I have," I lie.

"Easy, really." We come to office towers. Terry sinks lower in his seat to look up at them as they get higher and the streets shrink narrow. He's talking again. For ten years he has worked up there and there, been early, always where wages were good. At this time of the morning he would normally be taking a coffee break on the highest beam. The boss never bothered the man at the top, the one inching up with the scaffold, with the girders slotting into place, ready to construct another floor. This morning though, Terry is grounded to the passenger seat. The pain is creeping beneath his arms, around his sides to pierce his chest. It's painful to watch.

"Watch the road," he says.

"You okay?"

"Aey, fuck. This sitting causes stiffness. I've pulled a muscle. Doctor says different but fuck 'im. I've had this before so I know the symptoms. The doc's trying to confuse it with my other illness. That's if I've got another. Probably the effects of tests. They earn money from tests. Tests and bloody more tests. A money-making racket. Think I'm a soft touch, they do."

Terry doesn't know that I have never driven on the Continent before. I suddenly realise with perspiring eyes that I'm on the wrong side of the road in his expensive car. It wasn't a problem in the suburbs where I stayed in a lane and followed a Volkswagen. Now I'm lost at a junction, and beep, beep.

"Bart, for fuck sake, you're in the bus lane."

"I am of course. And why wouldn't I be? I've only ever come downtown on a bus."

"Left, left."

"Relax."

"Overtake these."

"That's a police car."

"Oh, yeh. Stay in this lane. See that building? Worked on that. Candy's right though. It's time to think about health. I need to get insurance policies, a pension. Quality time with my kids. I've got all that to come, Squire."

"Christ, it's suddenly busy." I'm driving across a big open space, following a bus or anything slow.

"Overtake this busload of moustaches."

That's what's in there, looking out. Dark faces with moustaches from the Balkans. Or they might be Kurds.

"Yeh," continues Terry, "couldn't handle a bus stuffed with refugees when I've got a bad back. Don't like immigrants at the best o time."

"But we're immigrants."

"You might be an immigrant. I'm an ex-pat."

"What's the difference?"

"Difference to me was Paddies were immigrants come to England for work while ex-pats left to escape the tax."

When Terry talks like this I know he has more to offer than advice at work. He's a tax dodger, an expert in avoiding the authorities. Just what a fugitive needs but there's a definite derogatory tone to the term Paddy. No doubt, Terry has laughed aloud at Irish jokes and at another time in another place I would have given him what I gave Scullivan. I don't worry about scratching his Jaguar now. And, I wonder, did they ever find Scullivan's car, which I dumped in Dublin? I overtake the bus of moustaches and Terry has his face to the window to look out at them.

"They're after our jobs. You should hear 'em talk. Can you imagine 'em wankers working on our site without a clue of what to do?"

I can of course, like myself, pretending for eight hours a day. For my sins, I'm driving Terry to a clinic, to earn a few moments of his time to ask questions about my job. His job. His buildings. His car. My time.

"It's okay for them," he continues, "they have nowt so they 'ave nothing to lose. I've worked fucking hard to be self-sufficient. Now they want me to support their social apparatus. And backdate it. Taxation is legalised robbery. Steal from savers and throw to spongers. I took nowt from their system, got fuck all. Asked for fuck all. Worked and moved. Honest as the day was long. Worked and moved. We had an' understanding, claim fuck all, pay fuck all. Contribute enough for an emergency, they said. So I did and paid my way. Now, I'm sick and the bastards demand that I account for it all or pay tax. Spend my savings on tests or they won't help me. The bastards are blackmailing me."

"O'Hanagan and myself were hassled. In Holland..."

"The Cloggies are the worst for bureaucratic bollocks. Hassling me for information. So piss off, I said to 'em. Go an' kiss my arse."

"So you didn't like the Dutch?"

"Fuck, made me fill in a form the size of yer phone book. I left a blank space an' bastards treated me like a fucking criminal. Ever had that? Ever know what it's like to be a criminal?"

"I do, Terry. Christ, I'm the same as yourself. Running from the taxman, hiding from forms and computer files. Isn't the world becoming an awfully small place?"

"Dangerously small. But stick with me, Squire. I know the score with these bureaucratic bastards."

Terry has his money to lose. I have my freedom to lose. O'Hanagan has only his virginity to lose. He's so innocent he has everything to gain. Maybe he's found it with Nicki, stupid in his work, carrying bags and boxes and standing guard outside her bedroom while she teases men. Nothing bothers the idiot and I'd be a happier man if I could adopt his attitude. Credit to O'Hanagan, he wouldn't expect payment for letting me learn from him. Not like Terry who makes me drive him to his clinic through Berlin traffic. But it will be painful for O'Hanagan when Nicki dumps him. So I had better find work for him too.

"Get in front of this wanker in his rusty bubble car. Look at 'em, four smelly turds in a tin can."

"You're as bad, Terry, as when you're drunk. Don't you like anyone?"

"Belgian bastards are alright, I suppose. They know the score. But worse than Krauts for not standing in a queue."

It's true enough. I could be accused of stereotyping Continentals but just look at them. They are all doing it, mobbing a bus. Can't blame the immigrants because the natives are doing it too.

"Just park here, an' stay with the car."

"You need a hand?"

Terry doesn't reply but struggles out to the pavement. He limps to a wall, and feels it with palms as he works his way toward glass doors.

There's a bitterness eating inside Terry. After years of cheating the system he's being caught by it. There's no doubt that Terry is an asset to any man on the run; a real tax evasion expert. He's a modern European urban nomad but from the time before the Maastricht Treaty, when EU member states were foreign countries. Euro contractors were allowed to roam as mavericks over borders, or at least tolerated, maybe excused but most probably encouraged. Companies welcomed flexible workers and governments connived and turned a blind eye; have an account and invest in our country and we won't say a word to your taxman back home. It was a gentleman's agreement. Now there's talk of Euroland and harmonisation and the swapping of information; backdated. There's a fear of betrayal. The likes of Terry are questioned while they're sick, forced to explain past existence, employment, account for current assets and ancient income that was received on a handshake. The only avoidance is to erase the past. But only the new poor foreigners can do that, people with nothing. Refugees.

Terry's resting. Maybe I should get out and help. It's a revolving door that's too fast for his feeble body. There he goes, walking cautiously to the other entrance, a sliding door that opens wide for him. I look in the mirror because I need to keep an eye open for traffic wardens, although I don't know what they look like in Berlin. Having a car is a liability. What happens if a policeman knocks on my window to caution me about parking illegally? Can I see some identification, sir? A simple question and suddenly I'd be caught.

18. Last winter's wild weekend in Amsterdam to celebrate our reunion and freedom and all things butterfly.

Where's our cheques? I asked, after O'Hanagan and myself were dismissed from our job in Rotterdam. I phoned the recruitment agent, Jim Kelly, but was put on hold. O'Hanagan and myself went to the office but there was no Jim Kelly or anyone else available on that day to deal with our query.

"Sorry, sir," lifting hands to show me his palms. "I don't speak English." There was no one there on the next day or any day. I complained, saying that they could speak English when they hired us, but they advised us to get legal advice. So we did, O'Hanagan and myself trekking the streets of Rotterdam to find the office. If you please, is what they said, fill in a form and pay a small fee. Then they concluded that we were not foreign enough so we must pay a bigger fee and answer questions about where we worked before and lived and held bank accounts. So I asked for the small fee to be returned. Sorry, they said.

"Anyway," O'Hanagan blurted, "it was a lonely old job up t'ere with not as much as a blade of grass or a goat." He had been sleeping in a mini bus. Each morning he would wake early and get out before the Scottish mob arrived, before they caught him. He walked around the corner and waited for them to pass so that he could hitch a lift to work. Eventually, the Scots gave him the job of watchman. They told him to sleep in the bus at night to deter villains because it was costing a fortune to change the locks. But villains still broke in while O'Hanagan slept and they drove him to the middle of nowhere. Then they threw him out through the back. As he was telling me, I watched his eyes, as big as his jaw and staring at my shoes. I did something that I had never done before, gave a man a hug. It seemed like a stupid thing to do because O'Hanagan was an awkward lump, solid and dumb. There was no response, not even a murmur to say it's okay or it's nice to be back. So I let go of him but decided to let him stay with me. We'd go together to Amsterdam for a wild weekend. I still had money from my previous week's wage, enough to get him a woman. It was great to have him back.

Amongst the debauchery and drunkenness of Amsterdam, Hanagan's behaviour or the nonsense he spoke did not embarrass me. With so many strangers about I did not have the normal sense of shame. It's not totally surprising because I was always more comfortable with O'Hanagan if we were with tourists. There had always been a feeling in the family that foreigners were oblivious to the *duchas,* an hereditary defect that was fuel for ridicule from neighbours. But in a metropolis pulsating with laughter and music, populated with addicts and ravers, the sight of O'Hanagan picking his nose had no impact. In the narrow streets, alongside canals and amongst the cyclists and stragglers, with sounds thumping through windows, O'Hanagan was just another tourist, or even a hard man in town to do a deal. The drug dealers who loitered on the narrow humpback bridges were baffled by his laughter. Unlike others, O'Hanagan was not intimidated. He was excited by things as simple as flower pots.

"T'em are grand flower pots, Bart, are t' not?"

"They are, O'Hanagan."

"I have never seen flowers on a boat before. Have you ever seen flowers on a boat before, Bart, have you?"

I supposed that I had not. It wasn't something I had ever noticed or thought about.

"And t'ey are grand flower pots, Bart."

They were indeed grand flower pots, painted in vibrant colours, like the barges along the canal. But O'Hanagan wouldn't stop the conversation. He said the same thing at every boat. If I responded he would ask more questions about the paintwork and dogs on the deck.

"Do you t'ink the dog thinks it's a captain? A captain of a ship. T'at would be a good one, Bart, wouldn't it? Wouldn't it, Bart, a dog for a captain?"

It was these persistent questions that would usually send me into a fury back home in Ballybog and I'd tell him to shut up. When I did it in Rotterdam Nicki was appalled, disliked my attitude and eventually dismissed me. But for most of the time in Amsterdam I tolerated O'Hanagan, let him carry on about flowers and pots and dogs. I had to stop him from talking to street dealers though. He was asking if they could swim as fast as a boat or as fast as a dog. The dealers retreated from his bulk and beaming pink face, like he was already reeling on drugs. I took him by the arm and led him into the red-light area. I had learned my lesson not to keep a loaded wallet, so most of my money was already in my sock. As for O'Hanagan, I would pay for him, a treat to celebrate our reunion. While he was inside, I would hold his wallet.

We had never spoken about things like this but I knew that he was a virgin. It was a great sin that I was about to commit but I was well prepared to answer for it on judgement day. I wasn't taking it lightly, introducing him to the pleasures outside of wedlock but I knew that no woman would ever marry him, or date him. With a head like his, and especially with green scabs of puss, he'd be lucky to get a kiss.

As I passed each window I'd almost stop to give myself extra time looking in. I had to practise because I still felt uncomfortable if they stared back with their brazen eyes. It was worse on quiet streets, just her and me. Red light radiated from each window and the orange glow from lampposts warmed the cobblestones. The breeze was essence of Amsterdam, bringing cries, laughter and the smells from a thousand restaurants. At a particular time, there were only them and us in the narrow street. O'Hanagan was always one window behind and so I had space to myself, like in a confessional. A thin screen separated her and me. I was gaining courage, standing longer, daring to meet her eyes. She was not like the others but wore a flowery frock and read a book. Sweet. Suddenly she looked up and frightened me with spiteful eyes. I moved to see another. It was like at school when we had to do the Stations Of The Cross, around the perimeter of the church, spending a few moments in prayer at each holy picture. In those days too, O'Hanagan would be lagging behind, saying his prayer awkwardly at each station. I could hear him mumbling but he'd get stuck on a word and would always start again. He'd begin the prayer each time he missed a word or even pronounced it wrong. For him, it had to be said ritually from start to finish without a hitch. He'd get louder and lose his temper as he repeated it. But he was okay this night. I glanced behind. He was two windows back, watching the ground. Red fluorescent flickered on his chin whenever he raised his head and dared to look.

It was a big shock for me when I turned again and I saw him being led away by a woman in a leather catsuit. Her body shimmered under the orange light and then her curves were caught by bolts of red from each window. I had no idea where she came from or where she was taking him. Two men were following, one watching them and one watching me. She wore sensible shoes for running away. O'Hanagan, I shouted. He tried to turn but she stopped him with her finger, kissed his nose and led him like a child around the corner. I ran. O'Hanagan, I was calling and the men stepped into my path. I had to force my way past, pushing to get to the corner. Without exchanging a word, our shoving turned to punches.

"O'Hanagan, watch your wallet." I was loud and girls came out to see the fight. The assailants were retreating, fleeing with the woman in her tight shiny skin. I ran after them, along the canal, weaving between bicycles until I wondered why? There was little I could do even if I did catch them. My lip was bruised, swelling, ballooning against my tongue. I licked it as I walked back to O'Hanagan.

Until that moment I had never heeded the warnings from the family about O'Hanagan being a danger. Even the murder was not real violence, not intentional but a fluke that the shovel connected accurately with Scullivan's skull. I assumed that they kept O'Hanagan up the mountain with the goats because they were ashamed of him. Embarrassed. His rages were talked about, and were the reason why he was expelled from school but I had never experienced one.

"You jealous fecker," he was saying.

"She was after your wallet," I replied, but he wasn't listening.

"You jealous fecker," coming towards me with long steps. Then he lunged for me.

"O'Hanagan, yer fecking eejit," but his fist sunk into my bruised lip, bursting it and the taste of blood spilling between my teeth.

"You jealous fecker."

I returned the punch. It was a powerful one straight onto the end of his nose. Although he was dangerously strong in a fight, it was easy to hit him because he was too stupid to defend himself. He came at me swinging an arm and I stepped back. The force of it nearly threw him into the canal. I had to punch him, to make him surrender but it had little effect. "You jealous fecker," and swung at me again. Onlookers had gathered around us and along the far side of the canal. They jeered and laughed, which provoked him. There was a hush when I cracked a fist into his face that eventually made him stagger back. But no surrender. Instead, he did something that I had never seen O'Hanagan do before. He ran. He came at me and chased me into the crowd. It dispersed with terrifying screams from the girls. "You jealous fecker," he continued, knocking over bicycles and trampling wheels into dismembered spokes. He didn't know where I was but lashed out at the crowd. A man tried to be a hero, swinging at O'Hanagan but was thrown into the water. Drunken men were laughing, running behind to kick him. Soon an arm had O'Hanagan by the neck, strong enough to hold while reckless boots and fists rained in on him. Eventually, O'Hanagan the monster was battered to the ground where the drunken mob drenched him with beer and urine before rolling him towards the edge. It was the screaming girls who intervened, to save him from joining the other in the canal.

I remember paying money to a man ready to have another fight. I just wanted him to go away so I paid him the price of a new wheel. He went but he did not take his bicycle. Then it occurred to me that it might not have belonged to him. O'Hanagan and myself were sitting in pulsating pain. We stayed there for a while, long enough to watch a boat pass and several bicycles. Sometimes as many as three people would be upon a bike. I loved the way the Dutch girls would sit on the back, sideways with their legs crossed.

"You jealous fecker."

I didn't reply for a while but turned to watch the reflection in the water. The lights from bicycles on the other side were darting along the canal and then dancing with the ripples. The flattest country in Europe, a state without a hill, yet lots of mountain bikes.

"You jealous fecker."

"She was after your money."

"She was not."

"She was."

"She was after me."

"She was not."

"She was, after me, to be away from people. To go for a walk away from crowds and loved it when I told her I came from up a mountain. Feckers like you, you jealous fecker. If she wanted my money she could easily have taken it." O'Hanagan patted his pocket where he kept his wallet. It was flat. Empty. He stood and patted again. He didn't feel the other pockets because he was a creature of habit. His wallet was always in that pocket. So he patted it again and again and then pressed his palm against it. Eventually, he put his hand into the pocket and turned it inside out. Despite everything I had said he could not believe that such a beautiful woman would take his money. "In the fight," he said, "they walloped me and took my money. You helped them."

"You're a fecking dipstick, O'Hanagan

19. Late morning and I'm driving Terry back from the clinic. But he drives.

An impressive building with a spacious foyer. I like the polished granite floor and the varnished wooden desk that's curved and long like a worm. Designer lights illuminate spots of space where I walk but leave the corners cosy dark. It reminds me of a cathedral, a modern monument to private healthcare that invites me to wander in to see the gymnasium. I think Terry said it was here. Health pools too, but I can't go far for fear of a policeman placing a ticket on Terry's windscreen. O'Hanagan would love this place.

"I really think you should go with the nurse," the doctor is saying. I assume that's the doctor in a suit and being insistent as he talks to Terry. "She has a bed ready for you and she'll be able to explain the procedure, the therapy..."

"A bed?" cries Terry.

"Sorry, I mean a room. When we say bed we actually mean a place to stay." The doctor looks at the paper in his hand. "Oh, sorry, actually, in this case it *is* a bed." Embarrassed, he looks up. "Sorry, but the accommodation is arranged by the insurance company. Of course, you don't need to go to bed. But it is better to settle in before you meet the therapist."

The nurse is ready to escort Terry to a bed in the middle of the morning. I *think* she's a nurse, in a blue cotton trouser suit. She has her hand near his elbow, ready to take it and coax him from the desk. It's ten o'clock, normally coffee time on the highest beam above Berlin. I look outside to where I've left the Jaguar illegally parked. Terry's getaway car is conspicuous, a shiny rebel's car in Germany where motorists are so law abiding. The owner's in here propped against the reception, unable to walk convincingly and escape in style through glass doors to his fast car. The doctor wants to go too, back to his office.

"What therapist?" asks Terry. He looks at the nurse with accusing eyes. She removes her hand from his elbow and looks at the doctor. They are both trying to avoid Terry's stare. "I'm not totally stupid," he continues. "I said I'm not paying for therapists an' more tests until I get answers. It's all to do wiv me not filling that form an'…"

"Oh, dear." The doctor, realising something terrible has to be explained picks up a folder from the desk. "Did you not read the results of your test?"

"I can't read German. Not yet."

"Schie...." under his breath.

"But, it's just a strained muscle," insists Terry. "I know the symptoms. Probably some side effects. It hurts when I walk but it's getting better, isn't it?" He's getting louder, demanding an answer in the foyer but the pain returns. "But I know it's getting better..."

"We suspect that it might be malignant."

In this silence, I'm suddenly aware of this building, not the structure but the spirit, the designer's mind wanting space for souls and sadness. They stare at each other until the doctor looks down at his notes and coughs.

"A malignant bad back?" asks Terry.

"Well, we're not sure. We suspect."

"Suspect?"

"We are not sure."

"Not sure?"

"We must do tests."

"More tests?"

"Please. Did your wife, girlfriend, sorry, what's her name?" The doctor goes through the paperwork awkwardly, trying to cope with fumbling fingers and a quivering tone.

"Candy."

"Yes, Candy. Does she read German?"

"Yes."

"Did she not mention the first results?"

"It's just talk, sales talk, from an insurance company. It's because I'm paying cash. What about those questions I asked?"

There's no more talking. A silence until the administrator speaks. "Well, if the pain gets worse, you're always welcome."

"Yes, please don't hesitate to call."

Candy wasn't able to tell him but she got up to cook his greasy English breakfast. She was drowsy and couldn't eat so early in the morning, but laboured at the cooker for her man. Of course she read the results. I saw it in her sleepy eyes struggling blind through paperwork while Terry chewed his bacon and boasted about past exploits.

"Here, I'll help you to the car."

"I'm okay."

His mother called Candy a good-time girl but Candy was always honest. I suppose she couldn't lie or want him for his money. She told him so this morning. A promise was a promise and things like that. She wasn't able to find a phrase though, to explain how he would die. The pain is getting worse. He must know it now and I have no idea of what to say.

"Will I fuck pay for another test," he blurts, going out to the cold. "Not until they answer my simple question. I'm not totally stupid."

"Well, if you can't trust your doctor…" I start.

"Yer can't, that's the fucking truth of it." Terry walks unaided to the car, provoking the pain to do its worse. "Is he fuck a doctor. He's an insurance man. And that tart at reception is painted up like a whore specialising in credit card payments and asked if I would like to do a cash transfer. That's an insurance company. They love people like us, Europeans when they need us but we qualify for fuck all when we're sick. We're too fucking rich or we signed the wrong forms, or contributed to the wrong policy in the wrong country. Spend my fucking savings on their healthcare bollocks programs or they tell. That's what it amounts to. And those sneaky gypsies come in here and get it for free. Why? Fuck 'em, I earned that money and not for writing blank cheques…"

"You're getting in the wrong side."

"It's okay, I'll drive."

Traffic crawls into town, latecomers competing and stealing space to inch a route into work. We're flying the other way with little regard for the law. It's lucky for locals who don't jaywalk because Terry's Jaguar is cruising carelessly. He has to stop at traffic lights, not because they're red but to save denting a car in front, maybe two or three as we career across the lanes.

"That's where Candy works. Used to work." Terry nods his head towards the club with flashing neon lights. Ridiculous to have all that illumination in the middle of the day but I expect they're getting ready to open for lunch. They probably need to lure businessmen in to try a tantalising dish. "She'll be in there now, collecting her things." He swerves across the junction without a care for others, or even a notion that bigger vehicles are on the road. Terry doesn't seem to hear the hooting horns or feel his pain. We are skidding into a space outside the door, like we were fired to here from a gun. Terry's car really goes like a bullet. I get out too and I'm considering joining the immigrants on the bus because, whether there's a queue or not, it'll be a safer journey home. Terry is striding now, daring the pain to do its worse as he enters the club. They're setting tables inside.

"Oh, Terry," says a waitress at the door, surprised and stepping aside. She's stuffed into a frilly frock. She's too old for its gaiety and the daylight shows her ugliness. The colours on her cheek and paint around her eyes don't fool him; Terry knows she's just got out of bed and hasn't had time to fix her hair. It's sprayed with coloured chemicals to suit a sleazy nightclub fashion. She seems alarmed as he walks past and into the dark. He goes deeper, along the bar and into blackness.

"Candy," he shouts. "Candy, Candy," sliding a hand along a rail to guide him through the dark and smoky smell until he comes to beams of sleazy light. Red and yellow spots are still focused on the circle, a circus for dancing girls, his darling Candy; the darkness for the ogling men.

"Candy, Candy."

"She's not here, you know she's not." Gently, the waitress touches his arm, squeezing it. "Come on, Terry," softly, "it's no good you coming in here," guiding him to the door, to the daylight and out to a winter sun.

"I wonder why she did that," he wonders aloud, bewildered. "Like a nurse, taking my arm." It was to guide him from the dark and out to the light. She was Candy's friend and he is Candy's man and so the waitress gave him a kiss. It was on his neck, as if she couldn't reach his cheek, and then she fixed his collar as if he were a child. Does she know? "No," he says, "I didn't know Candy wasn't there. Why did she think it was such a strange question?"

The morning has finished. Busy people in the middle of the day, even in the suburbs. Thankfully, he's driving slowly now, towards wide suburban streets, back towards homes hidden behind shrubs and bushes.

"How much were they asking for the tests?"

"I didn't ask," sighs Terry. "Just said I want questions answered before paying more. But he keeps coming the cunt. Telling me that if I don't fill in a form he can't help. But I *have* contributed. I've always paid something to the system. Even the bastard British. My own country. You know if yer miss one week's contribution to National Insurance, then the other fifty one weeks of the year count for fuck all? Lot o people working around Europe don't know that. Contributions paid 'ere are not credited there and vice versa. Suppose t be, they say. In theory, but yer tried to claim? They just bombard yer with questions. And y' can't trust Connor. That's yer first lesson. He won't pay your tax or contribution so y' may as well take the cash. As much as y' can get yer paws on 'cause yer 'ave to survive. Put it offshore. Because they discriminate against guest workers. If I stayed unemployed in England an' lived off benefits I'd have been better. But the thieving bastards have to check me out," suddenly erupting. "Wants a full fucking history before he can answer questions. Wants more fucking tests. Sent me back to reception ter pay my bill. But it's just a strained muscle, I told the bastard. Maybe something else but what about my back?" He stops outside his home and rests his forehead on the steering wheel.

It would be worse if he didn't have a nice home. Or maybe that's his problem; anchored here in suburbia watching for the taxman. He's too ill to uproot and drift into another country. It looks neat with shrubs and lawns, but it's on computers. Terry is just a number with blank spaces, waiting to be blackmailed by those in healthcare or social service.

I follow Terry to his front door. Their front door. But it's not their home anymore. Things are missing. Hats and frocks and shoes have all gone away, taken flight with her feathered frills. No good-time girl or her dancing boots. Vacant coat hooks are like the limbs of skeletons, stripped of their fur and sequin skin. She's done the washing one last time, left the house for his dying days. There's an envelope on the table. He won't open it now. An apology, a letter to say why she had to leave and let him know she never told a lie. Honesty, the highest virtue they agreed. She never wanted him for his money and now he shouldn't want her to be his nurse. And yes, I expect she'll say that she honestly loves him but to be honest she had to go away. Like the morning that has gone away. The best part of the day has had its time and all that's left is an afternoon. He sits to watch it fade into an evening grey. Soon the night will come and tomorrow morning, I fear he'll stay in bed.

20. Last winter, an angel was in the pub.

I know what it's like to lose a woman. Like Terry, I was torn and desperate for the comfort of the feminine touch. Just a kiss would have helped. Then she appeared, literally like an angel to aid me in a crisis. Then disappeared. She actually dismissed me, humiliating me before going away with O'Hanagan. It happened hurtfully and so rapidly that it came like a slap across my face. She did it because I reared up on him and it appalled her. It was impossible to explain to her how everything *really was* O'Hanagan's fault. Darling Nicki, is how I pleaded, Nicki, dear, please believe me. She allowed me time to say my piece, sat me on the floor in her penthouse suite. And please, I begged but still I failed to defend myself because I couldn't mention the killing and the problems he had caused. Also, I didn't want to say that we were in the red light area, and I found myself stuttering. It was, as always, impossible to explain to strangers O'Hanagan's irritating manner.

It was a pity because O'Hanagan and myself made amends after the fight in Amsterdam. We were drawing on our resources. Holland, the flattest country in Europe, has its subtle slopes. We found them at our peril. Sheets of ice were spread across pavements and at each dip, no matter how slight, our feet would slip forward until our backsides thumped the ground. We were doing this repeatedly as we navigated our way to employment agencies. In Holland they are called *uitsendbureaus,* which translates to out-send-bureaus. This is because they send people out to work but they were sending us nowhere, except away. The first question asked, sometimes before I had finished saying *goedmorgen*, was, do you speak Dutch? After a while I started to lie, saying, yes, I do, sometimes. And on a good day, O'Hanagan here is a lovely speaker of the language. They would study us before I said the only other Dutch word I knew, *tot ziens*, which translates to goodbye.

Amsterdam was bustling, merry and dangerous. Yet, it was sedate along the narrow streets beside canals. These were lined with houses standing tall like soldiers, shoulder to shoulder with pointed hats. Houseboats with flower pots, chimneys and dogs on decks were a homely sight along the water. But it's no fun in a beautiful city when money is sparse. Prices were set for tourists and all around was temptation and decadence. We encountered American tourists, English executives and Australian backpackers. They had cameras or maps, were interested in museums or nightclubs but couldn't tell us were to find a job. Learn the language, said a hippy, and he pointed us to an office offering help to foreigners. It was great a comfort to feel the heat and see the seats, the moment we stepped through the door.

"Goedmorgan," said the receptionist before we had a chance to sit.

"We're looking for help, for work." I was sorting words, ready for questions. There was a story in my head, about how our documents were burnt in a fire.

"You're English?" she asked, which was near enough for me.

"We are."

"Sorry, we're a specialist uitzendbureau. We are subsidised to help foreigners."

"But we are foreigners."

"Sorry, I mean our resources are limited to helping with the language, to help foreigners find work."

I looked at O'Hanagan and realised that we were both in the same dumb stance.

We went back to Rotterdam while I could afford the fare. I didn't try to dodge payment on the train because, with O'Hanagan, it would be too awkward moving seats to avoid the collector.

"Are we not proper foreigners, Bart?"

"We're English speaking Europeans, O'Hanagan, and we should be proud of it."

"Why?"

"Shut up." I was just making conversation because I needed repartee. As usual O'Hanagan resorted to questions. "I don't know why." I just said it because, according to a leaflet that the receptionist gave to me, we were allowed to work anywhere in the Union. I didn't think it applied to fugitives though, who refused to pour their history onto forms and sign the bottom.

In Rotterdam I walked and curled myself against the cold, aiming for the Brits Pub. The freezing drizzle came down the street like a paper shredder and through my clothes to turn my bones to crispy twigs. I needed a new coat because my one and only leather jacket was never designed for cold like that.

"Hot drink," O'Hanagan blurted.

"In the pub." I had heard Migael talking about the blackboard in the Brits Pub. We stepped into the warmth, looked up and there it was. It had jobs chalked up, vacancies galore. There was work waiting to be done at refineries along the river Maas, from Rotterdam to Europort. If a man wanted more money, then another more urgent job was waiting to be tackled in Germany. I reckoned they'd pay cash.

Itch Wool, the irritating fabric that sheds its bits of deadly razor dust, was well talked about on the last job. I had heard how it could eat through overalls, hats and gloves to claw a man's skin. Lagging is the filthiest job for desperadoes. Lengths of pipe, laboriously fat, frustratingly thin, and the dirty bends, all needed to be lagged from the cold. There would be places where a man might need to remove gloves and use a knife to cut the fabric to make it fit. The subtlest breeze could blow lethal bits up a sleeve and cause an itch to last a week. But we needed money, so yes, I said, we'll take the job.

"We'll have a job for you in the morning," said a tall Londoner. He towered over the others while he pointed to the men I'd be working with. "Wee Jock and your one from Liverpool." I couldn't see who he was pointing to but it didn't matter because the boss, a Scot called Duncan would come over during the evening to give me instructions. I felt better, knowing that money would be coming our way, cash in the hand and no questions asked. It was time to eat, and another drink to celebrate being employed for a while. It was just until a better job came our way.

"O'Hanagan, will you have a drink and how about a bite to eat?"

"I will, I will."

Nicki was watching us. We were near the end of the bar eating dinner and sipping beer. She was sitting at the corner, like an icon in the dark. An angel. I looked again and saw her move. She blinked her gorgeous eyes and smiled at me.

"Hello," I said. I was not trying to chat her up because she was from the realm of dreams and I was old enough to know that they didn't come true. I just asked to make conversation and because she was so near and watching with emerald eyes. Before I had time to think about what else to say, she was talking. Just for two days, she said. On business with a friend, a financial advisor who is at a meeting. Came in for a snack while it was empty and it suddenly filled with men. Slightly frightening for a lady alone. Workers from rigs and ships. And you, she said, pointing to O'Hanagan, you're a man on a mission. I am, he said, and what? she asked, don't know, he said, and we burst out laughing. She enjoyed us. You're a hungry man. And you, she said, touching O'Hanagan, you're a strong man. But were you fighting with a cat? No, he answered, it was she who was fighting with me. We burst into laughter again. As we bent forward my cheek brushed against her soft skin. Sitting up, we touched again with her silky hair on my unshaven face. She was so close without a care that I might scratch her with my bristled growth.

"Are yis the men looking for a start, a job on the lagging?"

"We are," I said, turning to see him.

"I'm Duncan. Half five the morning, outside here." He was gone before I had a chance to ask about wages. It was an early start. Very early, and while I talked to Nicki, I was wondering if he had booked us on a job in Germany. Maybe a three-hour drive and over the border. I didn't want to leave town the next day because Nicki was alone and like me, she couldn't speak Dutch. We practised words together, gargling them in our throat and as we laughed, we bent forward again, touching cheeks, and I'm sure she liked to feel my rough face. She was so clean and sweet and kissable. When she said, only one more day in town, I knew I could not go to Germany.

"Excuse me, Nicki, for a moment."

"Only if you promise to return."

"I will of course, Nicki, dear," and went away, pushing through the crowd of men in working clothes. The smoky air was filled with swearing and dirty laughter. The floor was puddled with beer and I had to kick an ashtray from my path, and then a stool. I had to step over it and then a body. No place for a woman alone. A lady of the finest style and patter. She must have been pleased to find two easy-natured men who didn't swear or cough or spit. I found Duncan at the darts board.

"The job's not in Germany, is it now?"

"It's not," he said, "more like Europort but further. Be outside for half past five or we leave without yis."

"And it's cash?"

"Half with half and fuck all if you're late." The men around the darts board laughed as if he had made a joke of me.

Nicki's hair was straight and dark to below her shoulders. Dark but alive with a shine when she turned to see me return. She reached for me, just a touch and then patted the seat where I should sit.

"I've kept it warm for you."

"Thank you, Nicki, you're so nice."

"I have moved to the middle stool to be between two big men. This one here," she laughed, "is a monster of a man. But the nicest monster in all the land," touching him. O'Hanagan had never been touched like that before, having his uncombed hair flipped behind his ear by a lady's finger. Politely she announced that it was bedtime and stood. That's a stylish suit, I thought, a chequered tweed that hugged her tight, and between lapels a white silk blouse. She reached for her coat, slowly waiting for the gentleman to help, and I did. I held her long brown Cashmere while she slipped her arms through the sleeves. It was a great coat for the cold, expensive and nice to feel, and as I folded it around her shoulders I almost kissed her hair, wanting to feel it in my face. I kissed her cheek. It seemed so natural. Behaving as if I'd known her for years. Then I escorted her through the crowd of dirty swearing men and I knew that she excused me for being like them, maybe smelly. Most had not seen her until we were leaving and I felt so proud. She was taking a taxi to her hotel.

"Up with the birds," she said. "And over there tomorrow night, tea for two." She pointed to a small café while her other hand rested upon my chest. It was a date and we embraced and kissed in the freezing street but I kept her warm with a squeeze and another kiss.

"You're so nice, Nicki dear."

"Eight o'clock, and please don't be late."

"I wont, Nicki, the gentleman will be there waiting for the lady."

Lag the pipes, itch and scratch. Get home, wash, eat and wash again and then it's out for a date with a beautiful girl. There was a great shower where we were staying, next door to the Portuguese gang. I picked the lock to get into the empty room and went to bed happy, to be up before the birds, raring to go.

21. Tonight, the long arm of the law seems to have snaked its way into here.

That's another day finished and it's time to wet my lips after work. Since receiving that letter from home I have stayed away from the Thatched Cottage. I have avoided all the Irish pubs, for fear of detectives waiting for me. But now I'm desperate to ask Terry about the job. Needless to say he's been in no mood to give lectures in his kitchen. My desperation is at alcoholic proportions, enough to drive me to the pub. I heard that he's in there every evening, wanting to talk to the lads about work. And I'm as keen as Terry to talk about the job. His job.

This week, the horizontal beams were positioned for the ground floor. The lengths of metal glided through the air, swinging from cables, and me with my boots had to kick them into place as they lowered to sit upon concrete pillars. Connor put two men working with me, and told me to keep them busy. Turks, I thought but Kurds they said with stern deliverance. Okay, I said, that's just fine, realising that they don't all have thick moustaches. We shook hands and they were away to get the nuts and bolts and fix the ladders into place. They even had power tools ready to grind some ends and drill the holes before I needed to give commands. Good man, I shouted, and gave the thumbs up without a clue of what they were doing. I suppose they had no idea of what I was saying. It was a stroke of luck that two out of the three of us knew what the job was about. I looked the part though, directing the metal beams into place. I was like a cat on a clothesline, walking along its length, and back again to detach the cable to let the crane go and get another. It's only the ground floor but the wind was in my face like I was fifty floors up. My heart was bouncing, ready for another floor, a higher one. Up I'll go to the top and meet the clouds. They won't catch me now, I was saying aloud, because I'll see them coming all the way from Ballybog; detective, solicitor or Scullivan's mother.

There's a healthy crowd in this evening, so early after work. I peep through the window to spy for a detective waiting in an Irish pub. That's how they'll catch me, while I'm looking in the wrong place, expecting them to wait for me at a table. Murder is too serious for the law to loiter in my local pub. They'll approach in some unexpected manner, like an actress at the bar disguised as a tourist asking my name. Then whack, I'm caught. So I scan all the faces until I'm satisfied it's just the lads from work. The Brits are in. I know their heads from around the site or in some other pub. Staggered lunch breaks mean we don't talk at work except to swap a word or two as we pass. Then at night in a drunken binge we talk at length about the rights and wrongs of the world, raising laughs and a glass.

This afternoon passed slowly because I didn't do a stroke of work since lunch but waited for the next instruction, which never came. The job's too easy to be true and I was wondering if I should be doing preparatory work while the crane moved loads for others. Obviously, I have to wait for the other trades to do their bit, I know *that* much. Men were busy from after lunch building shutters to take the concrete. The crane was lifting crates of bricks from a truck and lowering them into the basement. I went down to explore the site. Bricklayers were building walls, rooms for boilers and meters. Electricians were wrestling with a power cable like it was a snake. They forced a bend and were fixing it to a metal frame. It was dark and damp and drips on my head so I went up on top again, to see the sun.

It will be a tonic to talk with O'Hanagan this weekend, to ask about Nicki. And about himself, of course, but she keeps sneaking into my mind. Little chance that she'd want me for her boyfriend though. There's only space in Nicki's life for wealthy men naive enough to let her tease. That's what it's all about, luring men into the best hotel or to her table to pay her bill. O'Hanagan, the poor simpleton is having his time stolen. No doubt, she won't pay a proper wage and he won't know about rules and regulations. Yes, when he comes to his senses, comes to Berlin, I'll suggest that he works with me. It was a blessing in disguise when she told me to go away. Otherwise we'd both have been taken.

"Rita, a pint of stout. And do you have any post for me?"

"Nothing."

"And was anyone asking to see me?"

"No one loves you."

Good. I've matured a lot in a year. Life's an experience, learning new words as I listen to the Brits and Germans. *Arschloch* means arsehole. *Dickkopf* is dickhead or thickhead, and *scheibkopf* is shit head. The Germans swear too but in English. There's a distinct pecking order on the job with the locals at the top, and the East Europeans and Asians at the bottom. The English are in the middle somewhere, tradesmen but they don't know their place and wont follow instructions without an exchange of words. And the Germans don't stand in a queue. It causes a near riot in the canteen, or worse, in the engineer's office where there's a special coffee machine for the privileged few.

"You use the other machine," said a German. "Mad cows and Englishmen."

"Bollocks."

"Scheibe. Stubborn Englishman."

"Ah, the English won't do what they're told," I said, today. "Didn't the Romans say t'at they made bad slaves?"

"And don't you start, yer Paddy instigator."

We carry on like it all day, slagging each other. I feel much better for it, talking to folk. O'Hanagan would love it because there's nothing derogatory said about anyone personally, like back in Ballybog. It's just jokes about each other's nationality; racism some would say but good humoured enough and getting the job done. I'm probably the only one who isn't doing a day's work. It's too risky to ask Connor because he's a sub-contractor who has invested money putting me to work while sending others away. So I need to pick Terry's brain, what's left of it.

"A pint of stout,"

"T'anks, Rita, and has Terry been in?"

"He should be in soon."

His drawling voice will be in my ear all night but I need to know what to do next, and up I'll go to the clouds, singing with the lads, one of the mob and earning a decent wage. O'Hanagan too, up to the top we will go, slagging the English, Scots and Germans from the highest beams. And isn't it as good as up a mountain, Bart, it is, isn't it? It is O'Hanagan. All we need now is a bit of grass and we could have some goats.

Two men from some place in the west, possibly not far enough from Ballybog, are arguing. I need to eavesdrop, to check that they're not detectives.

"It's fine land, he has up t'ere..." the one is saying.

"Ah, Mat, it's up in the bog. Poor land."

"Ah, Pat, it's not. He's breeding fine cattle up t'ere."

"Ah, Mat, you couldn't breed caterpillars up t'ere."

There's no sign of Terry but I'm surprised to see Gunter, our stumpy German engineer who has never uttered a polite word at work. Whenever I hear him talking on the site he says *scheibe* in every sentence. Now he's drinking with the Brits, and even here, he has no easy way for talking. Instead of asking if I would like a drink, he shouts into my ear. I duck.

"Drink," he orders. "Drink and be happy." His rubbery face winks at me, and he gives me a friendly thump.

"A small one, then."

So I sip another beer, only a small one because I don't want to spend so long in an Irish pub. But I'll stay for this, and another for the road and I'll buy one for Gunter. I'm amongst a mob along the bar, talking nonsense and watching women walking in. Beer loosens tongues, and backs are slapped. Someone's telling Gunter that his speech at the last site meeting was a load of bollocks.

"Scheibe…" unleashing something in German to cause a laugh. This is an opportunity to fish for information. Gunter might mention something about the next stage of the job and give me a clue about what to do. This is better than enduring Terry's morbid monologue. Now Gunter's pretending to climb a ladder to ridicule the lads but makes them laugh. If he would stop for a while I could tell him about O'Hanagan, a great man for working on heights and lifting loads. A job up high with me will do O'Hanagan wonders. Him and Gunter would get on too. I can imagine the two of them having a conversation.

"Drink," Gunter would shout. "Drink and be happy."

"I will t'en," O'Hanagan would say, louder, "fair does to you, and I am happy. Why wouldn't I be happy? Happy enough."

"Good."

"You're right, it is good," shouting back. "It's great craic t'at we're having, Gunter. It is, great craic altogether."

The pair of them would be so loud that no one would hear the jukebox. So I'll offer Gunter a drink. I'll just squeeze between these elbows because there's a growing crowd, but he's already saying goodbye.

"And not late in the morning," he shouts to the English. "You understand?"

"Loud and clear, now fuck off for fuck sake."

"Scheibe."

That's why I want to keep this job, for the comradeship despite the slagging. If I go back to lagging pipes, a poor man's job, I'll be treated with contempt as well as taken for a ride, like on that job last year. Lagging, the dirtiest work, and I have an itch just thinking about it.

"So, got ya," and a hand lands on my shoulder.

"Christ," turning to see. "For feck sake, Terry, thought you were the taxman."

22. Last winter, two men went a lagging. To Germany.

It was before six in the morning when we drove out of Rotterdam. O'Hanagan and myself were in the back of the van. The fellow from Liverpool, Scouse, was sitting opposite on a bench seat. Wee Jock sat next to him with his head back and mouth hung open. Brown teeth, black at the back, rotten. My paranoia was gone and I had no worries about being caught for murder now. For the first time since the killing my mind was focussed on something totally new. Nicki. We were motoring along the ring road and then along the E25.

"This isn't the way to Europort." No one answered. No one talked for droning miles. There was no radio but wires were hanging like stretched guts ripped from the dashboard. Still dark but I knew we were travelling east. Soon we were on the E30 and I was confused. Duncan, the driver, was criticising other drivers, vomiting derogatory remarks. Our van was bigger and he didn't like being overtaken, especially by women. Lights behind would flash and he'd eventually move over.

"This is not the way to Europort," I said again. An hour had passed and from the signposts I knew we were travelling toward central Holland. At half past seven Wee Jock was awake.

"How's it going, big un?" he said to O'Hanagan.

"Grand," he replied.

Wee Jock stared with a menacing smile until O'Hanagan turned to look out through the back window. The Scouse woke up.

"Fuck. Fucking knackered. What's the time? We over the border yet?"

"What border?" I asked.

"German border, what fucking border yer expect, yer dumpling?" Wee Jock was talkative in the morning, calling me a dumpling. He also confirmed what I suspected, that we were going to Germany for a job.

"Hey," I shouted to the driver, "we going back to Rotterdam tonight? I have a date." They laughed at that, a hurtful roar that hit tin walls and the roof.

"Aey, the big un and him iz a right pair o' dumplings." Wee Jock eyed me, the way he did to O'Hanagan but I wasn't going to look out the back window. It was uncomfortable keeping eyes locked on his but to retreat would mean surrender and he'd give me a hard time on the job. Then Duncan spoke, giving me an excuse to look to the front.

"We're working twelve hour shifts. You no like it then get ter fuck out." That caused another laugh. It was freezing out there and as flat as ice on a canal.

"Fucking pair of dumplings we got wiv us todey."

Nicki was more than a beautiful lady, she was mystical in the way that she appeared, graced us with her company in that dirty place, and suggested a date. I craved to see her at eight o'clock, to touch her cashmere coat to peel it off and place the chair beneath her bum and taste her hair and kiss her neck. I couldn't stop the thoughts, a fantasy swirling around inside my head while we speeded to a job. As poor as I was, Nicki was more important than the work. There were more jobs. Lagging was easy to get. Employers were the ones running, begging men to work twelve-hour shifts, misleading them. Here in this van, O'Hanagan and myself were given the option to work or walk, virtually kidnapped. Wee Jock was laughing. The Scouse wasn't fully awake yet, his head was back against the window, watching the car behind. Duncan had a friend in the passenger seat. They were talking in low voices, and offered cigarettes to us behind. O'Hanagan was never allowed to smoke and so he didn't take one. I did. I was feeling bad, lost and expecting trouble from Wee Jock. The van was pumped with smoke and probably infested with germs because Scouse was coughing and spat some phlegm. A yellow dollop landed on the mat.

"Yer dirty basterd, yer."

"Fuck," he said and sucked the guts from the cigarette.

Wee Jock looked up at me and stared again, grinning. I watched the floor, a toolbox between our feet while the drone of a diesel engine came up through the rubber mat.

"What yer lookin' at big un? 'Ave yer done lagging before?"

It was almost eight o'clock when I said stop. I saw a sign for a service station and I could walk across a bridge to hitch a lift back to Nicki.

"Pull over you fecking donkey."

"Bollocks." Duncan passed the slip road. "We clock in at nine. We work till seven ter night. We start at seven the morrow. Seven ter seven. Day after, seven ter seven, and Friday we knock off early 'an back fer seven in Rotterdam."

Wee Jock was laughing when I went berserk.

"I'm not going to Germany."

"Of course yer no, yer here, over the border..."

Before he had finished I had Duncan by the hair and a screwdriver pressed to his neck. For fuck sake, they were saying, and slow down, and take it easy. I was louder, screaming orders and pulling his head from his shoulders, over the seat away from the road. He was looking at the roof, like in a dentist's chair. The van swerved and Wee Jock stopped laughing. The fellow in the passenger seat was stretched to the steering wheel.

"Go back," I was shouting, "back to Holland or I'll fecking stab ya."

"You'll fucking kill us yer fucking idiot."

"Fecking right I'll kill yer if you don't go back."

Duncan became a submissive wimp, taking his foot off the pedal while his friend steered us to the side. They were in a state of shock, getting out with hands in the air as if I held a gun. Wee Jock was the only one willing to fight and had picked up a length of wood.

"Come on, big un," he was saying to O'Hanagan, but thankfully Scouse was out the back and pulling his sleeve. While they reflected on my violent eruption I got into the driving seat and drove forward with such speed that Wee Jock was thrown from the rear.

The land was flat with streaks of shimmering frost strung out across frozen fields. Poplars had been stripped of leaves by the wind and were standing bare. It was cold out there and I lowered the window to feel the crispy air. I had to slow and eventually stop on the hard shoulder because I had an awful fright. It was a thought. Up until now we were just murderers on the run, unknown to anyone in Holland or Germany. Now, after threatening to stab a driver to steal a van, the limelight would be on us. O'Hanagan came up beside me. He liked sitting in the front, watching cars whizzing by. Most had Dutch licence plates and I doubted that we were in Germany. The men back there had not called the police yet. We had only gone a few kilometres and I could still reverse along the hard shoulder, go back to make the peace. O'Hanagan was silent, picking his nose while watching cars. He didn't ask and I didn't tell him why I was going back. I had my head out of the window and a foot pressed to reverse quickly. It would be seriously worse if the police stopped to help, to ask questions and arrest us all. It was easy to steer because the road was flat and straight, even when the land rose up. We came to an embankment and there walked the men, to a telephone I suppose. Their breath turned to foggy clouds in the crispy air and hid their faces. I saw their legs scurrying up the embankment, in case it was a trick. The cold was punishment enough and they didn't want to be run over.

Round two of the fight was different. The cold had awakened an aggression. The Scouse was the first to attack, coming down off the embankment with a spring in his heels as I came alongside.

"Yer fucking Paddy bastard," he said, firing a fist into the open window that knocked me senseless for a moment. It was enough for Wee Jock to dive in with his hands and clutch my hair. I drove forward but my head was dragged through the window as we accelerated. Wee Jock was like a terrier with teeth sunk into my ear. I expect it was the Scouse who was pounding fast and furious against my face while the dog hung from my ear. Yer Paddy bastard. I remember little else except for the door swinging open and my body swinging with it, hinged by the neck caught in the window.

O'Hanagan was too slow. He did eventually use his bulk to fight and try to help me. But they had chased the simpleton along the hard shoulder before he was roused into a retaliatory mood. As I recovered on the bloodied grass slope, I saw him dance. They made him dance by throwing stones at him. Yer fucking scabby monster, yer, and then walloped him with a lump of wood. He chased them into the van, and was chasing the van when I staggered to my feet. They had won the day, like children taunting a monster. The van moved slowly enough for O'Hanagan to keep pace with it, only the second time in my life that I saw him run. His shoulders came up to his ears with each pounding step, or stride, it was more like a series of jumps, from foot to foot. He was like a dwarf clown I had seen in a circus but bigger. They kept him running, the Scouse and Wee Jock at the back window making faces and showing their fingers. It was a good enough ending because they wouldn't be calling the police and we wouldn't be in custody for stealing a vehicle. At least I could go back to Rotterdam and have my date with Nicki.

As the sun climbed to the middle of the sky, the day warmed sufficiently for us to survive. Walking was laborious though. We were bruised again, but this time my insides were twisted or maybe snapped to bits. I would not work for a few days. There was not enough money to pay for a fare back to Rotterdam, and so we walked towards the service station to hitch a lift.

23. Today, I might get a clue about how to do the job. A possibility.

One person never argues, a spaced-out skinhead who has been sent to work with me. Keep him busy, is what Connor said. He said nothing else. But busy doing what? I was about to ask. I hope he knows as much as the Kurds. Unfortunately, they have gone and the skinhead is deep in thought, walking about without a safety hat on his head.

"Put your fucking helmet on," orders a safety officer. "Your last warning. Scheibe."
The skinhead walks away to find his hardhat, circling the site and coming to me.

"As if something could fall on yer head," he scoffs. "Haven't built anything yet." He has a northern English accent, picking his helmet from a bench. "Where yer from, mate?"

"Holland," I reply.

"Must be shacking up with an Irish bird, aey?"

"I was, but she had a temper."

"Aey, you've picked up her accent to a T." He walks away. I thought he was gone but he's back beside me, nudging me in the elbow. "Aey, mate," he says in a low voice. "Them two are a pair of pigs."

"Who?"

"Pinky and Perky," and he walks away again, without as much as a smile. I'm laughing but I'm supposed to be giving him instructions. Pinky and Perky the two little pigs. I used to watch them on television, years ago, when I came home from school. Yes, I decide, I'll ask the skinhead, what do you think we should be doing now? Try not to reveal that I'm a chancer on the job because I'm supposed to be the gangerman here.

"Excuse me t'ere," I shout at him. "Where you going?"

"No where in particular, just wandering until somone gives me a job."

"Well, we need to get cracking on the here. So, where would you like to start?"

"Shearch me."

"Well, what were you sent over here to do?"

"To help you."

"To do what?"

"Whatever you wants doing."

"Like what?"

"Preparation work."

"Well done. That's the answer."

"To what?"

"Scheibe," shouts Gunter. He doesn't stop but strides over heaps of mud, kicking lumps from his path all the way to the yellow office.

"He's got a big head," says the skinhead.

"Who, Gunter?"

"No, Humpty Dumpty."

I laugh again, and this time the skinhead has a bit of a smile.

"Bart," calls Connor, striding from the yellow office and I know by the face on him that it's my last day on this job. "What the feck are you doing here anyway, laughing to yourself?"

"Is something wrong?"

"Fecking right something's wrong. The concrete poured and you forgot the washers."

What washers? I don't know how to answer. I don't know what I've forgotten. I didn't forget because I didn't know. If I'm honest, I would say I'm here because I'm getting paid by the hour. I'm just here, as useless as O'Hanagan would be, and not an idea of what to say, let alone what to do.

"Well," he shouts, "are you waiting for someone to take you by the hand to show you what to do?"

"Connor, I haven't got a clue what to do. To be honest with you, I've never really done the job before. I needed the money..."

"Yer fecking chancer, yer bollocks."

"Well, I'm able to do other t'ings, a fair day's work for a fair day's pay, Connor. I could do the shuttering work, no problem..."

"Bart, the best thing for you to do now is get off dis fecking site before a big German cunt of an engineer comes over and breaks your fecking face for yer."

They *are* coming too, two men in suits and hardhats and unpleasant faces. I just want to leave now, over the heaps of mud, towards the street. The skinhead is standing on a hump and he's not wearing his helmet again.

"Are you finished, mate?"

"I am," I say.

"It's a pity," he replies, coming to shake hands. "Yea, it's a pity, because he's leaving Friday."

"Who, Connor?"

"No, Robinson Crusoe."

I don't laugh. Life is to be sad and hard again, especially the weekend. O'Hanagan is coming to Berlin, staying at the Hilton. I don't expect a date or even to see Nicki, but still I wanted money just in case!

24. Last winter, we had to follow metallic moonlit snakes into a frosty night.

Our money was gone when we arrived in Rotterdam, except for a few coins and a metro token. We spent sparingly that day on hot chocolate and cups of soup at service stations. We needed it to stay alive because, despite the sunshine, the day turned cold as we stood begging motorists for a ride. I'll always remember where I was when my thumb froze at the service station on the E30 motorway near the German-Dutch border. Even my ear, which had been chewed by Wee Jock, was numb. It was past lunchtime when a car eventually stopped.

"At last." I jumped with relief, forgetting about my battered body. A radiant pain zig-zagged through my ribs and limbs to remind me of the beating.

In the warm car we enjoyed a conversation with a German who talked about country music. He mentioned that he liked women singers. Then he said that he loved women at any time, so I mentioned Nicki. A lady of good breeding, I said.

"Does she dress well?" he asked. "Good breeding shows itself in a woman's style."

"She's the bees knees," I replied, and O'Hanagan repeated it, saying that it would be a sin to miss a date with Nicki.

"They have beautiful eyes," continued the driver.

"Nicki has gorgeous eyes, gorgeous."

"Beautiful big eyes," added O'Hanagan. "We were just eating our dinner and t'ere she was beside us. Watching us eat." O'Hanagan fuelled the conversation, saying she had the nicest eyes he had ever seen on a woman. Kind and honest eyes he called them and a good woman to bring home to the bog. "... And would you keep her for your girlfriend?" he asked me.

"I would, O'Hanagan, I would."

"She'd be a good one. No man back in Ballybog would have the likes of her and she's not the type to go with another."

"She's not, O'Hanagan, fair do's to you, you know a good woman when you see one."

"And she has black hair?" asked the German. "Dark and mysterious?"

"She does," said O'Hanagan, before I had a chance to answer for myself. I had never before heard O'Hanagan talking at such ease. "Shiny and silky," he was saying to the driver. O'Hanagan was leaning forward from the back seat, between our shoulders. He was not the shy socially inept creature that lurked around the mountain road back home. O'Hanagan was talkative and unstoppable. "A lovely lady she is with a fine head of hair like you'd see in pictures. Shiny and silky and wouldn't it be great to press your face against her hair? Wouldn't it, wouldn't it?"

"It would," I agreed, "it would."

"Shiny and silky. The shiniest and silkiest and softest. Twould be the best t'ing in the world to press your face against her hair and even have it in your mouth, to taste her silky hair and her silky skin. Would you ever do t'at, Bart, would you, would you, Bart, would you ever be kissing her so much that you'd be pressed against her and kissing and even tasting her?"

"I would, I would."

The German had a constant running laugh, listening to every word.

"Would you ever be kissing and tasting and pressing together?" continued O'Hanagan.

"Jesus, I would, I would."

The driver was slapping the dashboard and roaring with laughter.

"And would you kiss her inside her clothes, would you ever do the likes of t'at, Bart, would you?"

"I would, O'Hanagan, I would, I would, Jesus, I would."

"You would, would you?"

"I would."

"Well then, I'd say she'd be tasty enough."

The driver was in hysterics and needed to steer into the slow lane while he recovered. When he was able to talk again he declared that she must be a beauty.

"She is," I said.

"Shiny silky hair...." continued O'Hanagan.

But an hour later we were at another service station. The German was only going as far as Appledoorn and so we had to start again, stamping feet and clapping hands, begging motorists for a ride. My body had thawed in the car and a liquid ache was now dribbling from rib to rib, dripping and panging on every bone. The cold wind had followed us along the motorway and soon it would numb my pain again, turning it to dormant icicles. The warmest time of the day had gone and so an endurance, knowing that as evening came the winter would do its worse. Halfway through the afternoon a car took us to the next service station, an elderly man who felt sorry for us. He asked where we were from and how did we like Holland? But O'Hanagan replied that he liked well-bred women. They had nice soft skin and silky hair, he said. Then he asked the driver if he had ever pressed himself against a woman with the softest skin and silkiest hair. I had never heard O'Hanagan talk like this before, just rabbiting non-stop about shiny silky hair until we arrived at the next service station.

Any hitchhiker would think he was going around in circles because service stations look the same. We were surrounded by a panoramic horizon whipped with a winter wind. After a while I realised that the trucks made the difference. They changed the appearance of the parking lot as they came and went. This particular station had fewer trucks, and I realised there were fewer cars. It was a relatively empty place. It could have been due to the time of day, frozen in the afternoon. Buses came in to unload rowdy youths. Traffic droned along the autoweg, commuters going home, I supposed. Going home for dinner and unlikely to come in here for a bite to eat.

"Here, get a hot drink." It was the very end of our money, a few coins, hopefully enough for a couple of cups. O'Hanagan sauntered off to the foyer while in my mind I prepared a story for Nicki, to explain why I was penniless and dirty. Somehow, despite her wealth and style, I knew she'd understand. It was just to meet her and have a cup of tea, to talk and to arrange another meeting. A few days work, even on a filthy lagging job would earn enough to take her to dinner. There was no better woman in Europe to start a new life with. It was ridiculous because I hardly knew the girl but still the fantasy floated through my mind. Then it happened, a truck stopped and disturbed my dream with hissing brakes.

"Rotterdam," said the driver. "Naar Rotterdam."

"Yes," I answered, "Jesus, yes, yes but wait a moment, don't go. There's someone else." I forgot my pain or endured it, and ran into the foyer to get O'Hanagan. Youths loitered in my way, playing on electronic machines that were pinging and flashing. I charged up the stairs, through swing doors that nearly flew off hinges and knocked over chairs. He wasn't there.

"O'Hanagan, O'Hanagan." I fell down the stairs and people moved to leave space for a lunatic on polished tiles. In the toilet I was screaming his name, banging cubicle doors and pushing open others. I ran into the women's room and out again, slipped on the floor. By this time a crowd had gathered to watch me panic. O'Hanagan was in the newsagents, picking up stickers and holding them close to his eyes. He was lifting them towards the fluorescent light and turning them upside down when I grabbed him. A queue dispersed as I reached for him to bring him by the collar. I was like a frenzied farmer dragging a dumb animal past startled youths and pinging pinball machines, out to the cold. The truck was gone.

I watched the afternoon fade in the east. Darkness came along the motorway from Germany, drawing a hood up from the horizon and across the cold blue sky. The day was gone and it would get worse. Desperation possessed me, causing me to walk in front of cars. They swerved. I confronted truck drivers in the parking lot, demanding a ride, it was urgent, I had had an accident, fell from a van, was injured and needed a hospital.

"I'll call an ambulance," one replied. While he phoned I asked others until someone told me to jump in, he would take me. I crawled in, laboriously, and told O'Hanagan to shut up when he started talking about silky soft skin and shiny silky hair. I needed to rest and so I closed my eyes and waited for Nicki. I was dozing. There was no talking until O'Hanagan mentioned Utrecht. I awoke. Obviously, the driver brought me to the nearest hospital, in the nearest town. The wrong town.

"Jesus," I cried aloud. "Yer fecking bollocks..." I must have had a fit, cursed the driver and swore too much.

The day was gone but not the money. O'Hanagan still had it in his pocket. Simple people don't know the value of money in the same way that they seldom know their strength. We must have looked a pitiful sight, pushed up against the passenger door and a few coins in O'Hanagan's palm. The driver seemed afraid of us and he stopped at the police station instead of the hospital. He did not like people swearing in his cab, and told us to get out and report the accident. It was my fault. My attitude was wrong when I realised I was in the wrong town.

"And you have no right to take the Lord's name in vain," he added. "I would not mind taking you to Rotterdam if you asked but you told lies. You swear. You snap at a helping hand."

"I'm sorry." I must have been swearing very loud, blaming him and God. Added to this, O'Hanagan's size, scabby jaw and gawking stare must have been intimidating.

"I'm sorry, as well," added O'Hanagan, although he hadn't been swearing. He hardly breathed since I told him to shut up about shiny silky hair. He tried to pay the driver.

"It's all we have," I said, sounding as stupid as O'Hanagan looked. "We must get to Rotterdam." The driver took the pittance to count and returned it.

"Not enough for a coffee. One of the coins is useless outside Rotterdam. It's only a metro token."

The Dutchman was late because of us but as we were desperate, it was his Christian duty to help. He told us so as he steered the truck around, up the road and back to the autoweg. For his good deed of the day, he decided to take us to his destination, a container port on the Maas estuary. It was near Rotterdam so we could walk the rest along the tracks or get out when we liked. We went to the end, a frustrating journey in the slow lane all the way. Nothing was said until the driver suggested a prayer to make amends. Of course, I agreed, just a little prayer and then I'd sleep. The pain in my ribs was getting worse with the warmth. We said a Hail Mary and then the driver said it in Dutch and asked if we'd like to hear the Our Father.

"Yes," said O'Hanagan. "And what about a Glory Be?"

"A Glory Be?"

"Yes, a Glory be to God the Father and the Son and the Holy Ghost...." O'Hanagan delighted the driver with rhythmic prayer. I was between them trying to sleep when O'Hanagan started to recite prayers from his Confirmation. "Come oh Holy Ghost, creator come, from Thy bright heavenly throne, come take possession..." The driver loved it, especially when O'Hanagan started to sing hymns. I had never heard him sing before. Then he started to elbow me as he went clumsily through the sign of the cross. "I'll sing a grand hymn, now," he continued, and sang a Christmas carol, folding his arms as if holding baby Jesus, rocking it to sleep.

"Beautiful," said the driver, "beautiful."

This encouraged O'Hanagan and he sang louder although he didn't know the words. Part way through the carol he was just humming like an engine and rocking faster and faster. His elbows were flying back and forth across the cab, like windscreen wipers until he hit me in my damaged ribs...

"Christ almighty," I cried aloud, "will you fecking stop, yer big scabby bollocks ya."

When we arrived at the container port the driver told me he would say extra prayers for me, and that I should fight against the devil who makes me swear. The pain, hunger and fatigue were tortuous but we followed the tracks into town. Parallel rails, alive with frost and a shine from the moon, snaked into the winter night. We followed on a laborious trail. Eventually it bloomed with orange light from industrial sites and lampposts and illuminated buildings. Although I was late for my date, I went to the cafe to peer through the window. Nicki, Nicki, I wished. It was a cosy little tea room with rich yellow walls and chequered green tables. It was empty now. My body was labouring to stay alive against the window, like an engine wanting oil and each heartbeat pumping sand through veins. For a glimpse of Nicki, I would have suffered twice as much. I ached for a cuddle. O'Hanagan knew I was in more pain than he was and told me to keep the money for a coffee or a beer. He was going home to bed while he still had a place to sleep.

In the Brits bar someone told me something to make it worse, that we could have used the metro token.

"If yer walked to Hoogvliet, mate, yer would 'ave come to a metro station, near the end o' the line. Saved ya walking. How long it take?"

"Two hours."

"Christ, ten minutes this time o' night an' seats galore. Aey, she was in here looking for you. Long black hair an' dark complexion?"

"That's her."

"Aey, an elegant bit of stuff. About an hour ago. Beautiful bird, aey, yer screwed up there, mate."

25. Today, I'm meeting the man I sent away on a bus.

It's a strange feeling, wanting to meet the idiot who I used to hide from. But O'Hanagan sounded intelligent on the phone, telling me to wait a moment while he checked his schedule. O'Hanagan has an agenda these days, an electronic palm-top. It holds important numbers for Nicki and it's his job to look after it. Yes, he said, he could meet me here, at the cosy cafe around the corner from the Hilton. I'm really looking forward and there he is sitting in an alcove. He has a new flat hairstyle, rid of the fuzzy rust. There's an arch around him. There are arches over all the tables along the wall where people sit. But he looks like he's been stuffed into his.

I wanted this time with O'Hanagan alone, so it comes as a dilemma, seeing sweet Nicki in the next alcove. Despite having her in my mind for several days, I'm actually surprised, sort of pleasantly stunned. That must be Mr Financial Advisor sharing her table, with his back to me. She can see me but doesn't have the time to say hello. Unlike O'Hanagan she looks nice in her alcove, an angel in a grotto, a goddess demanding reverence, but I know she's a femme fatale beneath her silk and smiles. Well, I too have no time to say hello.

"Bart," cries O'Hanagan. "Bart, tis grand to see you," reaching excitedly to shake hands. It's good to see you too. She has him in a woollen polo-neck sweater, and it seems that she sent him to have his hair styled. It's not short but neatly longish to take the roundness from his face. They wouldn't know him back in Ballybog. His cheeks are still red though, a windswept mark from the bog. The table is too small for him, like it's a tray sitting on his lap. It moves as he stands, and a grin explodes upon his face, and now he's blabbering in his bog accent; some things haven't changed. "Bart, Bart, tis grand to see you. And tisn't it a grand day? It tis. For sure, Bart, tis great how we've met."

"It is, O'Hanagan."

"We came on a plane, Bart. Twas great craic. Have you ever been on a plane, Bart, have you?"

"Well, not since the last time I saw you." We're still shaking hands.

"Sure, there's little space for to be tying your shoes laces. And even smaller windows, Bart. Round ones. Great craic altogether with the clouds outside."

"Relax," and I try to reclaim my hand.

"T, tis, tis Bart," he blurts, reaching around the partition to tell Nicki in the other archway. The table rolls towards me, like a lump of wood washed up and the ashtray being tossed by waves. I catch it.

"For feck sake, be at ease."

He can't hear me in his turbulent mood but pants for Nicki to join us or invite us. Mr Financial Advisor acknowledges me with a nod. I'm in no pleasant mood to be nice to them. Especially Nicki. But Mr Financial Advisor is politely turning to extend his hand, breaking off his conversation with Nicki.

"I'm talking," she snaps.

"Sorry," he replies and obediently returns to his seat.

"Kevin, please sit down." She stands and holds out a lovely long arm that's gloved in silk to her elbow.

A calmness suddenly takes me, as soft as a cloud as I drift towards her. I want to undress her arm, peel it naked with lips and kiss, kiss, kiss from fingertips to her slender neck, her delicate ears that I was allowed to taste one night, which so suddenly crash-landed. I could crawl over her table now, naked over burning wreckage to…

"So nice to see you again, Barty. But sorry, we're talking business." She shakes hands, the slightest touch and retreats, thankfully before I've made a fool of myself, bowing to kiss her fingers.

It's claustrophobic in our alcove. Everything is too small, not just for O'Hanagan but for me too. I don't like the table. We're enveloped here. I push my chair back, far enough to see the next table, the back of Mr Financial Adviser. The partition walls don't go all the way up to the arched roofs; there's a gap. O'Hanagan has his face to it to see over to their side.

"Hanagan," I snap, and he sits.

I slipped a bit there. If I'm careless again, I might be spending another sweet suffering sum on the lady. And like the last time, I'm unemployed and unregistered. In a desperate state.

".... I want to go to the fun fair," I hear her say. "A roller coaster ride. Weee," she sings to Mr Financial Advisor, "weee..." Slightly drunk, I suspect, a beguiling beauty with emerald eyes and the cruellest manner, and for a moment she had me in her palm again. Well, not this time.

"Was mochten Sie trinken?" asks the waiter.

"A couple of beers."

"Not for me, Bart. Miss Nicki doesn't allow drinking while I'm working."

"O'Hanagan, you're with me now and you're going to have a beer." To spite her if nothing else. She has a spell on him, on me, even Mr Financial Adviser is on a string. But I'm the man to break it. "O'Hanagan, how would you like a job up high again...?" but he's not listening. He's standing to speak through the gap.

"Miss Nicki, would you like a drink...?" The table's tilting again and I'm just about to tell him to sit but Mr Financial Advisor is already saying it.

"We're fine here, Kevin," he says, in Queen's English.

I push my chair back farther, enough to see Mr Financial's suit, the cut of it. I could have had a suit like that after another week's wages. I was just about to find my feet if there were no deductions. Meant to talk to Connor about the lumps of tax but it was not the best time, while being run off the job. I saw nothing of the promised expenses paid in cash and, yet again, I'm in no legal position to fight for them.

"We're here on business," says O'Hanagan, taking out his electronic palm-top. He pokes buttons on the miniature keyboard. It was never designed for fingers as fat as his. His hands were made for working the bog and grappling with lumps of turf but O'Hanagan is persistent, obsessed with gadgets. Phone numbers appear on the screen. "Important numbers," he boasts. "If they need to contact someone they have to ask me." Suddenly he seems as stupid as always but a thin veneer of arrogance has been added. He presses another number to get an address. Tis in Brussels. "We're going to Belgium for business next week. Brussels is in Belgium."

"What business?"

"Big business. Deals." He stares as he says it, with eyes waiting for applause, expecting, demanding the perfect response. His smile still stretches across his inflated pink face. But that hairstyle will never suit him. O'Hanagan has always had a wild wavy mop of rust. Now it's ironed flat with flaps on each side and a fringe on a hinge. No, I'll never get used to it. Surely Nicki doesn't like it.

She's still talking about roller coasters and the fun of a fair.

"Coward," she says in her highfalutin accent.

"I am not," protests Mr Financial Advisor.

"You're too cowardly custard to come on a roller coaster..."

"So," I say, "how long are you staying in Berlin?"

"Not long." O'Hanagan presses more buttons as if the palm-top will give him a date. It displays the time and he shows it to me. "It's a clock. Miss

Nicki likes Amsterdam best, better than horses I t'ink. But we must do business in Berlin and next week we have bigger business in Brussels."

"We?"

"We're business partners."

"Well, O'Hanagan, it's not a proper business like t'at you have a…"

"Tis."

"Not exactly."

"Tis," he insists, standing and the table tilts. "Aren't we? Miss Nicki, aren't we business partners?"

"Kevin," she snaps, "I'm talking."

It humiliates him. He sulks, lowering his head childlike to look at his electronic toy. His hair falls forward and, God, what have I done, bringing him out of Ballybog? He doesn't have a clue.

"So," I say, "you've been busy."

"We are all very busy doing t'ings," pressing buttons and it replies beep, beep, beep. "We would be in Amsterdam but Mr Moore has to be here for a party and there's a casino tonight and he got us rooms in the Hilton hotel."

"That's great, O'Hanagan."

"It tis. Tisn't it?"

"It is."

"And, have you ever stayed at a Hilton, Bart, have you?"

"I haven't, O'Hanagan, not a bit of one."

"A grand place, it tis, Bart."

"And are you going to the party?"

O'Hanagan looks towards the other table, his lips quivering, wanting to ask Nicki.

"Two beers, sir."

"Danke."

"Well," she's saying to Mr Moore, "If you continue to be a cowardly custard, I'll have to take Kevin."

"Well, that's that." Mr Moore, her financial advisor pushes back his chair and sips his wine. I can see that much. I push my chair back to see more of them, to catch a glimpse of her emerald eyes. "See if I care," continues Mr Moore. He's scribbling and talking about business, loud enough for Nicki to hear, but more to himself. He's sorting out his schedule in his head.

"But darling," she cries, "I need you." She leans across to stroke his cheek. It's all I see, her teasing finger on his face, pleading, "Darling, darling, I need an arm around me when I'm up so high. I need you to cling to."

"But you just said you were taking Kevin."

"Henry, Henry, it's not the same. I need the great Henry Moore." She sings with the tune from the Robin Hood theme, "Henry Moore, Henry Moore, flying through the sky, Henry Moore, Henry Moore..." She's merrily drunk but not so much to spoil her cute and tipsy style.

"So, O'Hanagan, have you mentioned why you had to leave Ballybog?"

"I have not, not a bit of it."

"Good man. And did she ask?"

"She did not."

"But if she did, what would you say?"

"I'd say what you said to say."

"Which is?"

"I'm broadening my horizons."

"And, and?"

"And, ahmm." He stares at the palm-top. "I went with the lads for a weekend to Antwerp and was offered a job so I stayed."

"Good man. And?"

"And all my documents got soaked in beer." Remembering it delights him, grinning. "That's a good one, tisn't it Bart?"

"It is. And would you like a job with me?"

"I would not, Bart."

"What do you mean, you would not?"

"For sure, I already have a job."

"A proper job..."

"But Bart, haven't I got a proper job...?"

"O'Hanagan, listen to me, are you doing anything dangerous, like guarding money?"

"Only if we win. But sure it's not dangerous for me. I'm Killer Kevin. That's what Miss Nicki calls me, says I'm the best."

"It's dangerous."

"For sure, they'd get what Scullivan got..."

"Kevin," snaps Nicki. "You are naughty, drinking beer and you're working this afternoon."

I turn in my seat to see her behind me, to confront her. "I insisted," I say, rising.

"Well, we know that *you* are naughty." She touches me, forestalls my move with her silk-gloved finger softly on my nose. "Such a naughty boy, who stood me up, and then shouted at poor Kevin in Hotel New York. Everyone in Rotterdam heard you. I was so embarrassed and yet I still like you. But don't you think we are destined to cross swords, you and me?"

"I..."

"Please don't answer that," moving her silk finger to my lip. "I couldn't bear to hear your answer. I suspect I see it in your eyes. You don't like me." She takes away her finger leaving my head stuck in space. "Kevin," she snaps, "we're riding in the morning and you have my boots to polish. Again. You did a dreadful job. It's lucky I did my own packing and saw the state of them."

"Excuse me," I say, eventually standing to escape her spell, stepping out of range of her beautiful hand. I need some space to say my piece. "O'Hanagan and me are out on the town tonight…"

"You may be out on the town, Barty Baby." Her face is suddenly stern, contrasting with her fluffy pink coat. "But Kevin O'Hanagan is in my employ."

I'm about to vomit a flurry of words, but she stops my stream with a smile, stuns me with another touch upon my lips.

"Oh, Barty, you have not forgiven me for chastising you, siding with Kevin and having you dismissed; but really, you were a naughty boy. And shouting at poor Kevin about the socks, it gave such a bad impression, I really thought you were a nasty man. But now I know you're not. Please, walk me to my taxi, there are things I need to tell you." Nicki takes my arm and we drift towards the door. She stops and casually rests a hand upon my chest, as if to feel my bouncing heart, to take and fondle in her palm, to hold it like a little bird. She turns to O'Hanagan. "Kevin, wait here, I need to speak with Barty alone." I'm walking out with her, arm in arm through the door and Mr Moore is down the street to hail a cab. "Yes, you frightened me in Rotterdam, the way you shouted…"

"But, Nicki, anyone would shout…"

"Shush, my darling," placing a finger to stop my words. "Of course they would shout. He drives me nuts too and makes me want to rant and rave. But he's happy with the horses, and minding me on casino nights. Nothing dangerous, I hope you know. And now I know what a saint you've been." She kisses my cheek. "Must go." Touching, hugging and I'm paralysed by her scent while Mr Moore holds open the door. "But I'm delighted to have met you," she says, retreating. My arms are reaching as she slips away into a taxi. "You are every bit of the rough, rugged character that Kevin O'Hanagan described, and no doubt a rogue, but I'm tempted to know you, Barty. And I really am so very sorry that I had to talk business with Mr Moore all afternoon. It's very naughty of me to ignore Kevin's friend, but I do hope we will meet again."

I blow a kiss. "Brussels for a weekend. Maybe a roller-coaster ride?" But she is gone.

26. Last year ended, and a new one started as bad as the last.

Between that first meeting with Nicki, in the Brit's bar, and our next encounter, in Rotterdam's Hotel New York, I lived in agony. My poor body, after being battered, got worse before getting better. Christmas came during that depression that had me detained with pain to a bundle of stained and smelly sheets. I was in the room next to the Portuguese mob. At first they let us use their bread, and made us coffee, but I was so hungry that I had to crawl out to steal a little more. If I ever recovered from the nightmare, I would repay them. They were up and out to work each morning while I rested on a mattress. I heard their heavy boots trampling down the steep stairs. It was eight at night before they returned, often midnight. Then their drunken bodies on heavy hands and boots would climb the stairs as if it was a ladder.

The landlord would visit. Movements would send bolts of pain through my battered ribs. But I had to get up to the roof, the only place to hide without having to curl into a cupboard. It was difficult enough having to return the mattress to the bedframe that O'Hanagan was using. I would lay the blankets to make the room look presentable for letting. The stairs were long enough for me to hear him coming while I painfully inched along the corridor. Thankfully, there was a halfway landing with a toilet where he'd stop and clean. With all my possessions in a carrier bag, and O'Hanagan's in another, I'd be creeping along the floor above. He'd be banging the tin letterbin and flushing the toilet and swearing. From the sounds I had heard on previous nights there was probably vomit on the floor. Although I knew only a few Dutch words, swear words have a distinct tone and I knew he'd be in no mood to find a non-paying squatter in his house, and I was in no fit state to defend myself. He would be coming up the stairs and I would be climbing the fire escape, the plastic bags tied together and the knot between my teeth. He knew someone used the spare room. I expect the warmth of the bed betrayed me because he removed the sheets. O'Hanagan stole others from the washing line. We had to sleep with our clothes on, and on a very cold night, took the curtains from the window.

O'Hanagan had changed for the better. A new man. His scabby face improved and every day he was out early, just like back home when he went up the mountain. Sometimes he'd return late because he'd wait for shops to close and scavenge around the backyards. Hunting, he called it.

"I'm going out on the hunt for food and will be back with enough for a feast." He seemed happier. People didn't ridicule him here, although they probably kept a distance, especially when he had the scabs. O'Hanagan was twice the man, full of confidence, able to talk, telling the Portuguese not to tell the landlord. You won't, he bellowed, you won't will you? You won't tell him that we're here and Bart with broken ribs? They were probably afraid of him but they liked him; going down the stairs each morning and shouting up to him to keep the kitchen clean and not to eat their food. He brought them apples and oranges one night and I would have enjoyed being in the kitchen but I was crippled in bed with pain. They must have been rotten because they pelted him with fruit. Roars of laughter flowed from the kitchen and I could hear the apples and oranges splattering against the wall, and probably against that thick head of his. O'Hanagan loved it because no one ridiculed him in a cruel way. It was different to the fun they made of him in Ballybog when they splattered him with manure.

He was sad at Christmas. We had no money for stamps or cards or envelopes. I explained in vain that the post office was closed. Still, he went out to find it, to walk against a driving sleet. I followed him down the stairs to reason with him but he seemed numb with boredom or loneliness. He went out on Christmas day to buy a card and a stamp. The sleet passed horizontally and O'Hanagan bulking the other way. We had decorations though; O'Hanagan brought them back one night. The Portuguese were gone home and the heating switched off. The New Year will be better, you with your face rid of scabs, and my ribs healed and I'm ready to work. But still, we were sad. Back home, they would know for sure that we were guilty, having left and not even a card at Christmas.

"We could have phoned," O'Hanagan said.

"Phoned? And with what and not a penny between us?"

It was another disappointment when Migael and the lads did not return from Portugal. If they did we'd have some explaining to do as we had devoured their stock of tinned food. One week into the New Year and I had money to buy them a drink and return their food. The work was desperate in sandblasted carcasses of ships or upon the ribs of an oilrig. In a dry dock I was, snaking in and out of holes to lag pipes with Itch Wool, an endless length and a burning rash. I had to wrestle the deadly material into places it would not go. It stung me through my overalls, the finest slithers of dust penetrating to my underclothes. Itch Wool didn't just become part of the fabric against my skin but seemed to grow in it, especially around my cuffs and collar and under my arms. It lived in skin, reached my bones, slithering in my blood and tearing at the insides of my veins. It came like barbed-wire down my nose with snot, and even tears from my eyes were polluted with it, like bits of rust. Coughing up itchy phlegm caused my ribs to pound, so I swallowed it.

The landlord said it was great to see us back, not knowing that we had been there since before Christmas. The Portuguese are gone, and good for that, he declared, wiping the walls where they had been pelted with rotten fruit.

"... And they broke into the spare room and tore curtains from the window, and a bed on the floor and a smell like they'd been keeping a dog. You wouldn't behave like that, would you?"

"We would not, not atall," replied O'Hanagan. It was normally me who would reply but O'Hanagan's confidence had grown so much that it was difficult to shut him up. He'd reply to anyone and feed a conversation about nonsense for ages. "And that's a lovely smelling disinfectant you're using to wipe the walls. Tis, tisn't it?"

"It is," the owner would reply.

"Tis, tisn't it?" continued O'Hanagan, "tis a good one t'at, so it tis." Strangers were great for talking to, and O'Hanagan energetically helped them. If he saw someone struggling with a box or pushing a car he'd take over the chore, saying, it's a grand day, tisn't it? His mother would have been proud if she saw him, astonished to find him in the kitchen. Cleaning walls with the lemon fresh disinfectant became a nightly ritual. He was a different man to the village idiot who would shy away up the mountain road to the bog. It was a metamorphosis.

While O'Hanagan spent his evening asking the landlord stupid questions and helping to clean the kitchen, I was cleaning me. My skin was turning red, inflamed. I would look at my skinny blotched face in the mirror and see my jaw getting like O'Hanagan's with scabs around my mouth. Turning green beneath my nose. It was worse where the dribbles from my nostrils had set hard and caked the itch inside my skin. Hot showers and cold, soap and the creamiest shampoo all failed to remove the embedded bits. I rubbed hard with towels, turning the irritation to soreness that needed to be scrubbed. I used a toothbrush. The new towels lost their softness and became deadly sheets of woollen itch. Everything that touched my body became infected with the itch. Softness turned to bristle. The irritating fibre found its way into my bed, my body shedding it until the sheets were diseased too. It lived in my bed like it did under my skin; creepy crawling through the night. I scratched and turned, knowing that soon, at six o'clock I had to be up and out for work. The itch though, would stay in my warm bed, waiting for me to return from another awful day, to wash, eat and wash again. Then it would torment me for another night.

O'Hanagan was lucky, he was too big to get through the holes so he was put to work lifting loads. He loved it, showing off with hefty boxes. If he had met one of the fellows from Ballybog who used to ridicule his jaw, O'Hanagan would have lifted him up for a laugh. In Rotterdam, he was afraid of no one. We would visit places at the weekend, down dark narrow streets to see his friends.

"What friends?" I'd be asking but he didn't know their names. They were just strangers who he'd met when he went out in the daytime while I was resting with damaged ribs. "It's just to tell t'em I have a job." They were youths who loitered on streets, laughing when O'Hanagan lifted a gate from its hinges and put it on his head. They offered marijuana but O'Hanagan was already toking, sucking the splith and inflating his chest as he held in the smoke. He insisted on buying more beer because they were his friends but I felt uncomfortable. I was too old for loitering and drinking with kids in public. Now that I had money I could sit in continental cafes, like in movies where the jet-set made eye contact while sipping drinks.

"Come on, O'Hanagan, it's time to go," but he'd ignore me. He'd bought enough beer to last till dawn. We'd be in someone's house while their parents were gone for the weekend. Or they were illegal immigrants in a squat, asking would we like to move in and did we know how to by-pass the gas meter or hot-wire the electric? We'd spend hours drinking and smoking, O'Hanagan with his own packet of cigarettes and his face on fire with a beaming smile.

I had never before seen O'Hanagan toss something into the air and catch it. He had bought an expensive silver cigarette lighter because it was fashionable amongst his new friends. They could toss it and flick it. But O'Hanagan's thumb was too thick for him to flick it. Everyone laughed when he tried to do it. There was little conversation but bouts of laughter and words in Turkish, French, sometimes broken Dutch or English and more spasms of laughter. O'Hanagan would practise flicking his lighter because he wanted to be in their gang. As he got drunk he became vexed because he was too clumsy to flick a lighter the way they did it. They could toss it high and as they caught it, flick open the top and light a cigarette. When O'Hanagan tried it, he could hardly catch it, let alone light it with a flick.

I should have used another brush to clean my teeth. The Itch Wool got into my mouth and was growing like a fungus between my teeth and beneath my gums. On the fourth week I had the Itch Wool in saliva on the back of my throat. I used lengths of bread to drag it up to spit it out. At ten o'clock one morning I quit work and left O'Hanagan there lifting boxes, showing off. It was a great relief.

The river Maas is great for looking at. I sat for a while watching it, happy. It was a beautiful winter's day with enough sunshine to keep me warm while I gazed across to the Hotel New York. The Ballybog killing was well behind us now. The hard time, the hunger and my fiery skin, together with the sorrow of losing Nicki, were probably heaven-sent to help me forget about Scullivan's death. I had survived the ordeal in exile and now felt a sense of achievement. I was a new man with money in my pocket and it was time to explore the city, starting with Hotel New York.

It was an elegant redbrick building from the time of Atlantic liners. My body was numb with the itch in the river taxi, a boat that bobbed across the water to the door where the emigrants went decades before. It was their last night in Europe, en-route to America, the New World and a new life. Mine too. This day was the first in the rest of my life and although half of it had gone, it had gone right, with me having the courage to walk out of that dirty itchy job. I was intending to have a cocktail in the public bar to celebrate but while marvelling at metalwork I wandered aimlessly and arrived at reception. On impulse, I booked myself in. Never before had I indulged in such extravagance but the itch drove me to it. In my room I tore off my clothes, walked out of them forever and showered in creamy lotions. Every shampoo bottle was emptied, sachet squeezed and the soaps dissolved to extinction. The itch-infested clothes would never touch my body again. So I had dinner in the nude. When it arrived, I was wrapped in a soft towel, taking the tray, tipping the waiter. The food was on a cushion tray, padded at the bottom so I could place it on my lap while I lounged naked on the bed. It was the finest salmon with some unknown sauce, new to my taste buds. While my tongue explored new flavours my eyes pitied the workers, brought to mind by a ship cruising up the Maas. You poor immigrants, I thought, down there in the bowels lagging pipes. But not me. Never again.

It was just an idea at first, a test to see how clever O'Hanagan had become. The more I thought about it while stretched out across the bed in my new squeaky scrubbed skin, the more feasible it seemed; get O'Hanagan to bring new clothes to the hotel. My dirty clothes were in a bundle at the bathroom door, alive with the itch. So I phoned our landlord and asked him to tell O'Hanagan to buy me clothes, especially underpants and socks and to make sure they were the best of cotton. And a pair of trousers, just plain black, or blue jeans would do but nothing with a pattern or a stripe because I feared that he'd bring something that was fashionable with teenagers in Turkey or Morocco. Everything O'Hanagan spent money on these days was trendy with his new foreign friends. O'Hanagan was even buying their music although he had nothing to play it on. I was relived when he arrived with plain black trousers of a casual style. He had underpants too, socks and a souvenir T-shirt from the gift shop downstairs.

"Good man, O'Hanagan."

"Do you like the T shirt?"

"I do."

"Tis cotton."

"It is."

"And tis what you wanted?"

"It is."

"Grand." His face beamed with achievement. "And the socks, they're grand socks?"

"Just the job."

"There're cotton. Tis cotton you wanted. Twas, wasn't it?" When he didn't get an answer he looked around the room, at switches and the bedside lamp.

He had found his way to the river by himself and got on the river taxi, and by his account, had a grand conversation with the driver. Probably about nonsense and the driver pretending he didn't speak English.

"Did you come over on one of t'ose boats, Bart, did you?"

"I did."

"They're grand little boats for getting across to here, aren't they?"

I was never going back into my old clothes again so I decided to throw the lot into the bin while O'Hanagan talked about the riverboat taxi.

"Did you feel the way it went up with the water, Bart, did you, Bart?"

I couldn't even touch them with my bare hands. "O'Hanagan, shut up for a moment and put t'ese clothes into the bin."

He was still talking about the boats when we went down to the lounge. It was even better in the evening, another era. We sat at the bar and a bellboy came past with a chalkboard on the end of a pole. He had a message for a guest and held it high and rang a bell.

"It's like a bicycle bell, Bart, tisn't it?"

I was thinking, calculating how much money I had. A lot less after booking into a hotel and feeding myself on salmon but I didn't owe any money. What was in my pocket was mine. I had worked five weeks and paid the rent and there was another three days wages to come. Three days and whatever they would pay me for the few hours up to ten o'clock in the morning. I decided I would not give money to O'Hanagan for buying my clothes because he'd only spend it on music, silver cigarette lighters and beer for strangers who loitered on streets. He was still a bit stupid.

"What do you t'ink of this place?"

"Tis nice, it tis, Bart."

"Here, have a beer."

"I will, faith, Bart, I will."

I had enough money for a week or more, maybe two, time to find a better job, move to another town. I thought I saw Nicki in a mirror but didn't look around. It was no wonder that I'd see her because she had been on my mind since before Christmas, ingrained like the itch. And of course, the Hotel New York was a more fitting place for a lady like Nicki.

"Where's the money for the socks and t'ings?" O'Hanagan asked.

"Do you not remember t'at you owe me, t'at it was my money that paid our way down from Amsterdam and bought the food and things?"

"But where's my money for the socks and t'ings," he asked again.

"O'Hanagan, shut up." He was loud and embarrassing me.

"I want my money for the socks and t'ings."

"Shut up."

"I will not shut up. You shut up."

"Well feck off back to Ballybog."

"I will not feck off back to Ballybog. You feck off back to Ballybog and give me my money for the socks and t'ings."

"Okay, you want your money, you can have it on Saturday morning and then go and live with your friends."

In the wash room I threw water onto my face. Thank God I'd finished with that job. Never again, I swore, would I go near lagging work. My face was destroyed, burning, and when I looked in the mirror it was worse than it felt. The redness was raw and the scabs were alive with puss around my lips. When I went back to the bar, O'Hanagan, the lump, was sitting at a table with sweet Nicki. She was wearing a silk cardigan as shiny as her hair, opened and it slipped off her shoulder.

27. Today, I have a new friend.

Although he has a big mouth, Terry is suddenly my only friend. He has a car, money and he can take me to Brussels! As soon as I got word of a stranger looking for me I decided to leave town.

Admittedly, I'm exploiting Terry but it's on his way to England and he would enjoy the company; no one else wants to be near him. Purgatory. Listening to him talk about Candy will be hard but after this morning's news it's important to get out of Berlin, out of Germany. To where O'Hanagan works for Nicki.

"Come on, let's feck off while the going's good, while we're in the mood."

He isn't in the mood to do anything, especially drive to Brussels. It's the middle of the afternoon and he's only just got out of bed, or wherever he's been sleeping. He's in a dirty tracksuit and painfully creeping with delicate legs and an arm held out to feel the wall. This place is littered with bottles, bits of food and burnt-out spliths of marijuana. I follow him to the kitchen. He has to rest, put his head on the table. An empty whiskey bottle is on its side with vomit caked along the edge.

"A good night?"'

"Wow, what a night," he replies, trying to lift his weary head.

I suspect every night is like this. Terry wouldn't know. He wasn't home last night but crying in the Thatched Cottage. He was there this morning to tell some stranger about my job, and to boast about buildings that he had built. And with his big mouth he told the stranger what time I started work and where I sat to have my coffee. Luckily, I was fired and so I wasn't there. I escaped.

"Had some friends around," he continues. "Fuck." He puts his head on the table again, as if to go back to sleep. If the illness doesn't kill him, the drink will.

"Friends?" I ask.

"Yeh, from years ago," waking. "Yeh, we had good conversation, a few drinks, tokes, it was good to see 'em. They haven't been gone long, just took a cab, heard 'em go out. I was fucked, couldn't ger up." Terry likes pizza, there are flat boxes on the worktop and in the sink and about the floor. He must be eating pizza every day.

"Terry, dis place is fecking filthy. If you don't die of cancer, you'll die of some dirt disease. Come on, let's go to Brussels. There's more women t'ere, more than around here."

"I'm fucked," he replies. "And I ain't got cancer. It's not proved an' my back's getting better. Told them it would."

That was tactless of me to mention cancer, a rumour from the pub. He has stopped paying the rent. Although I can't translate his letters, the figures in red are obviously amounts that are overdue. I go through all his mail while he sleeps, reading invoices, demands and legal threats. If I was expecting to die soon, I suppose that I too wouldn't be bothered about paying my dues. There's one personal letter, from Candy. Very sad. I'm making myself familiar with his personal affairs. Like Scullivan, he has bank accounts offshore and accountants specialising in tax-free transfers. Some would say it's another bad deed that I will do but when he's dead he wont need these. It's not the money that I'm after. I'm not like Nicki sponging off Mr Financial Advisor. All I need is Terry's ID. While he snores with gasps and grunts in the kitchen, I pack his clothes. It's his fault that causes me to run again, him and his big mouth. But I'll make him breakfast. I move the pizza boxes to make space. Terry has an abundance of eggs and bacon in the fridge, the type of food for an Irish breakfast. Like his documentation, it's no use when he's gone.

I came here directly from the Thatched Cottage. Although I had decided to stay out of Irish pubs for fear of detectives laying in wait, I had two reasons for taking a chance: to get my mail and to get a job. It was early this morning so I felt safe enough to get a drink.

"A coffee, Rita, and do you have any post or messages?" To be honest, I was questioning myself about why I was still paranoid. So I pondered while she poured my coffee. Mat and Pat were there, arguing again, this time about a new farming technique.

"Ah, Mat, it would be a hard job to explain the likes of this technology to someone as simple as yourself. For sure, I don't suppose you would know what electrostatic precipitation is."

"Ah, Pat, back in Ballygilcash where I come from, we speak of little else."

There were two bits of mail for me, a postcard and a scribbled note. The card was from O'Hanagan. They're moving from Amsterdam to Mr Henry Moore's apartment in Brussels. That's where he works, he said. I supposed that Henry Moore, the financial advisor, had stopped paying hotel bills in Amsterdam. They are not poor, continued O'Hanagan's scrawl, they only had a cash-flow problem and this was normal for business people. On the other side it had a picture of a canal and houseboats decked with plants in pots. Brussels would be more of a business town, I was thinking.

"Coffee and a biscuit," said Rita, placing it on the bar. "That other message was left this morning."

It was scribbled on a memo square with a business name. I recognised the logo immediately. My heart leaped like a clenched fist up my throat. The same as I saw in England, which made me bolt from an armchair and leave the country. There was the same telephone number with an Irish code, and at the bottom, I was invited to contact their continental associates who would be pleased to help. They had an office in Berlin. I clenched my coffee cup to make it easier for me to read and digest its meaning. Please contact me regarding the tragic death of Mr Dermot Scullivan of Ballybog, Ireland, on the...

His death date frightened me. Although my mother would believe that it happened after I had taken the ferry to Liverpool, the writer of the note would have facts and figures. There was nothing to prove I was out of the country. Yes, it was a mistake to tell my mother where I was. Now everyone who wanted to know, knew I was in Berlin and had been using the Thatched Cottage to collect my post. The thorny thoughts returned and palpitations were so fierce that I had the shakes. Coffee was spilling out of my cup. I couldn't drink it. Couldn't lift it.

"Who left the message, Rita?"

"Some man came this morning. Tall, black hair, wearing a mac. Never seen him before."

"This morning?"

"This morning as we were opening. No one here except Terry. He told him where you were working. Told him everything, about your job, the building, every building in Berlin."

It was my lucky day. If I had been able to do my job they would have had me. I would have been a trapped animal, surrounded by heaps of mud and police armed with extradition orders. They are probably there right at this moment, questioning Connor and the skinhead. I would have been like a rat scurrying down to the basement, weaving between the half-built walls and into trenches, through pipes to the sewer. They would have had radios for communicating and a man at every hole waiting for me to emerge from a drain. A job in the basement was safer than on the highest beam in Berlin. There was no grass or bog up there, no place to hide or goats to keep me company. Even Ballybog would have been a better site, in and out of bushes and up and down the Boreen High Road where Scullivan met his awful end.

Terry moves to wipe a dribble from chin.

"They've been banging on the door," I lie, and I kick his chair.

"Who?" bolting upright.

"Bailiffs, I think. Came to t'row you out. Didn't understand t'em. They read something official, in German, an eviction order..."

"Fuck 'em. Fuck 'em all." He stretches bony arms and enjoys a yawn. It seems like enjoyment, a moment's pleasure with a healthy yawn because every other shift from his pitiful body is a painful sight.

I'll pour coffee. It was a beautiful kitchen once, when Candy lived here, with sparkly taps and enamelled sinks. She was creative with an array of pots and pans, herbs and spices, towels on rollers and recipes on shelves. Now the kitchen is streaked in grease, snot and vomit. A fungus grows in the corner and I wouldn't dare peep into the litter bin. The place is alive and needs to be doused in petrol and touched with a match. I put the breakfast in front of him.

"Fucking great, mate." He loves it. "Brussels, yer say?"

"Great place for women. On the way to England, if you're still t'inking of going back." I almost said, if you're still going back to die. He had said it himself, in the pub one night, talked for an hour about going back to die, to be buried there.

"I'm in no fit state to go anywhere."

"You might be dead tomorrow. Come on, get out and live a bit, who knows..."

28. Terry got going on fried egg sandwiches but kept going on and on and on.

It's amazing what a big breakfast can do. I didn't need to say any more. As he awoke, Terry talked and took command. After a while there was a drone in my ears that lasted till here. When we arrived in Brussels it was like letting a dog off its leash but Terry was lame and panting. While he marvelled at monuments, I phoned the number that O'Hanagan posted to me. When there was no reply my disappointment caused me to realise how desperate I was to hear Nicki or even O'Hanagan.

Terry has bank cards. So I'm leaving it all to him, to negotiate the rent and to sign the lease. He puts his name to anything, it doesn't matter, he won't be around to pay for it, I suppose. Terry's good for that. He could go anywhere in the world with his bank cards and a credit rating that could buy a house. The Jaguar is parked outside the agent's office and Terry's inside completing paperwork. I'll phone O'Hanagan's number again.

It all started with a burst of energy from Terry, after he finished the breakfast, which I cooked for him. I made him an extra fried egg sandwich.

"But fuck her," he said, getting to his feet. "Life goes on."

"It does, Terry. Fair do's to you, there's a new lease of life around the corner."

"Let's hit the road then and see some life, Squire."

It was just the tonic that Terry needed. Maybe I was manipulating him, using him and his family sized car but I was good for him. No one else would have endured his drawling lectures about health and life, stuck in a car motoring along an endless autobahn. My world was a prison cell for six hours a day, albeit a comfortable Jaguar with a moving landscape beyond the windscreen. We passed towns where Terry pretended to be interested in a shop or a church. He was probably trying to make himself interested, to take advantage of his new lease of life. Terry wanted to visit museums and see local architecture, anything but have a drink. He wasn't drinking and driving but living life to the full, and we had to go on detours to find open-air markets to buy local delicacies. We only found supermarkets that stretched for miles and were congested with long queues at checkout counters.

"Enjoy it," he was saying. "We might never come this way again." He would suddenly switch subject in mid sentence. He could get treatment in England. His sister knew how to help. She worked for the National Health Service, and Terry told me about her job, his job, how he had paid his tax and insurance while he lived in Britain. He told me that he was entitled to medical aid and it would be better to die in a hospital where people spoke English. "... Especially when yer're old. It can be hard work to say a sentence when yer're old. In the meantime it's important t' eat healthy. Appreciating life is important too, learning about history. Yer can tell a lot from looking at old houses, about how people lived, how tall people were. I like architecture, especially arches. Any old towns coming up?"

"T'ere isn't, Terry. Not a bit of one." Luckily, I was navigator for most of the journey, especially driving near interesting towns. While the map was in my lap I made sure we steered clear of them. I couldn't have endured a lectured tour with Terry.

There's no answer. But it's ringing. I'll have a walk and then phone again. I don't want to go back to the apartment and sit with Terry. The flat has two double bedrooms and a television with remote control but no telephone. I'm happier out here trailing the streets from phone to phone. Brussels has cobblestoned roads like in Antwerp, and flags fluttering from the walls of buildings. He was right about this place, it has some fine old features.

On the journey to here, it was easy to fool Terry because he liked to be in the driving seat as much as he liked to talk. I was manipulating the situation, suggesting that we only stopped at practical places such as service stations with moderate motels where I could wash, have a drink and get some sleep. Even at night, he didn't sip a beer but went outside to smell the air, sniffing at a bit of German countryside. And I thought, yes, you do that, go out there and have a look at those petrol pumps, and don't bother me. I just wanted to get to Brussels.

"I don't need friends," he said on the third morning. "You don't need friends. We're comrades, that's all."

"But, Jesus, comrades is good company for any man."

"Don't get me wrong, Squire. O' course it is. That's what I'm saying. We're straight wiv each other. I want nowt from you, and you want nowt from me. We're just happy wiv each other's company. We're doing an honest deal. You pay petrol money and I do the driving. If I get tired, you drive. We get to Brussels and that's it. We may never see each other again. Who knows, we might be dead. No one knows. No one knows anything. We might meet again. What's going to happen is going to happen. If we meet again, that's great, but if we don't, it's no one's fault. No big deal. It's just the way things are. Everyone has 'is own life to live. Look at Candy. She had to go. She 'ad her own life, her path to go along.

This is my path. We all 'ave to carry our own cross. That's life. What will be will be but we must go on, keep going while we can because we can't just stop. No one can do that. No one, no matter who they are, can just stop. Everyone 'as to go on. Me, you, Candy. Everything just keeps going. If I died tomorrow, would anything stop? No, nowt stops, it goes on and on…"

I wanted him to stop. He talked continuously about life going on and on and on. We were over the border so I mentioned it.

"We're in Belgium. Just crossed the border."

"That's a good example. Take a bird for instance. Does it stop at a border? Course not. It goes on. Goes where it wants. As free as a bird. That's nature, that's life, going on and on, striving for to get somewhere, like at work, going up and up. We have to be like the birds, up and away. You, me, even Candy, gone like a bird and I'm happy for 'er."

A few kilometres along the road he was talking about how she used him for his money. What else could one do with Terry? I was using him for his car. Like myself, Candy probably tried to make him a companion but he talked her into submission, enslaved for his audience to listen to a monologue. Until she rebelled and flew like a bird. A woman could only use him for sex and money, but a woman tires of the one. Maybe within a year, a month, as little as a week, or in Terry's case, I sneeringly thought, an afternoon.

"Terry," I interrupted, "how long did you live with Candy?"

"Ten years. Good looking but I was picking up a lot of nice birds them days..."

Here's another kiosk. O'Hanagan didn't say when they were moving. Maybe she's not bringing him along but abandoning him in Amsterdam. It's ringing again. I'll laugh aloud if O'Hanagan answers the phone, speaking French. I can not imagine that romantic language spoken with a bog brogue. It would have been fun to have had him on the journey to here. Until that awful drive, I have never craved for O'Hanagan's company. I often avoided him, crossed the road when I saw his hunched bulk with hands in pockets, plodding towards me. On one occasion, I pretended that there wasn't enough petrol for the car to bring an extra passenger, so O'Hanagan had to walk in the rain. Everyone back home walked away from him because he was an embarrassment. Sometimes I was stuck with him, everyone together in the pub, often locked in, drinking illegally to the early hours, like on the night of the killing. There were many good times when half the village was in there. We were like children hiding from the police, keeping quiet so they wouldn't hear us and O'Hanagan felt like one of the crowd. He would start talking aloud; isn't this great craic, Bart, isn't it? Isn't this great craic to be having? I would tell him to shut up. But *it was* good craic. And it would have been better with O'Hanagan sitting in the back as we motored to Brussels, saying this is a big car, isn't it, Bart, isn't this a big car? And that's a lovely door handle, and feeling the fabric and saying shiny silky hair. If he answers the phone now I'm going to say, sorry for all the awful things I've said and done.

29. Belgium life with Terry, fried egg sandwiches and Nicki on my mind.

Each evening, while Terry watches television, I'm out on the street telephoning O'Hanagan's number. Terry sits diagonally on a stuffed chair with his skinny limbs thrown over the armrests. It's worse when he wears his shorts and shows his bony legs. He's drinking again, a few beers to help him sleep, together with a fried-egg sandwich. A dollop of brown sauce. Living with him would be tolerable if O'Hanagan was here too, someone to make us laugh. I need entertainment after walking all day, looking for work in a town stiff with politics, business and multi-lingual aloofness. Brussels is a white-collar town for diplomats, translators and programmers. I'm looking for construction sites though, holes to be dug or walls to be built. Cash in the hand jobs. Today I wandered into a warehouse asking for work lifting boxes, but spoke in flimsy Flemish when it should have been French panache.

"Will yer shut the feck up?" I said this evening. Terry didn't reply but preached and drove me out to call O'Hanagan. I let the phone ring because I had nothing else to do. Alas I hung up because of the cold and walked to here, another kiosk and in I go to phone again. I'm wondering about the postcard from Amsterdam, the scribbled note from O'Hanagan. Maybe Nicki didn't want to live in Belgium. Maybe she was only using Henry Moore for his money, and when he stopped pampering her she returned to England. Still no answer.

It was wrong to speak to Terry like that so I'll buy him some beers and bits of foreign food. I don't know what I'm buying but it's better than anything we could cook. Fried egg sandwiches can become boring. On the way home I call again, from phone to phone, every kiosk until I get to Terry's door. All to no avail and up the stairs to our apartment. Terry's commandeered the easy chair again, sitting sideways with both legs over the arm.

"Alright?" he asks without turning from the television.

"A nice evening out there. Bought you some food. Beer."

He doesn't thank me but then I suppose I haven't thanked him for the drive to here. We sit in silence eating curried lumps from paper napkins and swigging beer from bottles.

"Terry," I suddenly remember, "I owe you money."

"It's okay, pay me another time."

"Take it for feck sake, ye mightn't always be getting it."

I might call Betty. We met her and her friend last Thursday. Two quiet girls. Terry asked to share their table and had disturbed their evening before they had a chance to decline. From that moment he didn't stop talking. It was his first and only night out on the town on a short lease of life. It happened spontaneously after we went out for fresh air and his enthusiasm for living was rekindled.

"Women," he suddenly said. "Let's hit the town and pull some birds."

With *you?* I cynically thought but we were riding downtown on the metro before I seriously questioned his suggestion. A spasm of confidence had a hold of him and it was difficult to keep pace with Terry in a whiz. It seemed that his back was better but I dared not mention it for fear of a monologue. He'd be saying, told you so.

"Fucking brilliant town, aey, Squire?"

"It is, Terry."

"Night life, women, Belgian beer. Fucking magic, mate." Terry was striding as if measuring the length of the pavement with his steps. He'd fall like a bicycle if he stopped. Then he veered into a café and shouted with panting breath for two beers. "Here we are, Squire. And over there, two spare bits on their own." He walked to their table. "Are these seats free?" he asked and was sitting amongst them.

Since then he's been recuperating here in front of the television. Some nights egg runs out of his sandwich to leave streaks on his sweater. He's been wearing it all week with his matching shorts. I'll suggest it tomorrow, that we do a wash. All the clothes together, towels and sheets and clear the smell from our rooms. He's sipping whiskey. Now a gulp that leaves him exhausted.

"Want a shot?"

"I won't, Terry, not right now."

His face is more wrinkled and he's uglier than O'Hanagan. It's a wonder that the women sat with us for so long last week.

"Aey, Bart, mate, yer know that I said my bad back was just a strained muscle?"

"Yeh."

"Well it is."

"That's good." I know I'm suppose to be more energetic but the dullness of this place deadens me. Brown half panelled walls and yellowed paper to the ceiling. "What's t'at you're watching, Terry? You're glued to it."

"It's a quiz." His skinny face stays focussed on the night's star prize. Only his arm moves to lift a beer to his quivering lips. He's dribbling again.

"Christ, I'm going out."

"Where?"

"To phone your one, Betty."

"No problem, Squire."

Betty was the shy one. The other had a bubbly personality that engaged us as we invaded their table last Thursday. But Terry bombarded both women with pathetic patter about their endearing smiles and the cosy environment and his impression of Brussels. Then he boasted about the buildings that he had built to the sky.

"… But can't do it anymore," he declared. "It's nothing for a man to be ashamed of, just because he's not doing that sort of work for the rest of his life."

"Of course not," replied the bubbly woman but Terry wasn't listening. He was talking about how life goes on and on and on, that she could be dead tomorrow, we all could be dead, so we should be free as the birds. I wanted to shout over to him and tell him to shut the feck up, like I would say to O'Hanagan.

Brussels is warmer than Berlin. I don't need my one and only leather jacket.

"See you later." I walk around the back of the armchair so that I don't interrupt his view of the quiz show. There are things I don't do to dying men, like disturb their television.

"Yeh," he suddenly says, "I should have had an insurance policy. Life would have bin better wiv kids."

"What?" I look back to see Terry struggling out of his chair; the quiz show has finished.

"Any more beer?"

"Two."

"It's a fact, they keep you young. Anyway, I'm still registered in the UK. Phoned my sister. Said I'm still registered. Just pins and needles," he explains because he's limping towards the kitchen. "Paid British tax and insurance when I was there. No problem. Yeh, she's going to send my National Insurance Number. How about it, are you coming to England?"

"Christ, Terry, you change from one subject to the other in mid sentence."

He reaches into the kitchen to grab a beer. As he returns, his white lanky legs stall in the middle of the room. "True what they say 'bout the Irish, aey? Thick. Do I have to stay on the same fucking subject all night t' give yer time to digest what I'm taking about? Just asking a simple fucking question."

"See you later, Terry."

Betty commented on it too. Your friend has a problem, she whispered. It was the sort of thing said about O'Hanagan, and I'd grin, knowing that it was obvious. It would often make me laugh but there was nothing funny about Terry.

"He's not my friend," I said to Betty, "we just shared a lift from Berlin. But yes, I t'ink he has a problem. Hopefully, he'll be okay." Last week, while sitting in that café I disliked him. He was telling the other woman about me, how I tried to do his job:

"… But Bart was useless and they threw him off the job." Terry was not like a big dumb O'Hanagan but an irritating insect buzzing in my ear, the way that Scullivan annoyed O'Hanagan. Persistent jesting about O'Hanagan's jaw, and now Terry's constant reminders about my failures. Gloating. I started to think again, about the murder, and wondered if Scullivan's cruelly persistent, irritating manner eventually triggered O'Hanagan to commit murder. Last week in the cafe I could have empathised with anyone who would wallop Terry's head with a shovel. The women tried to interrupt and eventually stood to leave.

"Bye-bye," they said.

"I'm sorry, we're not good company," I replied, following out to the street.

"You leaving?" cried Terry.

"Au revoir."

"I don't really know him," I continued. "We shared the drive from Berlin. He has an illness. I t'ink he's dying…"

"Dying?"

"Cancer or something. He doesn't talk about it."

"Cancer? Oh no." She slapped her hand to her mouth as if she had said something horrid.

I walk back around the armchair to get my jacket. It might be late when I get home. Gets cold at night but the later I get back here, the better. The way I feel, if I never see him again it'll be too soon.

"Where the fuck yer going?"

"Out to phone the shy one."

"Who?"

"Betty. From last week."

"Give 'er one from me." He crawls cautiously onto his armchair, tucking bony knees up to his chest. I go down the long stairs, open the door and step out to Brussels. Streets are lined with tall terraced houses. Some have six or seven floors, balconies, arches and sculptured pillars. Orange street lamps illuminate the hotchpotch brickwork. Between the Flemish facades there are modern blocks in concrete grey. I'm getting to know this town better than Berlin. I know each kiosk like the flat. Before phoning Betty, I'll try O'Hanagan one more time. Hello, is anyone there? The ring is familiar, a lonely electronic pulse calling to no one.

"Bonjour…" startling me.

"Hello…" I cry with excitement, screaming at a recording. It's only a machine speaking French and I catch my breath. Now she speaks in English:

"Hi, I'm in Brussels, either busy or in bed but do leave a message." Nicki has a delightful voice, in French or English. Even though I've called her a bitch I want to talk to her, carry on from where we finished in Berlin.

"Hi, Nicki, tis Bart, O'Hanagan's friend. Guess what? I'm in Brussels too, hope to meet you. Just booked into an apartment, no phone yet but I'll call again. Maybe we can go to the funfair, a roller coaster ride." As I replace the receiver I feel a smile stretch across my face.

Brussels is suddenly cosy orange, warm with the glow from lampposts. The red brick houses are homely and I step out to feel the breeze on a beautiful night. I ponder about the fair and what we'd do. Suddenly, I feel ridiculous; I hardly know her and I forgot to ask for O'Hanagan.

Betty! I forgot to phone Betty. Yes, do it now because I'd rather speak to a human than return to Terry in his morbid mood, stuck in his chair and his leg hooked to the arm. I know it's bad of me, even to think of what to do if I find him dead. They'd have to break his legs to make him straight and fit him in his coffin. I've already decided to buy him the best of wooden suits to show respect. It's only right to send him home in style after I use his hard-earned money. The phone's ringing.

"Hi, Betty, it's Bart, from last week, remember?"

"Of course."

"I'm on my way to the James Joyce, t'ought I'd give you a call while I'm in the neighbourhood…"

"That would be wonderful. I can meet you there soon."

It was Betty who mentioned the James Joyce first, last Thursday. It's an Irish pub near the European parliament, where politicians meet to have a drink, a talk, or do a bit of trading. It's rumoured that, although the treaty for European integration was signed in Maastricht, the debating was done in the James Joyce. It's a place where a tradesman can have a drink with his Euro M.P. or a stranger could find a job. Same as in Berlin, writing numbers on beer mats, but I sense that I need a suit in Brussels.

Unfortunately, I left mine in Ballybog. It was a wise decision to wear my leather jacket. Cooler now.

French always sounds sexy to me, Belgian French too, or even English spoken with a French accent. It has everything the bog brogue lacks. The sounds ooze with panache, poetically strung on vocal cords and gargled in throats, accompanied by musical tones from the nose. But Betty is flat. She speaks as if it's going to be a terrible day, a depressing monotone to suffocate sounds and extract any spice or sparkle from a phrase. Whereas Terry's monologues decant his mind, Betty is raiding mine for information. This is the first time I notice her mousy shoulder-length hair of no particular style, like her plain skirt and sweater. I suppose she's seen fashions come and go, and no longer cares for dressing up.

"How are you enjoying your first week in Brussels?"

"Good."

"How is your friend Terry?"

"He wants to go to England. He's getting worse. I don't think he could drive t'ere on his own."

"And what does he do?"

"Watches the telly…"

"And what do you do?"

"I'm between contracts."

"What business?"

"Engineering."

"And how long have you been in Brussels?"

"Not long."

"And are prospects good…?"

Interrogation. Extracting information to assess my financial potential. While she analyses me I'm pondering about a roller coaster, up and down and swirling around. Nicki, dear, what's your relationship with Henry Moore, the financial adviser? We could have a foursome. Talk to each other's partner. Betty could ask Henry Moore about prospects. I'd take Nicki up and down and around we'd go and Betty's asking another question.

"Sorry, Betty, you were saying?"

"I was asking if you were staying in a hotel?"

"No, not atall. An apartment."

"Long term?"

"A flexible monthly lease until the situation is more steady."

"I'm sorry, it's time for me to leave." She should say sorry for being so nosy. "And you?" she adds as she rises.

"Me? Me what?"

"Don't you have to be up early in the morning?"

"I do of course. But first, let me walk you home."

I don't want to go back to see Terry so I'll return to the pub as soon as I've said goodnight to Betty. Then I'll think of Nicki and drink to better times to come. I have learnt my lesson and I won't repeat the mistake I made in Rotterdam. I was in a mean mood as I came out of that washroom in the Hotel New York. O'Hanagan was sitting with Nicki. It was certainly the beauty and the beast. She was chic with her silk cardigan slipping off her shoulders.

"You can ride a horse?" I heard her ask. I was watching the way a man would, wanting to reach towards her cardigan. It slipped a little on her silky arm. Her kissable shoulders.

"Sure," said O'Hanagan, "I can ride a horse, why wouldn't I?"

It was true, O'Hanagan could ride a horse. His mother had even found him a job in a stable, the only job he ever had. It lasted several weeks before he had to leave. His temper frightened the horses and made them bolt. The other stable hands were to blame, making fun of O'Hanagan, pretending he was one of the horses and trying to feed him hay. Scullivan was there in those days, before he inherited his land. No doubt, he was worse than the others for flicking manure. They would aim for O'Hanagan's jaw because it was so big and you could hardly miss. A dollop of it caught him in the mouth and O'Hanagan had a fit. The panicking horses hit the roof and O'Hanagan was sent away. Now that I think of it, Scullivan caused it, and I dare to wonder if his killing was not accidental but a deliberate and accurate blow of revenge. I watched O'Hanagan in the Hotel New York that night, fumbling with his new silver lighter, trying to flick open the top and light the lady's cigarette. Nicki had a long elegant cigarette holder and she was waiting for the light. He fumbled again and I knew he was too clumsy to ever strike an accurate murderous blow. Then he tossed the lighter into the air, not too high, just a little to impress her and as he caught it, flicked open the top to light the lady's cigarette. Perfect. And I wondered.

"Bart."

"Sorry," turning to see where she's gone.

"I live here."

"Of course."

"Are you okay? You seem distant. In fact you were walking away into the…"

"It's the late hour, Betty. Time for bed." We kiss cheeks.

As I walk back to the James Joyce, I retrace my steps that night in Rotterdam. I approached Nicki, butted into her conversation with O'Hanagan to kiss her cheek.

"Excuse me," she said and turned back to him. "That's very kind, but really, it's so expensive."

"But we will pay," beamed O'Hanagan.

"That's so kind."

"Give me my money for the socks and t'ings," he said to me.

"O'Hanagan, quiet."

"Give me my money for the socks and t'ings."

"Shut up," I snapped.

"I will not shut up. You shut up. And give me my money."

A phone kiosk and I can't help but call and listen to Nicki's sweet voice.

30. My poor dying friend, have a fry-up for the road.

Now I can spread myself like an octopus in the armchair. Eat biscuits and let the crumbs litter the floor. The carpet is sprinkled with them and ha, ha, I laugh aloud. It's a great life. I have a long finger biscuit, holding it like a cigarette and knocking off crumbs to miss the ashtray. A delinquent causing a mess and my boots upon the arms of the chair. And farting, yes, and who wouldn't be farting, eating junk food stuffed with greasy bubbles? I hated Betty's healthy rabbit food. It was forced upon me like Terry's monologue, obliged to eat and to listen and to answer questions and fill in forms. Now I have this place to myself while Terry's in hospital, time to sort out his affairs, his bank accounts and things like that. And I can do my own washing, Betty, dear, I'm not an invalid. I just need space in life.

Occasionally though, I feel guilty. To think of the torment I suffered in overcoming Scullivan's death, and then last week I found myself silently asking, complaining that my flatmate was still alive. The same man who paid the bulk of the rent, and didn't bother me for a contribution towards the petrol to get us here. I ate his food and promised, lied through my teeth, that I'd be out on a shopping spree. But, Terry, I have problems with my off-shore bank account, wouldn't you know? Of course, he was empathetic, in the same boat, and started a monologue about finance and tax evasion. I tried to accommodate his droning lecture that went on and on and on and I wondered, aren't you ever going to die?

Next, I'm going outside on this sunny day to post a letter. I'll just scavenge around Terry's room for spare coins for the phone. Make a call in the sunshine. Maybe a phonecard for convenience, the sort of thing Terry would invest in. It'll be a treat to listen to Nicki's voice. And here's a stamp, enough for the letter to my mother. I wrote to say that I have moved and to say that I forgot to pay my tax. So I must move fast, Mommy dear. I'm healthy and my memory is in fine form now. I forgot to mention it in my last letter, about how I fell and forgot it all. And of course your phone number but now a full recovery. And yes, O'Hanagan followed me, and he's a better man for it. Did they not get his postcards? He tried to call but these foreign phones and I forgot the number. That's what my mother would want to hear; it's great that we're together and I'm getting away from the taxman. Don't give my address to anyone, I said. Wrote it in big bold letter so she'd not forget. No one. Because they put it on a computer. And they're foreigners with no sense of justice but to be treating tax evasion as a criminal offence.

The sunshine's coupled with a piercing wind. There's a film of ice on the dark side of Terry's Jaguar. I was hoping to have it until he recovered, to relieve me of laborious footwork when looking for work. But he took the keys with him to his deathbed, and I'm thinking about a dead man's grip. He might be right about his back though, a great improvement but still he'll never reach England while his other illness eats his guts. He eventually talked about it, unleashed a droning monologue of medical terms, explained in painful detail the procedure his sister used to arrange emergency treatment. It was worse than filling in forms but I listened respectfully, secretly hoping that he would die soon so that I could have some peace. God forgive me but he was virtually saying it himself; passing on, is what he said. On and on and on because life goes on and on after death. 'The other world' is how he phrased it with panting breath. He was standing but had to hold onto the doorframe, almost hanging from it in his effort to deliver a speech. I stopped listening when he started about state benefits and a place to die in dignity. I cooked him an egg sandwich, and then proceeded with bacon and sausage. It was his turn but I insisted that I treat him to a British fry-up with brown sauce. In any case, I couldn't get out of the kitchen with him hanging like a rotting corpse across the doorway.

"Terry, a feast for the road. And may you be in heaven an hour before the devil knows your dead." He didn't worry about fatty food. It was swimming in grease and dollops of sauce to bring a smile to his faded face. The English are not keen on wakes but what harm to bring some healthy features to his bony body, to have him presentable in his coffin? Just in case.

Here's the postbox and there's the phone. I have called most nights to hear Nicki's voice. So sweet. For me, the telephone is the link to the other world, a land for longing and me lonely, listening to Nicki on the other side. It's the same tune; five long Continental rings.

"Hello." The word springs into my ear and like a ghost it stalls my heart, sends me stuttering into the corner. "Hello," she sings again in her angelic tone. "Anybody there?"

"Tis me, Bart."

"Barty baby, why so quiet?"

"Am, well you seem so alive after all the times I've talked to your machine."

"You *are* silly, Barty. What a wonderful surprise. But please don't ask for Kevin right now. It's taken all my day to organise him, to make him earn his keep. I have him up a ladder to paint a wall. If he stops right now

I'll never get him started again. He's so good at carrying things but I'm afraid that's where his talent stops. Even with the horses, he was such a disappointment."

"Oh no, I just phoned to suggest a roller coaster ride."

"Weee," she sings down the phone. "Barty, baby, you remembered. And can we have dinner and can we go mad? I'm already mad. Travelling and packing and unpacking and Kevin drove me crazy. But, Barty, you remembered."

"That's the end of my money..."

"Barty, it's so nice to hear from you, really is, especially as I was so rude when we met before. Please, do call again, you've really brightened up my day..."

31. Thinking of Nicki while sitting with Betty.

Words in my head, wanting to invite her but this time I should remember that I'm really phoning O'Hanagan. Play it cool, not get drawn but let Nicki suggest the roller coaster. Make her beg a little, maybe sing the Robin Hood theme, like she did for Henry Moore, Henry Moore, flying through the sky, Henry Moore, Henry Moore. Yes, business first because she is too beautiful and a man could easily forget his reason for making the call. Composing a phrase has become an ordeal. Now there's a loiterer in the phone kiosk. Not to worry, there are plenty of phones between here and Betty's place, but I feel as if I'm cheating. It seems wrong to go to Betty's home for a date while I dream of Nicki at every step. When I'm with Betty so stern and still, I long for Nicki so sweet to smell. That kiss in Berlin, her finger touching behind my ear.

When I was with Terry, I thought of O'Hanagan, how ugly he is. It's possible to be ugly and awkward but still funny. Terry was just ugly. *Is* just ugly because I expect he's still alive with lanky limbs dangling from his deathbed. I'm feeling guilty again, for not being kind to him while he withered in the armchair, waiting for him to set stiff like Scullivan. I'm even planning to take his car, like I stole Scullivan's for our reckless drive to Dublin. Woke up this morning thinking about sneaking a screwdriver into hospital to prise open his hand to extract the keys. It's worse I'm getting since recovering from Scullivan death.

Right, I have it all set out in my head. A little nervous as it rings. Must remember that I'm phoning to ask for O'Hanagan and to refrain from being swept away by Nicki's sweet voice.

"Feck," the answerphone. I'm choked and now I'm muttering. She probably knows it's me on the other end holding my silence. I slam down the receiver. "Feck," hurting my fingers. I hate technology sometimes; frustrating devices that bring my ear so close to her lips and then switches off. It's like a slap in the face but the poor girl has done nothing wrong.

Betty's done nothing wrong either and I'm going to show my appreciation with a bunch of flowers. It's amazing what I was able to buy with a few discarded coins that I found in Terry's room.

"Bonjour."

"Bonjour," I reply, singing into the intercom. "It's me, Bart."

"Push."

Number four is where she lives, along a carpeted corridor with front doors, brass knobs and knockers. Apartment number four opens before I get there. Her eyes scan me, like security cameras pivoted on needles inside her head.

"Some flowers."

"Merci." She takes and sniffs them. "Please, come," and kisses my cheek.

I kiss hers and step into her nice clean flat. Betty talks excitedly as she leads me into her clinical lounge. Yes, I'd be more at home alone in Terry's flat. There's no armchair here but a designer sofa assembled from a flat pack. The white's too bright, unnaturally and intimidatingly clean. And Betty's talking at my face.

"Pardon?" I ask.

"Shoes."

"Oh, sorry. I was just stunned by the light. Lovely big lamps."

"Thank you. Drink?"

"Not right away, Betty."

"Were you looking for work today? Did you phone the company on Avenue Louise?"

"I did, Betty, of course." But I did not phone any company on Avenue Louise or any other avenue. Betty thinks I can work for one of the international companies, assumes I'll have my own office and a car and expense account by the middle of next week. If she's not naive, then she thinks my blarney could sell sand to Arabs and ice to Eskimos. I'm a fugitive without references or bank account. I don't even have an address but a flat registered in Terry's name. Betty likes men to be proper professionals, to wear a suit, a tie with their white shirt.

"And?" she asks, waiting for the answer.

"And what?"

"What did they say?"

"They will send me an application form."

"The man across the road is English, an engineer but he's different, works with artists, and he makes wonderful lasagne. Why don't you learn to cook?"

"Now?"

"Of course, it must be difficult, having to learn French." A smile snakes across her face, demanding a reply. I can't bare it. Betty is not bad looking but she's mostly two prying eyes on a nosy face, and lips that interrogate me.

"That's a grand idea." Now, I hope she'll go away and put the flowers in a vase.

Teleconsumption has never been one of my vices. Although much of it is in English I'd still choose any alternative, especially when the woman next to me has the remote control. Betty just sat down and switched it on. We're flying though channels, occasionally seeing a compelling scene that quickly aborts to the news or to an advert and I want to snatch it from her hand.

"Is there anything you wish to watch?"

"T'ere isn't, Betty."

"Pardon," turning to check me. Inspect me with those penetrating eyes.

"I mean I don't mind."

"But don't you have any interests?" she asks, accusingly. "There must be something you wish to see…"

"I hate quiz shows, Betty."

"Me too," and for a moment a smile shines, like a glimpse of sun and now it's dull as she points the remote control at the screen. An Australian soap opera shouts out at us; neighbours arguing. Rather than watch them I let my eyes roam along bookless shelves, stopping at ornaments and redundant bookstops. There's a ceramic dog, a wooden giraffe, and a boomerang inscribed with love from Australia. It would be enjoyable to visit Terry now, in his deathbed. Join him in morbid conversation. Should I speak and disturb our night? There's probably a proper time for talking, like visiting hours in a hospital.

Wrap an arm around Betty's shoulder to break the stillness. She has wooden shoulders as stiff as her wooden giraffe upon the shelf. Here's a woman who needs a massage, to be touched or pinched and brought to life with probing fingers but no response. Now my elbow aches while I look around her home for something to inspire a thought.

"I really love t'at lampshade." I don't really. The whole room has been transported from a furniture shop window. Minus the tags: do not touch. My elbow's setting stiff like Terry's knee.

"Are you okay?"

"I am, Betty, happy enough."

"Are you sure?"

"Well, a little tired," bringing back my aching arm. "The walk, wouldn't you know?"

"The walk?"

"Interviews I mean. From place to place to discuss a job."

"But don't you take a taxi? Or at least the bus."

"I do, of course. It's just a figure of speech when talking about a hectic day."

"You can stay the night, if you like."

"Are you sure?"

"Only if you want to." She turns back to watch the screen, taking my hand. "You'll enjoy this if you relax a little. I'll introduce you to the characters and when you know them you will have empathy. It's an excellent show. You have not seen if before?"

"I have not, Betty."

"You will love it."

So we hold hands watching television in her one-bedroom apartment. I'm sure that I won't enjoy it with my hand sandwiched flat between her palms upon her lap. I'll stay the night and think of Nicki. I'll have to if we go to bed together, to get an erection.

32. **Today, I get post and a drink and an offer for a job**.

Since moving here I have received no mail, until this morning when I get two letters. One from Ireland. It has my mother's telephone number alongside the sender's address. The other is from here, Belgium, and addressed to Bart. Could only be from Terry. Time to put the kettle on. A cup of tea while I read my post.

Mom's delighted that I've recovered from my fall and that my memory's back to normal. She writes her telephone number again and says I'm right about computers, they have almost taken over the world. If one computer has my address, they will all have my address. And no one has more computers than the taxman. She understands the situation and assures me that she'll be too clever to give away information. *Don't forget to send a telephone number. And what about O'Hanagan? There's been people looking for him too, on the phone and at the door and not a word of what they want. Would it be the tax, do you think? And does he have a phone? Do any of you have a phone or what sort of a backward place are you living in?*

A sip of tea before opening the big square envelope. It's a card with a blooming bunch of flowers. I fear the worse and guilt rides up, dreading that it's a begging letter: please, please come and visit your dying friend. Terry's right. I can hardly bare to look, opening it wide to see a scribbled note from…

So I start again, reading with a pounding heart. Oh, Nicki dear, what lovely loopy letters you do with a swirl of your pen. And, yes, my dear, you're so right, I was horrid to leave messages galore for Kevin O'Hanagan, and not one for lonely Nicki, forsaken in a foreign town. Not as much as a hello, and I had promised to take her to the funfair. She still sends all her love. Her whirling hand invites me for dinner. And please, Barty, don't be late.

Of course, she is right. It was utterly horrid of me to ignore her. She's a saint who has already apologised for her behaviour. It's more than I have done. Like everyone else, I have often ignored O'Hanagan, and would have treated his friends as she did but he had no friends. It's obvious why Nicki appeared so rude. She was only being wary. And what woman would not be cautious of O'Hanagan's friend? Anyone who was friendly with O'Hanagan couldn't be right in the head, she'd think. And me, his cousin, a relation and travelling companion. But Nicki was kind and beautiful, the only woman who ever let O'Hanagan sit in her company, and bring along his friend whom she'd only met once. Twice, when I made such a bad impression about money for the socks and things. Last time, she was sincere and forgiving and gave me the nicest kiss when we parted. She touched my neck with her finger. And if that wasn't enough, she apologised in Brussels when I phoned. It is the least I could do, take Nicki on a roller coaster, let her cling to me as we fly through the sky; Bart Rabbit, Bart Rabbit, flying through the sky, Bart Rabbit, Bart Rabbit, with his new girl friend. She's a nice girl. Yes, I'll take her for a meal, to thank her for all that she has done for O'Hanagan. Apart from his mother, Nicki has done more for O'Hanagan than anyone in the world. He's seen some fine places in Europe, the best stables in Holland and slept in Hilton hotels in exciting cities. It's better to be a servant in a fine house than a village idiot in Ballybog.

Happiness is a wonderful experience, best taken in bed. I want to savour these moments while I read it again. Then I'll get up to go hunting for a job. So I slip back under blankets and open the card. Dear Barty, is how she starts, you are indeed an awful man, to phone and tease and not call back.... A knock disturbs me, a policeman's knock! The front door swings open and a lively pair of legs is coming to get me. Feet pounding up the stairs as if they own the place. My bedroom door pushes open against the pile of clothes waiting for the wash. If it was night, I would have thought it was a ghost. It's beaming Terry as bright as day, out of hospital and full of beans.

"Feck sake, you frightened the life from me."

"Told yer," he sings. "Aey, what the fuck did I say? Just a strained muscle. A few other problems but this body, they said, hasn't been beaten yet."

"Yes, it's amazing what modern medicine can do." To bring a bag of bones back to life, but I won't dampen this cheerful occasion.

"The doctors were really impressed at how I'd bin fighting it. Biggest problem was lack of nourishment an' too much booze..." Terry talks excitedly about his treatment, with arms moving like windscreen wipers. Not just the medical treatment, but the fuss the staff made of him, "... Brave fighter... and they're able to prolong my life to pension age. Of course, 'ave to return to have my batteries recharged. But it's mostly down to lifestyle and diet. Sitting around boozing is bad for anyone..."

It seems that he can live like this for years, stretching out his life to spend another month in the apartment, talking conversation to death while doctors experiment to make incurable ailments a relic of the past.

"Tat's grand, Terry. And it was lonely without you…"

"We should have a routine for the shopping and cooking. Have fresh fruit and vegetables in the kitchen. If it's there we'll eat it, a bowl of fruit." My bedside table is suddenly littered with leaflets about medical research, and a Pan European charity for sufferers. "It's a self help group really," he says. "There's a campaign. Gettin involved. Brussels is a great place for lobbying politicians. Make 'em listen. Do yer know how much public money is spent on arms compared with cancer research? …."

"Tat's grand, Terry. But I have an interview for a job today. And a date tonight."

"I'm talking long-term, Squire. Wiv bin eating too much shit. I'll get some shopping in…"

"Good man, Terry, I'll talk to you later."

I'm going to the phone this minute to tell Nicki that I need to escape tonight. Dinner for two at eight o'clock and don't be late. Terry's too excited to notice that I've left my leather jacket in his bedroom. He's going through his papers, unaware that they've been read and digested by his flatmate.

"Need a filing system," he decides. "H for health. L for lifestyle…"

"Terry, shut up a moment." I take his hand, and give him a hug. "No, it's grand to see you alive. Feck sake, I was beginning to feel bad, t'ought you sent me a card begging for a visitor. Sorry I didn't make it…"

"Agh, bollocks."

"No, really."

"No time for visitors in there, Squire. First I was filling in forms and then I was in for tests. Told yer, that bastard in Berlin had me by the bollocks. And this bad back could have been triggered by stress an' strain they say…"

"Terry, before you start your ranting, I've stole all your loose change, had to…"

"No problem. What's a few bob amongst mates?"

"Bought you flowers but I gave t'em to Betty."

"Still seeing her?"

"I am."

"Got your leg over yet?"

"I did, the other night but my mind's on another, a real beauty. Did I ever tell you about the one O'Hanagan was with - Nicki?"

"Some nice birds in that hospital. Best part of the therapy, Squire." He walks out to the kitchen. A happy man. I'm happy too. I pick up my leather jacket; it could turn cold out there and I might be gone all day.

The disadvantage of using Irish pubs for finding work is the cost. But I'm only having one drink today. A toast to Nicki. A toast to Terry too but I can only afford one drink. I'll make it last and loiter near the door to catch the few heads that might be in for lunch. They're a useless lot. The international community in Brussels is a different ilk to the rowdy crowd I knew in Berlin or Rotterdam. Brussels becomes more distant the closer I get. Even London was chattier with their mouths sealed closed with nothing to mutter except in a queue to say get to the back. These made-to-measure groups here would know nothing of casual work unless it came as a directive from the European Commission.

"A beer, please."

"Which?" asks the barman; he expects me to take a stout.

"Just a tap beer," I say. "Grand day." There's no response, and just as well because I'll be saying that I need to save my money for a date tonight. Career folk in cliques are what I see: boisterous businessmen and antics from administrators. In the corner, a couple are having discreet words over a drink.

"One beer," says the barman, placing it on the counter. Froth spills over and runs down the outside of the glass.

"T'ank you." I take it to the door, to look out at blue sky and drink to Terry. And Nicki, I'll be on the phone soon to say, yes, of course I won't be late.

"Hello, there."

I turn to see who's shouting into my ear. He's a chubby man with curly hair and the froth of beer on his upper lip.

"Oh, hello," I reply, to the familiar head who laughed about a cat one night. Now he's sober. I'm sober too and unable to recall why we laughed so loud.

"Grand day, so it is."

"Tis," I reply.

"You didn't see a ginger-headed bastard come by here?"

"I didn't."

"Jaysus. Second time this week." He tilts back his head to empty his glass into his mouth. "Can't get reliable men in this town."

"And what line of business are you in?"

"Computer-cabling. We have an office to wire up the weekend…"

"Of course," I say, "we were talking about work the other night."

"Were we? Christ, there's so many nights I can't remember what I was talking about."

"Aren't I in the same business? Just finished the project in Antwerp…"

"Ah, Christ, I remember you now." He wipes his lip with the back of his hand. "You wouldn't be free to take on another bit of work now…?"

"Ah, I wouldn't," I say. "Work up to my ears and jobs galore and my first day off in months."

"Shite."

"Of course, I'd consider it if there was cash in the hand. But all my tools are packed and off to Rotterdam for mountain of a job. Although, we're not starting work until…"

"Don't worry about tools and come up to the bar. And what was your name again?"

"Bart."

"Bart, of course, I remember you now. I'm Paddy," offering to shake hands. "And what will you be drinking?"

"A pint of stout, one for the road. But first, I must phone to confirm a date." Yes, it's my lucky day with a letter from home, a date tonight and a job lined up. Computer-cabling sounds easy enough. "Paddy, I have an important call to make, you wouldn't have a coin for the phone? The apprentice is away with my mobile…"

"Here, use mine."

"You're a gentleman."

33. Tonight, I have a date.

It might be raining but for me it's a sun-drenched night. Orange sodium light spills from lampposts to soak the city streets, on cobblestones and tarmac, up brickwork walls to parapet points. Wet like rain but diluted with flaming juice blown in from sunny Spain and settled like snow. Not so deep, just a veneer, a matt varnish, coloured but translucent so that every twig and rock keeps its shape. And a glitter in every crater where a puddle lives, like diamonds embedded in stone, twinkling, winking at me to say good luck. In a taxi I'm happy with Nicki, looking out at Brussels in orange streetlight.

"Oh, goody," she said, when I phoned, "so glad my card found you. All those messages for Kevin O'Hanagan but not even a hello for me."

"Nicki, Nicki," I was pleading.

"Naughty Barty," she replied and said she'd be ready at eight o'clock, and to wait in the forecourt so that the taxi won't run away. So I waited till nine, worrying about the cost and then the driver asked for more money. But it was worth every cent and moment of my time. The front door opened and Nicki came out into the night. She was an angel in a long frock coat, chic and unbuttoned and I caught a glimpse of crimson silk and pink.

"Barty baby, have I kept you long?"

"Nicki, Nicki," is the best I could say, "Nicki, Nicki," nervously trying again. She was stunning with emerald eyes that zapped me to the ground, but she was kind and allowed me to open the door for her.

It's a beautiful city. A beautiful night. Beautiful trees. Everything is butterfly and I'm seeing places where people live. Not like Berlin where I had only travelled from city-centre bars to industrial estates and back to my bedsit home above a shop. Here with Nicki in the south of the city, where residents work in consulates or jet out to do deals and home again to walk their dog.

"Oh look, Barty, aren't those the most magnificent towers?"

"They are." She loves architecture and so, driver, I order, drive around again, and again to wherever she wants to go.

"And look at that, all lit up at night, Barty dear, can we see it all again?"

We can, of course, Nicki darling, Nicki kitten. Driver please, around again. And again. Three times we circle the arch so Nicki can see it all again. It's a happy time in my life, flying through Uccles, into Brussels to show Nicki all the sights and now we stop at half past ten.

"Time for dinner, Nicki, dear."

I take her coat, peeling it from her silky arms and surprised to see she isn't wearing a skirt. She's so fashionable, ahead of her time in designer frills. I ogle her thighs in embroidered lingerie, pink panties or bloomers, whatever they are. She's sweet in fluffy socks and crimson booties. No woman would dress like that in Ballybog, chic in cheeky pink and a silky top, while wondering about nibbling chicken drumsticks.

"Excuse me, sir," asks the waiter, "would you like me to take the lady's coat?"

"So, Barty, here we are."

Yes, here we are, me with a beautiful lady, and not a bit spoilt as I thought, or over-pampered. Not pampered enough, so champagne, I say, or was it her? But before I know there's a bottle on our table.

"Let's drink to a wonderful time."

Yes, yes, let's drink to a wonderful time for tomorrow we may die. So we drink to a wonderful time, as if things could get better, up to the clouds all the way to the top, like Terry said, on and on and on. It just keeps getting better. She touches my hand and I nearly die - reached across and felt my pulse just to say she's so happy.

"And can we come again?" she asks. "It's so nice, and you're so nice."

Yes, indeed so very nice, the two of us between cosy creamy walls, and warm lights above our heads. She still has her fingers on my wrist. Long slim and slender with manicured nails painted in the deepest tone. I stroke them, lift her hand and kiss.

"Excuse me, sir." The waiter is a penguin with jet-black hair swept tight around his ears. He doesn't converse or joke but places our meal upon the table and "Bon appetit."

We have fillet. I don't know what, but it's definitely fillet of the best. The best in the world, Nicki said, and creme caramel and coffee Cognac, and at midnight I'm the happiest man in Brussels.

Terry, my dear dying friend, you were so right, so perfectly right, life goes on and on and on after midnight.

"Dancing, would you like to go dancing?" I'm carrying her coat because it's such a warm orange night although so close to winter. Nicki looks cool in crimson and pink. Dancing, yes, she's a dancing doll, dressed to live the night but;

"No," she says, "not tonight, Barty, dear. I'm with you, to wander and talk, to get to know my gentleman friend."

And so, poor as I am by this late hour, I hail a taxi for another tour of town and out to suburbs and pass an airport and soon we're in the dark, motoring to some distant place. We have gone so far and it will cost so much to go cruising through the night.

"And is it far?"

"Oh, not so far. But Barty baby, do not fret. It's just a little place for you and me, to spend the night."

That sounds grand, off into the night with no care for the fare or time or how I will ever get home. All I know is Nicki, sprinkled in scent and gloved in silk. Infatuation. I'm mentally numb from my brain to below my throat. Not a word, only my lips quivering. I bow, as if she is a queen. She is, because I'm on my knees to kiss her hand, her silk sleeve, kiss and kiss up her lovely long arm. These slim shoulders. I nibble them all the way to her neck and feel her flesh, taste Nicki's skin to lose control and touch with fingers. Like an excited dog slobbering against her cheek, I press my mouth to her gorgeous goddess lips. I'm so ashamed as she retreats, her stern face studying my appalling manner panting like a filthy mongrel. She places her long majestic finger upon my lips.

"You're rather naughty, Barty."

"Sorry," I whimper, "sorry, sorry, sorry," whispering with little kisses on her finger, following it down to her side, rubbing my cheek against her thigh. Now a kiss, and another, kisses and kisses along her arm so slender and endless to feel her silk and smell her scent all the way back up to see her emerald eyes.

"I told you, Barty, naughty, naughty." She sits back and uses her finger to send me away.

Now it's torture. We're out of Brussels, away from the orange, northbound on a motorway into the black.

"Driver, music please."

"Nicki, I'm sorry, I amm, n- n- not a bit of what you t'ink..." My stuttering is worse than O'Hanagan's brogue. I'm desperate to say my piece although lost for words and switching midway through sentences, persistent like Terry. So I stop and start again, "Nicki, I'm sorry, I'amm..."

"Please, I'm listening to the radio."

There's not a clue in my head as to where we're going and I'm too frightened to ask. Not even a murmur while she listens to music. Like her obedient puppy I sit, longing for Nicki to touch me, with a finger, her beautiful long fingers, her hand, wrist, kisses, kisses, kisses all the way up her arm to her silky shoulder to smell her scent and see those emerald eyes...

"Barty, I will not tell you again."

It becomes orange again. Nicki does not comment on the town with quaint little houses and a humpback bridge. It could have been so romantic but she's busy giving instructions. She has an address written on paper, directing the driver through some unknown town, through the centre, suburbs and back to the black, to a country club.

"Darling, darling," cries a voice in the forecourt, "where have you been?"

"I've been to Brussels to see the sights."

While I pay the chauffeur, I hear the most beautiful French accents, the Queen's English from Hooray Henrys', and American laughter. The international jet-set is dressed for dancing and flirting in designer clothes, and a big sign says, members only.

"This is my escort," sings Nicki to a group at the door. "A very fine gentleman. Took me to the most delightful restaurant, didn't you, darling? And we've been to see the sights."

I'm standing on the terrace, looking like O'Hanagan just back from the bog, dowdy amongst the bright creative folk. Nicki's friends are looking at my one and only tatty jacket. It's a mild night and the guests are strolling along the terrace. Nicki giggles, somewhere around the side and down the steps in the garden. I'm still holding her coat. Brussels in the distance is radiating orange lamplight that curdles with billowing clouds in the night.

"Can I help you, sir?"

"The lady's coat."

"Oh, yes, I'll take it. For Miss Nicki, is it?"

"It tis. And is the bar in here?"

"It is, sir, straight on and to the left."

I drink an expensive beer; the cheapest item on the list. I sip it slowly and wonder how I'm getting home, while watching the big hand on the clock do an orbit. The barman seems to know that a woman has taken me for a ride. He places complimentary nuts on the counter. They're too salty and soon I need another drink but have to count my pennies. I can't afford another extravagant taxi ride. Hopefully, I can walk back to the quaint little town and catch a bus to Brussels or hitch a lift.

It's much too cold at half past four. Guests come in to feel the warmth, Nicki amongst them. She's laughing and telling a blond Australian that he's very, very naughty. But she allows him to take her hand, to kiss. Kisses, kisses up her silk sleeve but he doesn't get as far as me. He doesn't even make it to her elbow.

"Barty, baby, where have you been?" She comes to kiss my cheek. She's drunk but kind again. "I thought the taxi had taken you away, stolen you."

"Oh, I was looking after the lady's coat, keeping a seat warm for you, for when the night turned cold."

"Barty, I love you. You are so considerate." She swings around to address her friends with a drunken speech. "This is Barty, O'Hanagan's friend from Ballybog, the bravest builder in all of Berlin, who came to Brussels to buy me a drink, so Barty baby, please buy me another," and as she swings, she loses her balance and falls into my lap. "Take me home, take me home and tuck me in, Barty, Barty, Barty baby." She kisses me on my lip, the littlest kiss, and we gaze into each other's eyes. Green, the deepest but brightest, dangerously murky but daringly sparkly, while all about us is orange and languages and musical accents.

"Yes, sir," interrupts the waiter.

"Champagne," cries Nicki, coming to life, "Champagne and make it pink." I order a beer for myself, the cheapest, an expensive local brew that takes the last of my money.

Nicki spills her champagne while dancing with the blond Australian. He's bought her another but she wants a cocktail, something blue and jazzy.

"Blue, blue, Belgium blue," she sings, and sends him back to the bar. He takes much too long and as the poor man eventually brings the blue cocktail, Nicki wants something green. She's not sure, she will have to think about it. In the meantime she's sipping something yellow. It's big and bright with a slice of orange. Now Nicki dances with a French man in a silver suit, waltzing out through the door and into the night. It's black out there and I watch it dilute to grey, a slate blue grey getting brighter.

The fields grow green and as I walk into the village, the sodium light above the city fades. In the east beyond Brussels, there's a morning sun, bright like the slice of orange in Nicki's cocktail. But clouds are coming to make it dismal like my night, to turn it grey. Pouring rain but I'm on a train without a ticket, going down underground, into town with a crowd, through the dark, the black, commuters and tourists. When I get up there'll be grey mist from the bog, all the way from Ireland, dismal, very depressing. But not to worry as long as no one asks me for a ticket.

34. Tonight, I'm determined to celebrate my reunion with my old friend,
O'Hanagan.

Two days ago I thought Terry would never come through the front door again. I assumed that O'Hanagan, when I found him, and myself would have had the apartment to ourselves. But Terry is back and alive with intensive conversation. And touching; I hate the way he paws me. Back to normal, he says, as he wraps an arm around my shoulder and calls me friend. Drugs have killed the pain and injected life causing him to move in an erratic and an irritating manner. His lanky limbs that hung for hours over the arms of the chair are now swinging and carrying him around the room.

O'Hanagan has been a dumb lump since arriving here. I went to get him because he told me on the phone that he got lost. In a park that was a circle, he walked around and around until he returned to where Nicki lived.

"Stay where you are," I said, "and I'll come to where you're at." He was outside her apartment. I had no desire to speak to her or even ask for her. I hurried through the park and towards the big houses in Uccles to see the bulky idiot who had followed me for years and then departed with Nicki. O'Hanagan was standing at the entrance with his hands in pockets. He was wearing blue overalls that bulged from his unbuttoned brown coat. It was too cold for his coat to be open like that but he was too big for it. From a distance I could see the smile break on his face, stretching to his ears. Then I saw his teeth. O'Hanagan had bright teeth despite his neglect for personal grooming.

"Bart, Bart, tis grand to see you, it tis..." taking hands from pockets and starting to walk. He suddenly stopped to correct himself, put his hands back into his pockets and took them out and put them back while deciding whether to wait or run towards me.

"Grand to see you," I shouted, the most alien phrase to come out of my mouth. Not because I had not spoken it before but because I had never greeted O'Hanagan sincerely in all the days I had known him. Now it was different and he responded with frenzied excitement, striding towards me with a hand reaching to shake mine.

"Tis grand, Bart, it tis, t'isn't it? T'isn't it grand that we've met. Tisn't it?

"It tis."

"Tis grand t'at we've met in Belgium, Bart? Sure, tis grand to see you…"

"O'Hanagan, slow down. You're going like a helicopter." Sputtering like an engine, he wiped his mouth with the back of his hand and started again, shaking my hand. "O'Hanagan, you've got spit on your hand. And now on my hand."

Of course, I had to stop him, like I had always done but I refrained from swearing or calling him a donkey. There's nothing wrong with excitement when a man has a bulk of a body like O'Hanagan's, able to withstand the vibrations. I couldn't though, and my arm ached after shaking hands with him. I just told him to relax, and that we'll go back to Terry's flat. On the way to here I told him about Terry, warned him.

"O'Hanagan, this man likes the sound of his own voice. He antagonises people."

"Is t'at something to do with atoms?"
We stopped to buy some of that foreign food and bottles of beer with the money I took from Terry's pocket. That's how bad it is, actually stealing from my flatmate. I had to after my date with Nicki. But I promise with all my heart that I'll pay him back. I stole only coins but I'm determined to celebrate O'Hanagan's return.

It's good to see his grinning face eager to join our conversation. Never again will I exclude O'Hanagan.

"So," I say, escaping Terry's drunken clutch, "what do you think?"

"Tis a nice flat, Bart. Tis."

"It is, O'Hanagan. Is it as good as Nicki's?"

"It's not t'at good." He pokes a pastry into his mouth and continues talking with puffed cheeks, chewing words excitedly but only crumbs come out.

"Fuck," says Terry, "he looks hungry."
Terry's right, O'Hanagan's scoffing food. I had forgotten how questions excite him. He stutters and splutters pastry.

"Fuck sake," cries Terry, "you having an orgasm or what?"

"Well, lets all have a beer and the craic," I say, to defuse the scene.

"Yea, I'd better take one of those before your mate shoves it all in his mouth, bottle an' all."

I can see that Terry's the same as on our first encounter. Hospital has helped him enormously but it's not made him endearing. He's an annoyance. And he's drinking again. Of course I encouraged him, offered him a beer to celebrate my reunion with O'Hanagan. But Terry's celebrating too, on his legs and around the room to make a speech and his arms around our shoulders. It's a tonic to witness his recovery, no matter how temporary it might be. Said so myself, cheers to good health, and cracked open the beers. No sooner had he sipped alcohol, though, than an antagonistic tone was dancing from his tongue, spitting at us like the crumbs from O'Hanagan's mouth. Terry's making a session of it, poking our chests with his bottle to emphasise a point.

"...Not a cure," he's saying, "but it's hope. Enough chance to live a few more years. Shit, few years ago when I was workin on those heights, no cunt would 'ave give me a chance to live till now. The number of blokes killed in construction is staggering...." Terry's drinking whiskey again, just reached into the kitchen to grab the bottle by its neck.

O'Hanagan's smiling, listening attentively and fears a scolding. I see it in his eyes darting towards me for help whenever Terry's offensive manner spills over. We're reprieved for a moment while Terry goes back to the kitchen. He doesn't stop talking but returns with a glass. "Aey, fuckface, look. See? See how clean this glass is? That's 'ow yer clean glasses proper." Terry's almost shuving it up my nose. "Yer mate's a fucking useless wanker at washing," he tells O'Hanagan. "You ever had to live wiv 'im?"

"I, I don't know," stutters O'Hanagan.

"What, yer fucking lost yer memory?"

O'Hanagan looks to me.

I have seen that plea in his eye before, begging for intervention while being bullied by Scullivan. My response was to ignore him, let O'Hanagan fight his own battles. I could justify it because he was big enough and at other times he'd be as bad as Scullivan, finding spiteful pleasure in my misfortune. On our last night in Ireland in that drunken dump in Ballybog, O'Hanagan gloated while Scullivan flicked peanuts at me. He raised the chorus of laughter, pointing at my restrained face while I suppressed an awful anger. We were surrounded by an immature mob that night. The more they laughed the more frenzied O'Hanagan's eyes became. The attention - mayhem - that he managed to raise elevated him from idiotic status. My reaction was to snatch an ashtray from the table and empty it into Hanagan's face. That moved the focal point of the fun back to him and caused a bigger laugh amongst the immature mob. And now, on this drunken night I'm afraid that fear is being evoked by Terry's cruel persistent manner.

"I was living with Miss Nicki," O'Hanagan eventually says.

"Nice bit of stuff, is she?" persists Terry. "Well? Nice bird this Miss Nicki?"

"She is."

"Well, don't keep it secret." Terry grabs a wooden chair. "Here, sit down, for fuck sake, yer're making me nervous."

O'Hanagan glances at me before sitting obediently.

"Terry," I say, "relax."

"Just getting yer friend te socialise a little. Ain't that right?" he says to O'Hanagan. "So this bird yer shacking up wiv, nice bit of stuff?"

"She's my girlfriend except t'ere's no room for me to live t'ere."

"So where have you been living?" I ask.

"We had cash-flow problems. T'ere was no room for me at night and no hotel because they had cash-flow problems. But it's just until the end of cash-flow problems." O'Hanagan's speaking up to me, as if being interrogated by me at his side and Terry bending down to intimidate his face.

"Cash-flow problems," persists Terry, "that's what yer get wiv birds." He stands straight to sip some whiskey. "Bin shafting 'er?" bending again.

"Hold your horses, Terry, for Christ sake. Move. O'Hanagan, tell me, have you had a bed to sleep in since coming to Belgium?"

"Tis only until the end of cash-flow problems."

"Where were you sleeping."

"She gave me blankets."

"You mean that bitch threw you out penniless?"

O'Hanagan stares at me. He knows my scathing tone but I don't know that desperate look in his eye, something new and worse, a strain that has festered since leaving Ireland. He doesn't like me calling her a bitch, so obvious that it's bulging in his eyes like a wart on a tree.

"Yep, we know about bitches," continues Terry, "lived with one for years. You got to wise up and be alert. The bitch will take you to the cleaners."

O'Hanagan doesn't like Terry saying it either. Worse, and a spasm of loathing radiates. I see it on his brow, red with hate. It's an explosive recipe when mixed with love for sweet beguiling Nicki.

Since my all-night date with her she's been erased from my mind. I thought of sleep as I trekked home in the morning rain from the station, congratulating myself for the trickery in avoiding ticket collectors. It was a small consolation but essential that at least something went right. Into bed without a word to Terry. For him, a merry morning mood is to boast about his ability to rise so early. I ignored him as he heralded the day's schedule. I stepped aside and sunk into slumberland. When I awoke, I went out to phone while he was asking if I had got my leg over. I never muttered her name but told the answerphone that I was calling for O'Hanagan. I waited until he picked up the receiver to blurt, Bart, Bart, down the phone.

"Will you pass round the whiskey," I shout, before too much else is said about her. "Pass round the whiskey, yer mean bollocks," reaching for the bottle while walking away from O'Hanagan sitting in the chair. I pull Terry with me.

"See," he cries, hanging onto the bottle "see, see what the fuck I've got to liv wiv. No wonder yer went off wiv that bitch."

"Terry, shut up for fuck sake an' pass the whiskey." I wrench the bottle from him and pretend to look for a glass. "O'Hanagan, pay no heed to this bollocks. It's a pain in the arse he is."

"Fuck sake, just 'aving a bit o' a laugh."

"Aey, I'm having a bit of a drink here, like to have a sense of occasion with my countryman who…"

"Aey, no problem, Squire. Don't you Paddies be ganging up on the Englishman now." Terry throws an arm around O'Hanagan's shoulder. "Aey, we go on like this all the time. Just friends."

There's whiskey in my beer. Wholesome food is what we need but I don't have enough money to buy a postage stamp. So we drink ourselves sick, listening to Terry lecture about women, about Candy, about how all wives are glorified whores. O'Hanagan's grinning while being told to shut up.

"… For fuck sake, you with the scab on yer jaw."

As Terry turns his back, O'Hanagan gets up from the wooden chair and goes to the window. It's been a long time since he has had to endure torment. I too have forgotten how to handle the drunken likes of Terry. He's showing off now, trying to convince me that he's an able-bodied man, clasping my hand in his.

"I show ya this, Bart."

"I have little interest…"

"Na, na, na, listen. Do yer self a favour an' listen," shaking my hand.

I'm wondering about the thoughts that had settled in my head before Terry's return. About finding him dead on the sofa while the television shouted to a stiff. Guilt would have been redundant while I felt for a heartbeat and my other hand searched his pockets. He has an expensive watch and wallet, credit cards too. Terry doesn't know that a penniless flatmate was waiting like a vulture to rifle his pockets and bankbooks. I didn't know it myself but suddenly realised my disappointment today. It felt dirty stealing his coins. O'Hanagan is obviously poor and stupid, unemployable and a potential burden. But me? Guilt overwhelms me in my drunken stupor because Terry is alive. We're holding hands in the middle of the room. If he died naturally it would have been reasonable to pick through his coins and notes and the books from his bank.

"Come on, yer cunt," he says.

"What?"

"The table."

"What?"

"We'll arm wrestle."

"Away an' fuck yourself, Terry." I pull my hand free. "You're pissed."

"Aey, an' yer're not?"

We're fugitives, something else that Terry doesn't know. Of course I'm guilty about being disappointed that he's going to live so long.

"Look at this body," he continues, tensing muscles. "Admit it, Bart, you were not able to do that job. That's why they fucked you off, before the building even got off the ground." He goes to O'Hanagan and slaps his back, "Aey, Jaws, did you hear that they kicked his fucking arse off the job. Aey, come on, yer're a big one, let's see how you would cope." He takes O'Hanagan's big flabby bog hand. "Come on, ye big scab." It's an old trick using a twist of the wrist, something for insecure men to play on big ones to impress onlookers. O'Hanagan looks to me. He's like a large dumb animal again, wanting me to rescue him. For our penance we are living with a creature worse than Scullivan.

"What do you say, Scab?" Terry's an unctuous persistent creature.

We have to get away from him. I can do nothing because I'm penniless and too drunk before I know it. It's a horrible night with music blaring from a radio and everyone having a bad time. It might get worse because O'Hanagan is in love with Nicki.

35. Tonight I'm looking for a bed because a man came asking questions.

Betty is delighted by the good news, opening her door wide to see me. I phoned an hour ago to boast about my new job and to say that I am moving into a luxury apartment next week.

"Oh, it is heavenly," she sings, and claps her hands. She kisses my cheek and I can feel her excitement in fingers that touch my shoulders. It causes another wave of guilt to rise through me because I have just fed her a pack of lies. "And how is Terry?" she continues, inviting me into her home.

"Oh, he's gone to England." Another lie. "Just as well because the lease expired on our apartment. I'm looking for a hotel for a few days but I was wondering if I could leave a few items here. It's only until next week..."

"A hotel," she cries. "Oh no, that's too expensive. Please, have a key. And what kind of work have you found? Is it a career or just a job?"

"Management. International trouble-shooting, a back-up team for multinationals..."

"But the language?"

"English is essential. Working with Yanks, wouldn't you know? T'ey can't even spell in English let alone mutter in French. Yes, a job with a suit. My clothes are on their way from Germany. Would it be okay to use this address?"

"Of course."

Honesty is wasted on the poor girl. She has no appreciation for reality. What she heard is what she loves to hear; an eligible man is moving in and he has a career in management, and wears a suit, and he's suitable for showing off to family and friends. Optimism is what she gets from my lies. I am spoon-feeding opium to her, fuelling her fantasies. Of course I benefit too because I'm desperately seeking survival; I need a bed tonight.

I need sleep after racing from the metro this afternoon to Nicki's apartment; hiding in subways and stations like a rat and scurrying out to daylight and across the park. I had to catch O'Hanagan before they caught him!

"Come here, you big bollocks," I said. He was loitering outside her door. "Now, listen. Something terrible has happened. T'ey know where we are. A man was at the door."

"What door?"

"Terry's door. And they phoned Nicki, asking for you."

"Who."

"Christ," I pleaded to the sky. "I don't know who. A detective, solicitor, I don't know who but t'ey know us and t'at we're from Ballybog. And they know about the killing."

"Sure, Bart, we can stay with Nicki. She won't tell…"

"We can not."

"We could if Henry Moore would let us in. It's him…"

"O'Hanagan, you bollocks, I have a safe house for us."

"I am no bollocks. You're a bollocks."

"Okay, sorry, sorry," and raised my palm. "Come on, you can see Nicki another time." I tugged his sleeve to make him come, and pretended that Nicki might visit us. I had to, to keep him happy on the long walk back to here, to Betty's flat.

Betty is already making space in the wardrobe for her man's suit. She's cleared a shelf for my soaps and talcs and aftershave, things I don't possess; I've been using Terry's.

"Betty, dear, you're much too kind."

"It's so important for a man to feel at home. Stability relies on it."

I peep through the window, to check if O'Hanagan is still standing across the road. I told him to wait at the bus stop until Betty goes to her weekly aerobics class. Then I can bring him in here for a bath and a bite to eat. He smells of booze from last night's reunion, and spent the day hungry, loitering outside Nicki's apartment. We both need washing, and then something hot to fill our bellies because we have work to do. When it's dark we're going to steal a pile of copper scrap and then ferry it from across the street. I can see a glimpse of it now beside the big white house, and in my head I plot our crime, to scurry with pipes upon our heads or try to hold the twisted lengths beneath our arms. It'll be an ordeal with clumsy O'Hanagan but I should remember his success in Rotterdam, scavenging around the back of shops while I was crippled with broken ribs. Yes, we can do it. We have to do it because I must now stay out of the Irish pub and say goodbye to my computer-cabling job.

"Bart, what are you looking at? Please don't do that with the curtains."

"Oh, sorry," moving away from her window. "I was just checking the weather."

When Betty smiles into my face I have to smile back, holding it as if squeezing the last bit of toothpaste.

"Wouldn't you like a home like that?" She points to the big white house across the road. It has a large Flemish façade and majestic steps that lead up to a door with a polished brass knocker.

"Yes," I say. "Lovely." But tonight I'll settle for the heap of copper scrap that's piled around the side. "And Betty, isn't it time for you to go to aerobics?"

"Well, I thought maybe I should cancel this evening's class." She touches my arm, a gentle loving clasp. "We should celebrate."

"Celebrate?"

"Yes, celebrate you starting a career in Brussels."

"Well, yes, but as you know, in Brussels, one gets a job because of who he knows, not what he knows. Tonight I must pay the debt."

"You mean buy him a beer?" She drops her hand as a cloud descends to distort her face, a blanket of disapproval. I can't bare her piercing eyes.

"No," I surprise her, "he doesn't drink. A lawyer of some reputation. I t'ought a meal, a vegetarian and he likes his tea. He's so keen to know how I got on."

"These are the people we should be mixing with," nodding her head bright with hope again. Thankfully she's not touching and staring me out. I find it so difficult to respond when I'm cornered.

"Yes," I agree, moving away, "a little old but I'll suggest a foursome for the future. Him and his wife. You and me." I step further for fear that she'll smell my sticky skin, perspiring with last night's booze. I had a sweaty run this afternoon, after escaping without a wash.

Even if I weren't going to steal scrap from across the road, I'd still be too tired to cater to Betty's needs this evening. Last night's drunken reunion exhausted me. Today didn't start until this afternoon. Terry had been up with the birds and came into my bedroom to tell me that the morning was the best part of the day.

"Terry, feck off." It wasn't that good because he had gone back to sleep by the time I got up. When I struggled to the toilet he was snoring in his room. There was a leg in the bed and his other on the floor. The stench and bottles reminded me of our binge last night. While I made coffee I decided that I did not like Terry. My brain didn't labour much to search my conscience before walking into his room to steal from his wallet. His socks were alive with odour that ate the air. I checked the bedside table, the floor, and patted his jacket pockets. He was still wearing his trousers but I checked by pressing fingers against the denim and his bony body. Desperation drove me to it with brazen thieving fingers. His clothes were baggy and pockets loose and the wallet slipped out.

I used to do my thinking while I had a beer, a night-cap, but I have recently started thinking in the mornings while waiting for the coffee. The evenings were good for reflecting on what progress I had made during a day, and for making plans for the next day. But life is now going nowhere, and so this morning I started thinking earlier to predict what a terrible day it would be. I could see a pattern emerging, a step forward to earn a pittance, and then back to square one. After all the success, for the few times that it happened, everything had returned to a familiar dire situation; I was skint again, O'Hanagan was back, he had scabs again, and there were no jobs. Now we were in the wrong town for casual labour.

While Betty collects her kit for aerobics I peep through the window, careful this time not to touch her curtains. O'Hanagan is still there, at the bus shelter where I told him to wait. I told lies to him too, promising that we would meet Nicki later. I had to, to make him move. During our walk to here I noticed other desperadoes with shifting eyes just like mine. O'Hanagan doesn't have a shifty look because he's in love and oblivious to his desperate state. I feel it though, being sinisterly-sighted for the sake of survival. Like birds of a feather that flock together, my eyes locked with theirs, other poor people loitering near junctions and stations. I would not have seen them or known their illegal status if it was not for my own abysmal situation. Being suddenly exiled from Irish pubs again, hence losing my computer-cabling job, made me aware and empathetic; I was destined to join them on the street as a wandering immigrant. Unless I found a woman to exploit, with a home like this.

Of course it looked worse this morning because I was suffering, my body paying for last night's reckless drinking. I put plates and cups into the sink to wash away the dirty sight. Gushing water seemed to ease the thumping pain in my head. But it really was worse because O'Hanagan's in love. This morning I lacked the energy to stop him, not enough breath to utter a few words of advice. Like every other morning since he arrived in Brussels, O'Hanagan had to find a phone to report for duty, just in case she had a little job for him.

"I must call Miss Nicki at eleven o'clock," he said.

"But it's almost one o'clock."

"I still have to phone. Anyway, she doesn't answer. It's just a machine so maybe she will t'ink it is still eleven o'clock."

"I'll talk to you later then. I'm too tired now."

I was actually straining, stopping myself from calling him a stupid bollocks. You're a donkey is what I wanted to say but I also wanted things to be nice and peaceful. A madness was needling inside my head. My skull was collapsing like a battered coastal cave, falling into stormy waters as each option was washed out to sea. I thought meeting O'Hanagan would help. It hasn't. It's brought memories, bad feeling, the thorny thoughts riding in on the tide to pierce my brain, my mind bobbing up and down with waves.

He went down the stairs to the front door. He banged it closed and it sent a thump through the apartment and through my head. You big bollocks, I called him, talking to myself at the sink. Then the doorbell rang and drove needles through my brain. It rang again, and again. I supposed that he had forgotten something. Or was entertaining himself.

"I'm coming, I'm coming." It was hard work going down the steep stairs. My mouth was dry and my head dancing with the doorbell. Anyway, I figured, it would be good to get down and out to let in a burst of freshness. The whole apartment needed to be flushed, my head too, to expel the numbness. The smell of booze and socks seeped down the stairs behind me, following like a herd to the street. I gasped at the daylight.

"Bart Rabbit?" asked a man in a suit.

"Tis."

"Bart Rabbit from Ballybog, Ireland?" It was too bright. It was too late, they had me. I suddenly realised that I was talking in English with a stranger who knew about me. About Ballybog. His face focussed and I tuned into his English accent. "... And so we phoned this number," he continued, "and the lady there said that Mr O'Hanagan might be here. With you. Oh, and she said to say sorry if I saw you..." He was talking about Nicki.

"No," I suddenly said. "He's gone. Him and O'Hanagan," retreating and shutting the door. I ran up the stairs, slipping down steps on my shins. When I finally got up, I limped through Terry's room and peeked through the window. He was still down there. Not a sign of uniformed police but the doorbell rang again.

"What the fuck's happening?" Terry turned on his bed. "Aey, what yer want?"

"Taxman is outside. Got me cornered."

"No kidding. Taxman from Berlin or one from England? Or Ireland? Where the fuck he come from?" Terry rolled off his bed with ropes of blankets around his legs and thumped onto the floor. His lanky body rose with enthusiasm, kicking to untangle his feet as he danced to the window.

"Will you get the feck back from t'ere?"

But he ignored me, trampling blankets that clung to his ankles, and flung open the window to shout down to the street.

"Aey, mate, yer speak English?"

"Oh, shit, ye fecking English eejit." I ran to the back, an escape route. I was getting out. Terry was starting another of his monologues, asking what jurisdiction did he think he was in. I could hear the man in the street calling back. Then Terry was calling me, telling me that he was not a taxman but wanted to talk to me about an accident, which occurred in Ballybog, in Ireland last year.

Accident! That's a good one. Come here and stand still while we talk about an accident. Then it's an incident, a little illegal event called murder, might be able to refer to it as manslaughter if you come quietly and plead guilty. I was scrambling down a pipe while Terry called me back.

"Fuck," he was saying. "Shit, you must owe 'em a packet."
There was a dog barking. I was up on a fence, climbing over and it wobbling between my legs and me riding it like it was a drunken donkey. Then it tilted and down we went and the dog going berserk. It fled. I fled, kicking open a gate and down an alley to the street. To the metro station, down steps, under the road and gone like a rat.

Betty loves the idea and goes to her aerobics class a happy woman. I wave to her, through the window but careful not to touch her curtains.

"Thank fuck for that." Now I'll get O'Hanagan from across the road. Drag him inside here for a bath and a bite to eat. A long time might pass before we get the likes of it again. Then I can look around the back yard to check the garden shed. He can sleep in there with the scrap. Lengths of the finest copper are waiting to be carried across the road tonight. It came to mind while standing over there with O'Hanagan.

"Do you hear me talking to you?" I was saying.

"I do, Bart, why wouldn't I hear you?"

"Well, wait here by the bus stop. When she's gone to her aerobics class I'll call you in."

"Tisn't that a fine bundle of copper, Bart. It tis…"

"Shut up and listen…" Then I saw the illuminated pile of precious metal. A peak of a pyramid, the tip of an iceberg was protruding above the fence. I wandered closer, along the side of the big white house.

"It has fine chimneys too," O'Hanagan said. "Tis a big house."

"Faith, tat's a nice pile of copper."

"Fierce big chimneys, so they are."

"Heavy gauge pipes."

"Ah, they are, fine chimneys, so t'ey are."

I was peeping through a gap at a manicured lawn. The owner was obviously a man who didn't want a mess in his garden. We would be doing him a favour if we went in and removed his bulging pile of junk. It was neatly stacked but still its belly was ready to burst and spill about his lawn and flowers.

In any case, it doesn't matter, we need to survive. Some hot soup for us workers before we go thieving from the neighbours. Betty has a well-stocked pantry. Tins and tubs and twice as much again in the fridge. What I took from Terry's wallet would not buy a fraction of it. It's just as well that the Irish pub is unsafe because I have little money to be spending on drink. But a pity to lose my contacts there and that computer-cabling job. Now I'm relegated to the league of illegals, destined to loiter on streets with immigrants on the run, refugees who have absconded, delinquents doing deals and tramps in the park. I saw them in the station, rats like me wary of the authorities.

Now, I had better phone Nicki. Just business of course, while the phone is free. And before O'Hanagan gets here.

"Nicki," I say to her machine, "I got your message but please, please," I plead "don't send anyone else to see me. Or O'Hanagan. Much too busy. Business deals, like you know. I'm such a busy man and can't afford time for strangers looking for me. Just salesmen selling junk, so don't believe anything they might say, nothing illegal, ha, ha. No time for them." Just time for you, I almost said, all my life I would give to you, madly in love and holding the receiver with two hands. I'm just about to kiss it and want to feel her silky shiny hair but stop. "Yes, Nicki, much too busy, business and t'ings...."

"Barty."

"Oh, Nicki."

"Barty, what a pleasant surprise. I was just coming out of the shower and there you are again, on my answerphone. And I do hope you've forgiven me and you weren't going away without suggesting a date."

"Ahmm..."

"How about half past eight tomorrow night?"

"Well, really, Nicki, I'm not happy with how you flirt."

"Of course you're not, and I *was* a flirt and you are just the man to put me straight and spank my bum, an Irish stud twice the man O'Hanagan ever was. Barty, dear, forgive me please, it was just a drunken night with friends from long ago. You, them, I forgot my manners. I'm so sorry. Barty, are you there?"

"I am, Nicki. But Nicki, dear, I have big problems in my life."

"And what are they? Can I help? A friend in need is a friend indeed."

Yes, she could help, of course she could. "Yes, Nicki, yes, maybe you could help."

"Well, tell me tomorrow…"
I kiss the receiver pressed to my lips.

It's a lovely night again despite the chill. I hope O'Hanagan is as content as me. I'm sure he's not and he'd be worse if I told him about my most recent call to the girl he loves. Here he comes, his bulging belly in the night. The less said the better.

"Now follow me and as quiet as a mouse." On the way into the building, I remove the bulb from the lamp above the entrance.

"Tis a lovely flat, Bart." He walks along the hall, pushing each door with a finger to peep into a room.

"Remember t'at a woman lives here, as tidy as your mother." I direct him to the bathroom. "Get in there and I'll go heat some soup." Betty's kitchen is clinically clean and blazingly bright. I'm suffering from a nervous disposition as I open the soup for fear that I spill a bit and cause a spot.

"That's a good one," he shouts from the bathroom. "Bart, tisn't it? Great craic, tis."

"O'Hanagan, yer big bollocks, will you get your big hooves off it before you've squashed it." He's sitting on the toilet with his trousers rolled up and his naked feet in her foot spa bowl. They're filthy feet and it's a plastic basin that he's trampling to death. The delicate device is for feminine feet, smooth and slim with a lady's toes. It's the kind of thing she likes to have, gadgets for the modern woman. It comes with a matching set of towels and flannels and a mat.

Everything in Betty's bathroom comes in sets. Tubes of paste have matching brushes. Bottles in gift-stuffed baskets are wrapped forever in plastic paper. Lids with heads. There's oil for skin and cream for lips and spray for hair and something for shoulders and another for bums and a lotion for legs. Pacific Pink for perfect skin, Atlantic Blue for blotchy bits and Pine Forest Green to clean her toilet.

"And isn't that a lovely mat, Bart?" A fluffy pink mat to match the cotton-wool balls in a jar. "For sure, Bart, tis better than a tickle. Did you ever do t'at, Bart, did you, walk on gravel and the stones tickling the bottom of your feet?"

"O'Hanagan, will you get up off your arse. No, yer donkey, don't stand on it."

"But, Bart, tisn't it a grand yoke and the coloured water. For sure, Bart, I bet she has a lovely set of feet on her. Did you ever see her feet? For sure you did, I'd say. Do you see the waves t'at it makes and it'll turn feet to flippers."

"Yis, donkey." Water spilling out, oilrig grey from filthy feet to swamp the fluffy pink mat.

"I'm no donkey. Tis too much water that's in it."

Never leave kitchens unattended while heating soup. It could have caused a mess while I was in there with him. But luckily I forgot to switch on the cooker. Feelings from the old days are back, when I would lose my temper because O'Hanagan was near me. I want to shout at him but O'Hanagan is a new character now. He challenges me with a vexed face because I call him a donkey. I can't help it when I see the mess he makes. Now he's stubborn in the bathroom refusing to wash, just his feet and putting them back into dirty socks. I hear a car in the forecourt, outside where Betty normally parks.

"Come on," I say, just in case, "get the feck out of here." I lead him towards the back door. "Christ, like a donkey. Come on." His eyes focus on mine, not flinching but boring a hole. "For feck sake, O'Hanagan, get the feck out."

"There's no need to be pulling and pushing."

I close the back door to shut him out and decide that I'm better on my own. Now the front door opens and stuns me.

"I was so excited that I forgot my pass." Betty comes in with such chaotic haste that my panic attack escapes her. She sweeps along the hall and I retreat to the kitchen. "Aren't you going to be late?" she calls back.

"Oh, oh," I stutter, leaning cautiously around the doorframe to see where she's gone. "I was, ahm, cleaning." She reappears and stops to kiss my cheek and hurries away before I can get to...

"My bathroom," she screams.

"There's a leak, Betty, calm yourself."

"Get out, please, leave my home."

"But Betty..."

"Please go."

"But Betty, it's a leak. And I found where t'at smell was coming from. If I wasn't here it would have been worse..."

"What smell?"

"The smell. The smell tat is always in your bathroom. At last I found it..."

"There was no smell..."

"Betty, darling, t'ere has always been a smell. We just never talked about it. I t'ought you were embarrassed, and what girl with a lovely home like yours would not be embarrassed. But we have it solved now."

"It was not there before." But she smells it now, O'Hanagan's feet.

"Of course it was. It's just worse now because I had to flush it out. But have no fear, Betty dear, and leave it to me, a few moments to show my appreciation for all your good deeds. Let me fix your plumbing. Aerobics, yes, it's time for your aerobics class. You'll be late. And when you get home all will be clear."

"Bart," she sighs, "I'm going. But I need my own space tonight so please come tomorrow. We need to talk," and away she goes without a kiss. "Please turn out the lights when you leave."

Not even a thank you for all the hard work that I have done in her bathroom. Of course, I have done no plumbing but she doesn't know. Thank God for Nicki. And what about the simpleton outside?

"O'Hanagan, will you shut up?" opening the door.

"You shouldn't be shouting like t'at. As if you are more important than me."

"Well, I am important if you want a bath and a bite to eat."

"Bart, for sure, why would I want a bath and a bite when I can go to the hostel?

"What do you mean yer big bol - what hostel?"

"Where I stay with homeless people. Just until the end of cash-flow problems. Nicki arranged it with the money."

"What money?"

"'Tis money for filling in forms."

"What forms?"

"Sure, Bart, don't be shouting at me."

"I am not."

"You are."

"I'm not."

"You are. Sure, I'm not deaf."

"What fecking money? Yer big fecking bollocks. And what fecking forms have you filled?"

"I'm no bollocks. You're a bollocks. And Nicki said I have rights because everyone from Ireland is a European citizen. And she has a bank account t'at changes my cheques. Nicki said it was my right to claim."

"O'Hanagan, you're an even bigger bollocks than I t'ought."

"I'm no bollocks."

"You are a bollocks."

"I'm no bollocks. You're a bollocks," his face reddening and watery eyes fixed on me. If I call him a bollocks again he'll either burst into tears or erupt. This new continental creature could lose control. "And why were you phoning Miss Nicki?" he suddenly demands.

"When?"

"A few days ago."

"Because I was worried sick looking for you, yer donkey." I'm ready to batter him with Betty's broom if my fists can't do the job. It's a swish-styled gadget with a matching bucket. It's near the kitchen door and in my anger I kick it. Pine Forest green suds hop out to soil her immaculate floor. "All fecking day looking for you, you big fecking bollocks of a donkey." I don't care a bollocks or a donkey what I call him now. I've done my penance and this is the end if he says the wrong word. Go on, I dare, just you tell me not to call you a big bog bollocks with a lump of turf for a brain. "All fecking day looking for you. Up all fecking night driving to Dublin. And phoning around all because of you. And hiding you here in my girlfriend's bathroom."

"That's something else you didn't know, t'at I can transfer my medical record from Ballybog. Nicki said. You t'ink you're important but you didn't know t'at. And I'm going out."

I don't need him. I don't need Betty either or care for her beige wall-to-wall carpet. And it's not my fault that murky green soapsuds are about her sterilised floor. Pine Forest footprints follow me from her shiny kitchen to her vacuumed lounge. It was an accident, not the murder but walking onto her carpet with green footprints. But yes, the murder too, that was an accident. Anger makes me careless. Folk would say that I'm mean to exploit Betty and abuse her home. I tried to be clean but it's so pukingly purified. The coffee table is in my way so I kick it. Just a little kick but burning with an Irish temper, my boot thumping the leg of it. It's a big round glass table with a rim the size of a circus. Not sharp but it hurts my shin. Provokes me to make me kick again, this time I really kick it like I'm giving the lounge and all the matching bollocks a good kicking. It gets my boot up between its legs and crystal splinters to the ceiling. They come down raining javelins and I'm lucky not to be stabbed to shreds and blood on the carpet and glass and Pine Forest suds. "Feck. Agh, Christ, no, no, sweet suffering mercy please." I'm praying or something. Just a killing though and it could have happened to anyone. There's no way out, O'Hanagan's saying, for sure there isn't. I listen. It's him insisting that there's no way out of the garden except over the fence. I step over the puddles to the back door.

"There's no way out for sure t'ere isn't," he says again. I open the door wide. He's in the dark, on the lawn. "I haven't come back, Bart. I just haven't gone yet. I could climb but was t'inking I might not."

"Come in, for God's sake."

I take a deep breath and wait a while. The waves in my head are settling now, the tide retreating to leave a mess. I gaze at the storm-damaged glass and puddles of green suds. Talking might be good, even to O'Hanagan.

"Listen, will we not be fighting?"

"We won't," he replies, beaming again. He's brought in mud with his boots to dilute in green puddles. It doesn't seem to matter now; it's beyond redemption.

"We won't then, O'Hanagan, we won't fight. What would we want to fight for?"

"And for sure, you're right, Bart. What would we want to fight for." That smile grows across his face, like when people back home would speak to him as if he was normal. "And will we be going to get the copper scrap?"

"We will, O'Hanagan, we will."

"And isn't t'ere a rake of it up to St Peter's Gate?"

And there is. O'Hanagan's behaving as if nothing has happened, oblivious to the disaster in Betty's lounge, kitchen and bathroom. I will try to clean it while he carries the copper junk on his own. The shed behind Betty's flat is good enough for hiding pipes. Of course I'll need to remove the lawn mower, take it to a shop to sell.

"Good enough for gun-running," says O'Hanagan as we go out to the night. Streets in this district are quiet. We stroll across to the big white house. An image of normality is needed, easier done at night. If it were daylight the neighbours would see my red-flushed face. It feels like a beacon, pulsating as I open the side gate. It's a huge garden to complement the size of the house, stretching into the dark. Lawn lights though. Yes, that will be a better-looking garden without the junk, thanks to us. I help with the first load, across the road and in through the front door of the apartment building. Lovely lengths of copper pipe that will fetch a decent price. Thick-gauge like thick-cut marmalade and not the tinny stuff.

"T'is great craic, for sure, Bart, tis, isn't it?"

I almost said it, shut up you big bog bollocks. It's difficult but I restrain myself from calling him a donkey, which he is, like a mule hauling a load in the dark. Sssh, is all I say until we're inside Betty's flat. Now, don't make a mess and follow me. He does, along the hall and out through the back door. We stack it in the shed and now O'Hanagan works on his own while I clean the mess in Betty's home.

That was a good idea, to remove the bulb from the lamp above the entrance. It wouldn't do for someone to see a bulky figure carrying copper pipes into the building. It's an easy job for O'Hanagan. For sure, I remind myself, wasn't he out on his own in Rotterdam around the back of shops while I was dying in my bed?

"Good man," I say, as he comes through the hallway with the second load. He loves it. "Not a sound now. And don't cross the street if you see as much as a shadow."

"I won't, Bart. I'm as sly as an old fox."

"Good man, O'Hanagan. We'll have money for a feast."

She's not going to like it but accidents do happen, even in Betty's perfect home. But not to worry, I mumble as I clean, picking bits of glass. Betty dear, I will buy you another, a better one, or maybe, darling, you would like to choose your own. I can only peck like a hen at crystal bits that were swallowed by tufty carpet threads. And please don't worry about the money. You've been divine in your immaculate flat so let me buy you a house and be your hen-pecked husband for the rest of my miserable life. I'm going mad doing housework, a mental breakdown while she's out at her aerobics class. Homeless in a woman's home, picking splinters buried in beige. I crawl along the hall wiping puddles with a cloth. Shreds of paper in the wet!

"O'Hanagan, yer bollocks." I wait awhile and here he comes with the third load. "O'Hanagan, be careful. You're tearing paper from the walls."

"I will, Bart, I will," stepping over me. "I will of course. Why wouldn't I?"

It's a useless situation and I continue with my crawl and my cloth to clean the puddle from her bathroom. But it's gone. All that's left is a fluffy mud patch. Nicki, Nicki, I'm suddenly saying, I won't be late for my date. Let me come back, he's driving me mad. And Betty the bore, I never liked her, was just here because a man came knocking on Terry's door, from Ballybog. I killed no one but only kicked Scullivan like you'd kick a glass table or a bucket of suds, kicked the bastard for harassing O'Hanagan and now he's driving me mad.

"What?" he says.

"Feck."

"Bart, you're on your knees and t'em wet."

He's right. O'Hanagan's at the door looking in at me. I'm kneeling in water, praying to St Nicki, patron saint of lonely men, to have mercy on me, pity me... "What?" I shout. "What the feck d'yer want?"

"Don't you shout at me."

"I'm not fecking shouting. I'm busy."

"You *are* shouting. You t'ink I'm no fool but I am."

"And you suppose you're not shouting, yer bollocks?"

"I'm no bollocks. And I'm not taking pipes to the junkyard. And you can put back the lawn mower yourself because you took it out. And it's not my fault if there's no space in tat shed for it. And it's not my fault..."

"O'Hanagan, yer bollocks, feck off."

"I will feck off, t'en. And you feck off and it's not my fault tat soup is boiling in the kitchen and spilling over..."

Streaks of it caked to her enamelled cooker. The saucepan is a burnt-out volcano. It's partly her fault, I reason, for failing to test her smoke detector. The gumption for housework has gone from me now. It's all a burden too far and everyone's a nuisance. Except Nicki. A friend in need is a friend indeed, she said. There's no hesitation but to limp with knees pierced with glass to the phone.

"Nicki, Nicki," I plead and I'm just about to beg her to pick up the receiver when she answers.

"Barty, baby."

"Nicki, darling, I've had the most awful day."

"Have you?"

"O'Hanagan has driven me mad."

"Of course he would."

"But it's worse, not just now but always, all the way from Ballybog. And a woman."

"A woman?"

"Not like you, Nicki dear, not a friend but a housewife looking for a husband with a career to help keep clean her house."

"You poor thing, Barty baby..."

"Nicki, darling, can we meet tonight?"

"And not tomorrow night?"

"Tonight, tomorrow night, any night, but tonight I need a friend."

"Well," she ponders, "well yes, I suppose. I started cooking but... Yes, lets meet tonight and treat ourselves, a bottle of red and fillet of the best. Please come in a taxi, then we shall fly off to the most amazing restaurant with food to cheer you up."

I walk against the wind on my wet knees, my poor pierced skin stabbed with glass and my shins battered by a coffee table. Yes, I say, good riddance to the big bollocks.

36. One poor man and his bottle waiting for a lady.

The poor immigrants approached me but I walked on, virtually barged past them. They were only asking for money, and who wouldn't, living in this expensive town without the right to work? But I can't handle child beggars with pleas on cardboard while their mothers supervise from a distance. Then a desperate adult in layers of coats came towards me with her cup, obstructing my exit from the station. Her rigid arm refused to yield and I almost had to take the cup to push it back towards her. I didn't really see her because I was not obliged to look at her pitiful features that peered out from beneath her hood. An arrogant manner possessed me. Although I can't speak languages like they probably can, I still qualify for European citizenship. I have rights like O'Hanagan, eligible for employment and health and to walk without harassment. All the rights bestowed by treaties if I fill in forms. I have chosen not to but I am nonetheless beyond loitering on corners and caring for foreigners and feeling their fears. It's essential to suppress dismal thoughts to maintain a pleasant mood. And not to be late for my date with Nicki.

Now I'm waiting for her. It's a bistro, her local place to nibble when money is tight. That's what Nicki said after learning of my dire situation. Did she push me away? I think she did, setting a distance by placing her finger upon my nose to say stop right there. Yet she was alluring, dressed for the night. I was ashamed that I couldn't afford the best and I caused her to cancel her favourite restaurant and choose this instead. But this is nice, her local bistro. It's packed now with a bustle at the bar but it was not so full when I walked in. She sent me in here, on my own and told me to wait. A table for Miss Nicki, I said, the best, s'il vous plait. So they gave me this table and I'm here with a bottle. Beautiful, I say again, and sip some wine. She was in pink and oozing with power and panache like she owned the world and the taxi and the driver and me. A little more wine for a toast to a lady.

"I'm sorry, sir, are you intending to order?"

"I'm waiting for Miss Nicki. She had to go back home to change. She won't be long."

"Oh." He smiles knowingly. "Maybe she will."

I suppose I *was* a little late. I had to walk, across the park in the dark to get to her door as quick as I could. It opened and there was the world's most beautiful lady.

"Barty, baby, you took so long?"

I did of course because I walked. Nicki was dressed in pink like Jacqueline Kennedy. Was it the same suit that the First Lady wore while she cradled her dying husband? The president's blood trickled onto Jackie's coat and she was still wearing it the next day. Nicki in outrageous pink with a designer-stain in the deepest claret. Of course she was overdressed for this little place. That's why she wouldn't come in here, not until she changed her clothes, to dress down to my level. It was for my benefit, to help my appearance blend with the crowd. So a little drink while I wait.

"I'm sorry, sir, are you sure she's coming?" The waiter has dark Latin features and greasy black hair and an annoying stare. He's refusing to budge until I reply.

"A few more minutes, if you please."

"Where's the taxi?" is how it started. She was shocked to learn that I had walked so far and then no money to go downtown.

"Nicki, dear, I have cash-flow problems."

"Not again," lifting eyes to the sky. She sighed and pulled closed her lapels to keep out the cold. Feminine and delicate so I gave her a cuddle. "Bart, please stop. You seem deranged. And dirty."

"D- d- didn't I tell you on the phone...?"

"I wasn't listening." Her words were as cold as the night but she was as calm as the breeze. Not a breath of breeze but just the sting of a frosty night. Still, I craved to touch with fingertips her skin so smooth and her face too stern. She stepped closer and held me with icy eyes. "What exactly did you say on the phone? I couldn't hear you because of the television, except that Kevin was driving you mad. But I'm sure you invited me for dinner."

"Yes, Nicki, of course I did."

"So? Are you going like *that*?" She was appalled, retreated for fear my scruffy attire was contagious.

"Ahmm..."

"And you have something on your knees."

"It's blood. Glass on the floor. Nicki, you wouldn't believe what awful trouble I've been through."

"Are we going for dinner or not?"

"Of course we are."

"But *where* like that?"

"Actually, I didn't mean dinner. Not tonight, tomorrow night. I'll have money then, cash galore. But tonight I'm having a bad time. I need a friend. And you said a friend in need is a friend indeed."

"You're poor?"

"Cash-flow problems. Tonight I need to talk, just a friend. I'm alone in town. I need company, someone to trust. You'll never believe the trouble I'm in...."

Nicki's right, the house wine's good. A bottle of red. What is it again and I tilt the bottle to read the label. It's almost empty! Has the wine gone so soon or has she been gone so long? I've drunk enough to make me laugh at her vacant chair. But what man wouldn't drink on his own in this awful town? It's actually a beautiful city and this is a busy place. The body of hungry bellies bulges from the bar. They're hungry for tables but this is for Nicki. A cosy bistro, she called it, something cheap and casual. But the diners are big suave businessmen and women are chic and the waiters too formal. I am a slob possessing a whole table. Lovely stone walls and I make a face in this cosy crowded room. Heads engraved in stone. Stained glass windows in arched frames. But how could I tell her that I was unable to get home for a change of clothes? Isn't it obvious that I have problems? Lovely wine though. Another sip before I get thrown out. It's increasingly likely that the lady has changed more than her clothes. It was in her mind I suppose, to take my money, Terry's money, for a taxi home. Desperation's an awful ailment. She saw it in my beseeching eyes begging like immigrants at the station, pleading with her not to go. Wanted for murder, and I was about to plead my guilt about the forecourt when a taxi arrived. It's that sort of place where she lives, where neighbours come and go in taxis.

"...It was O'Hanagan's fault."

"Of course it was. Bart, here's a taxi. Please get in."

"Did he tell you?" I opened the door for her. It was thankfully warm but Nicki stayed cold and sat by herself.

"Did he tell me what?"

"Why we left Ireland."

"Can't remember. Remind me."

"Yes, but let's have a drink."

"Yes, Barty dressed to shame me, let's have a drink and dinner and let me listen to your confession. Driver, into town. Now, Bart, where exactly do you live?"

"Why?"

"To get your clothes, for God's sake."

"But they're in the wash."

"All your clothes?"

"Or on their way from Germany."

"So you *really were* taking me on a date like, like…"

"Well, O'Hanagan..."

"Always blaming poor Kevin," she snapped. "I get dressed for you, looking good for my man. I come out of my cosy home, travel in a taxi at my expense, to come and comfort you. To listen to your problems, to be a shoulder wet with tears, to pardon you for your sins and then I have to dine with a tramp."

"No, no, Nicki, please, I'll have money tomorrow..."

"Money," she shouted, "money like I'm some whore?"

"No, Nicki, please, I promise, you're a lady..."

"Well, say it right." Suddenly silent, she turned towards the window. Sulking to give me hope.

"I'm so sorry…"

"On your knees."

"I'm so sorry, Nicki, dear…" kneeling on pierced skin to kiss her hand but she kept so far, far away.

"You're very naughty, but a horrid naughty. I'm going to have to teach you a lesson." Anything, I wished with all my heart but bring me home with you tonight. "Driver," she called, "take me back, to the bistro on the corner." She placed her gloved hand upon my hair. "You're much too dirty to go downtown. We'll go to my local bistro for nibbles. Go in there and ask for the best table. Tell them it's for Miss Nicki and order a bottle of Claret."

"I don't have much money." I took the pittance from my pocket, the remnants of loot stolen from Terry's wallet.

"This will pay the taxi," and she scooped it from my palm. "In there and don't move until I return"

"How long will you be gone?"

"As long as I like. I must change into something casual. Might change my mind. Remember, I'm a lady not a whore. Now go."

"But I have no money."

"Oh ye of little faith. And if you fail or flee oh feeble one, you'll be punished. Driver, please, take me around the block." Away she went without a kiss.

So here I sit and drink it all and here he comes with greasy hair.

"I'm sorry, sir, but I'm sure there are many men waiting for Miss Nicki. Now, would you like to order? We are very busy tonight."

"The gentleman is waiting for the lady."

"One hour and a half?"

"T'at long?"

"Much too long, to sit and drink and not order food, my friend."

I'm not his friend. He's treating me with contempt and now he's taking away my bottle. Ha, I smile, not so fast and I have a hold of my wine. He pulls it hard and out of my hand.

"Okay," I concede, standing, "let's go and see where she is then." I walk penniless to the door and out to the night. Too quick for him. There's a fine drizzle out here, dancing on my face. I'm drunk because I'm too happy despite my troubles and thorny thoughts and burning knees and being alone. The waiter follows so I run away. It's just a trot but he's no fool and was ready for me. I run faster but he's sprinting and grabs my collar. Now he's speaking French and turning me around to shout at my face. That's your big mistake and I butt him on the nose. He returns a punch so I give him what I gave the coffee table, a good kick up between the legs.

I suppose I tried to do the same to Scullivan the last time we met. Yes, I kicked him. That's all I did. It's my boots that cause the problems; kicking people and things, Scullivan, a coffee table, the bucket of green water all over Betty's polished floor. I'm ashamed really, like a hooligan instead of a gentleman with his fists. It's no good trying to start the fight again, to do it right because the waiter's down and Scullivan's buried. So I run to the junction where immigrants loiter.

Where do illegals go at night to survive the cold? Some have homes I suppose, squats or maybe boxes in the metro station. There'll be scams for food or at least some crumbs, a common cause for survival. But the station's closed so where do the families go late at night? Only men along this street but no one asks me for money. I look too poor and it's O'Hanagan's fault, or Scullivan's. Maybe mine for starting fights. If I meet poor people I'll stop to talk, share our thoughts this drizzly night. Might laugh a bit but they stay away.

"Bitch," I cry aloud. I'm a drunken man wandering city streets shouting at the world. "English rich bitch whore."

37. PC Nicki from Pillow Street Police is coming to get me.

Terry was right, mornings are great. It's a beautiful time although there's a mist today. It's just a patch of it here on the slope because over there birds are singing. I think I hear seagulls cry and am I going down to the sea? It seems like the Boreen Low Road from Ballybog. I'm coming down from the mountain. My boots are laughing. Toe-caps are coming away from the soles, like mouths chattering as I walk. They are bruised from trailing streets and kicking a waiter. And a coffee table to bits. The same boots I used on Scullivan. They're laughing, flipping open with each step and my toes for teeth. Toenails like fangs through the holes of my socks and gasping for mouthwash. The damp air comes in and soothes my feet, better than Betty's foot spa. What do you think of that, O'Hanagan, if you were here and my boots laughing their heads off because I'm talking to myself? I thought I was at the sea but I am not. I'm in a car park. This is not Ireland or anywhere like it. This is a very steep slope down to a road busy with buses.

There's nothing more potent than rush-hour traffic to bring a wandering mind back to here. God, that was a bad day yesterday. Or the day before or whenever it was. Memories are elasticised knots inside my battered twisted head. Today is for repenting and reconciliation, to come to terms with a troubled time. I shall apologise to everyone. To poor Betty, to Terry, O'Hanagan, Scullivan, the waiter, and yes, even to the carpet men.
"Bonjour Monsieur," I sing, in my merry morning mood to a passing stranger. Not a murmur in reply but no harm. It's good that at least one of us is civil in the morning. First, I will go to Betty's place to apologise for the mess. Then to the restaurant to make my peace with the waiter. Rather a phone call to say sorry from a safe distance. A fine wide road this, space for a speedy wet breeze to wipe my face and dampen the rumble of traffic. "Bonjour monsieur," I sing again. He ignores me like the other commuter going to NATO headquarters. It's over there behind a fence. Cars going in and out, soldiers and diplomats. Peace to the world. Yes, I'm definitely going the right way, back to town against a breeze that disperses mist. In a bout of brightness I see a crowd spill from a bus. "Bonjour," I say to the body of bags and brollies and busy faces. They're a pig-ignorant lot en-route to work. God help the world if they're employed at NATO At least one of us is good humoured in the morning. Motorists don't like to stop for pedestrians in Belgium. Fair do's to the English despite their bad deeds, they were polite enough to stop at a crossing, even the lunatics in London. They were nice people, and Terry, poor dying Terry with your withered limbs. I wonder if he's still alive, pumped with drugs and

vitamins to keep him full of beans and talking like a politician. Yes, a card for him too, to say sorry and get well soon.

"Bonjour!"

I've gone several steps before I realise that someone's just said hello to me.

The carpet men battered me this morning. It was easy to steal into their van last night because they didn't close it properly. The carpets were too long but lovely for sleeping on. No one so desperate as me and wet with sweat and drizzle, stained with blood, snot and bits of glass in pulsating knees could resist the lure of carpets. Rolls of them the length of the van, longing for a drifter to fall in and stretch aching limbs from end to end. I was snoozing this morning with arms and legs stretched to the four corners of the world. Then he grabbed my hair. Wakey wakey. Dreams lured me back to carpet valley. I was a stream dilly-dallying along. I was Pine Forest Green Dream, a liquid cleanser flowing over Betty's carpet, to ease away the most stubborn stains. Then he was hitting me, had the hair pulled from my head. I was suddenly outside in the wet and the breath walloped from my belly.

There's no more bleeding. It's turned crispy; bits of dried blood up each nostril. I recognise that landmark in the distance and I'll pick my nose as I go to it. A little pleasure, pick a bit and flick it on the ground. Nice buildings set back from the road, Art Deco blocks with semi-circle balconies, saucers that were thrown like discs into the wall while the concrete was wet.

"Bonjour," I say but it seems useless now because the streets are busy. Can't go around saying hello to every soul in Brussels. Mothers bringing children to school, big ones on bikes, ting-a-ling. Big but not rich enough to be asking them for money. A few spare coins because I have lost my way. "Bonjour," I say because this one was looking at me. She might have unwanted pennies burdening her pockets. "Excuse me." But she quickens her pace and lowers her head and is gone away. My dirt and grit and crispy scabs repel them all. First, I'll have a wash. Make sure I don't disturb Betty's Pacific Pink collection or leave a gritty ring around her bath. Give it a wipe with Blue Lagoon. A bite to eat, her healthy rabbit food on a wafer. Can't nibble it though, not like her. No, in it goes, bread, biscuits, a lumpy lot. No fear of crumbs, I'll be her vacuum cleaner sucking up biscuit bits. It's not exploitation though, not a bit of it, and I'll explain it to this redheaded stranger coming my way. It seems so strange to be shouting in suburbia. "Hello. Excuse me, I've lost my wallet... Sorry, I mean I've lost my way..."

Don't worry, Betty, I won't be a burden. I'm leaving after my coffee, and cleaning crumbs and writing a sloppy note on her pink perfumed pad. And have a fart in her bathroom. No, no, just a joke. Can't resist a bit of devilment because she's so prim and proper. Miserable but I'm definitely leaving after cleaning her house. There it is. The mist has cleared now, and the street comes alive with sunshine. Brightness blooms on suburban walls and windows ablaze with the reflection. A beautiful day.

"Agh, feck it," and I suddenly stop, stalled stiff in the street to see the man from the big white house. He's with the police, following a trail of copper debris across the road. The sun is burning now on shiny lengths of pipe. O'Hanagan, you big fecking useless bollocks, yer. Scraps of copper lead the way from the man's gate, across the street to litter the forecourt outside Betty's home. Now they've found another bit by her door. You're some donkey, O'Hanagan. Left a mess the size of donkey turds right up to Betty's door. My merry morning mood evaporates like the mist. Time to go, before I see Betty wearing shiny handcuffs. I meander the other way, towards the metro to get advice.

A sweat beneath my clothes, my skin dribbling with a dirty coat of it. What would Nicki think, Betty or any woman? A growth on my jaw like a bramble bush, and my hair thick with urban grease. Even O'Hanagan was cleaner than this. He managed to get a shave somewhere, the sly fox. I'll just look in here. Down I go into a litterbin for a dirty bite to eat. Get out of it you dirty little bastard fly. No, nothing in here. I'll look in another. Empty. Just newspaper. Plenty of places for dumping rubbish but the dustman has done his job. Over there where they loiter outside chicken bars and hamburger stalls. Kitchen smells are in the air and packaging in a bin. A tasty piece of paper for me to lick. Now I've got my tongue inside a carton to catch a taste.

"Shite," throwing it back. "Wouldn't do to drop it on the floor," I say to a polite couple forcing smiles on their distorted faces. They retreat to dump their rubbish somewhere else. Nice people are disturbed by the poor. Poor people can lick their packaging. I'm tongue-tackling another tasty delight. Stuck down inside a bin, tearing a carton to bits, like an animal with no mercy for its prey, ripping open the belly to devour a strawberry yoghurt. I've got the blood around my mouth, strawberry flavoured bits on my beard. It's on the back of my hand because I don't have a napkin to wipe myself clean. What would they think of me licking yoghurt from my sleeve, yes, my sleeve? Got it everywhere, my sleeve, my face, neck and hair because it burst strawberry blood mixed with milk when I went in for the kill. Bit into its belly and out it came, guts and all.

Reduced to a disgusting tramp and I killed no one, and that simpleton is getting fed with homeless folk. And he has had a shave.

There's an illegal immigrant from the east, sauntering across the street. I know he's one of them because he wears two sweaters, maybe three or four. It's never been a fashion in the west except to serve against the cold. He's too fat around the chest to fit that coat so I'll go over to say hello. These are the people to be mixing with to get advice, not deranged dealers on the street. Here's a dirty depressing man looking for work, one like me recovering from last night's weather.

"My friend," I say, "how's it going?" I'm offering my hand, stretched out for him to take and be my friend. He won't even look at it but pretending to be busy. Now, look where I'm at, a credit to my boots, all the way to Terry's door. But I'll not be caught by detectives waiting in a car. Ha, ha, with a photo of Bart from Ballybog. Is that your man? they'll be saying, him with a strawberry yoghurt beard, get out and arrest him. Risk it for my clothes, a wash and food, a tramp on Terry's doorstep, come to see his dying friend. But I'm too clever for them, walking around the block checking cars and doorways to find a loitering policeman. Empty cars and immigrants are all I see, in long thick coats or padded jackets and one with a blanket on his head. Yes, I'm sure that's what they are. Don't talk then because I've come back to Terry's door and I have a key to let me in.

"Shit," says Terry from up the stairs. "The fucking state of you." He looks a lot healthier than myself.

"Food, Terry. I need food," pulling myself up along the banister.

"Where the fuck yer bin, Squire?"

"Have they been here?"

"Who?"

"Who? The police?"

"Why, what's yer done?" He steps back to let me pass.

"The murd... the tax." Nearly said it: murder. I had forgotten that I'm supposed to be running from the taxman.

"Shit, yer must owe 'em a real packet if they're sending in the fuzz for ya. And yer smell of something."

"Need food, Terry. Lumps of it and vitamins, nourishment and t'ings to feed a horse. I never t'ought t'at I'd be at death's door before you."

Terry's a grand feller cooking me an English fry-up while I empty the biscuit tin.

"It's coming, Squire, for fuck sake."

"I'll still eat it, Terry. Everyt'ing."

Heaps of sausage, eggs, bacon, the lot swimming in grease. And toast.

"No beans."

"No problem, Terry. A magic bit of cooking, Christ, you're a credit to your kind. You'll be rewarded in heaven."

"And where's yer mate, Jaws O'Hanagan?"

"Gone with the faeries." Black pudding too, from Lancashire. Lovely cup of tea. And carpets from Pine Forest Valley. Lovely long green carpets the length of the high street. First time in Pine Forest? Own the place and the carpet factory and the carpet cleaner...!

"Bart, wake up for fuck sake."

"What?"

"Yer fell asleep in your plate."

"Oh, I was dreaming of cleaning Betty's carpet." I lift myself from the table and wipe an egg from my face.

"Yer need a wash."

"I need to sleep."

If they're going to get me, they would have had me by now, had the place surrounded with police and dogs and I'll be in Ireland before I'm awake. Great, sleep. No need to panic. The police have enough problems in Brussels and no time to bother me in bed. They probably couldn't find me under these fluffy blankets. Lovely in here, better than carpets. I can stretch a bit, not too far because they might see my leg coming out of the bottom of the bed. Wouldn't want them to know that I was in here. Snug as a bug, don't let the bedbugs bite. What's this, a note under my pillow? From my legal advisor, done a deal! Mr Financial Advisor, my legal advisor wants me to sign it, here in bed and Nicki is coming over to my side. Just sign it. It's to promise that I will never kick the coffee table again. I do hereby swear that I will never kick, so help me God. Okay, I'll sign it. There, so I get a suspended sentence. Is that it? Yes but you must report to O'Hanagan each day at eleven o'clock. I am not allowed to phone Miss Nicki without his permission. I am not allowed on her side of the bed. And there she is between pink silk sheets and dangling shiny handcuffs to take me home to her padded cell, detective Nicki from Pillow Street Police. Won't get away now and has me stretched out to search for evidence and look at the mess I've caused, enough for a holding charge and stains on the sheet and everything Betty said is true. There she is in the witness box, upon the wardrobe. And Scullivan poking through the top, his white withered head playing Punch and Judy with her. They can see it all now, pointing to the mess. What a mess, says the judge, and how could this be poor Mr O'Hanagan's fault?

38.   Terry's right, mornings are great but please don't start a monologue.

"Morning," sings Terry.

"What time is it?"

"Nearly seven."

"Great sleep. Weird dream." I throw my legs out of bed, a dirty pair of trousers. My socks too are on my feet. I fell asleep fully clothed so I need to peel them off, like pulling paper from a sweaty gluey wall. There's a coat of sweat between my thighs and beneath my arms and I need to scratch the itch from my hair. Terry's right, it's the best time of the day. A credit to my flatmate who done the washing and left a clean towel for me.

"Best time o' the day," says Terry from some other room. "When I was working in Berlin, I'd 'ave an hour's overtime in the morning. Best productive hour of the day…"

"Terry, I'm having a lovely day, don't spoil it with a speech." I'm determined to stay rational today and sort out my life. Into the shower to wash away the last few days.

"Tea in the pot."

"Grand, Terry." Steal some of his toiletries. He won't mind. He has all this stuff, a bit like Betty. Bottles of bollocks in every colour. Shower gel to bring a tingle to my skin.

"Aey," he shouts, "don't be fucking nicking my stuff. 'Bout time yer bought yer own."

"I'll be going shopping today, Terry. To buy a heap of stuff. We'll be needing more shelf space."

"Here's that letter," flicking it into the bathroom for me. "That bloke who came to the door. He left it for you." The envelope lands on the floor, an innocent piece of paper on the tiles, yet awesome.

I'll open it later, a daunting task when Terry's gone. He goes out for morning walks to live life to the full, tram spotting or something, God love him. I take back everything I said about the English eejit. He was here when I needed him and my own countryman has deserted me just because I called him a bollocks. And Terry cooked a fry-up to feed a horse and not a murmur from him. Not even a monologue. That was in the past, when he was nearly dead, and what man would not crack up with death knocking on his door? Look at myself, gone to pieces just because a man asked for me. I'll open that awful letter after I've shaved. Do it while my hand is steady, before retarding into a nervous wreck. A clean sharp razor against my neck is sheer luxury. Each therapeutic stroke slices away a carpet of growth. And now a splash of aftershave to sting my skin and bring my face fresh alive, revitalised for another today. Thanks to Terry I can slip into clean clothes.

"Fair do's to you, Terry, you done all the laundry."

"Some cunt 'ad to do it."

"You'll be rewarded in heaven." Clean clothes are a tonic for the skin. I pick the letter from the floor, opening it, unfolding paper with a subtle shake.

"Looks official," says Terry, coming to my shoulder. "Yep, they're solicitors, written in English as well..."

"Don't you have an anorak to be getting into?" That's what he wears, like a real train-spotter from the North of England. I move before he has the chance to read about a murder.

The first thing I focus on is the site of the killing, printed in seemingly bold letters. It's really ordinary type but the Boreen High Road, Ballybog, Ireland seems to bounce off the page. My hands tremble. I can't read but only glance from word to word, zig-zagging across the page to fatality and O'Hanagan's name. Please come to our office, it says..

"Terry, will you stop gawking at me and put some coffee on?" I need space for pacing about. Around the flat I go, from room to room while I read again. Accident! Inheritance!

It could be a trick, to trap us but it's true enough that Scullivan was a distant cousin of O'Hanagan. I'm a cousin myself and know something of the family tree. We are both distant cousins but Scullivan was closer to the O'Hanagans. He was also an only child, his father lost at sea and mother too old and the land has to be inherited by someone. That's the way it is in Ireland. An inheritance.

"But what accident?" I'm pacing about like Sherlock Holmes.

"What accident?"

"Precisely, Terry. What accident?"

"Well, just go and ask."

And what would happen if I walked into their office, asking about an accident and an inheritance? An Irish detective is waiting with a warrant and a one-way ticket to the backside of Ireland. What better place would there be than a solicitor's office for reading my rights, and making an arrest and sorting out the extradition with the minimum of fuss? Look at the letterhead, a fine address on the same street as the Irish embassy. The associate companies are listed too, with an office in every capital. No doubt, they are just the people for finding fugitives running over borders.

"Oldest trick in the book, Terry. Lure a man in to get an inheritance and then slap him with a tax bill."

"Inheritance, you say?"

"Inheritance or not, Terry, I am no man's fool when it comes to tax."

"Well, do what I do."

"And what would t'at be, oh clever clogs?"

"Phone."

It's a brilliant idea. It's Friday, business hours, and so I'll race down to a phone.

"Here, use this." He pulls a slim mobile from his top pocket.

"Oh, you have a new phone."

"No, the same one."

I wonder where he's been hiding this, the sly fox.

Nice music while I'm being transferred to another office.

"So, Terry, where's the coffee?"

"Tea?"

"Coffee, Terry. Coffee in the morning." I don't really need coffee but get him out of here, send him to the kitchen so he can't hear.

"Mr O'Hanagan?" asks a woman down the phone.

"No, this is his colleague. Unfortunately, Mr O'Hanagan is travelling, on business. I look after his affairs and received a letter this week..."

"Oh, you're Mr Rabbit?"

"Amm..." I don't know if I should admit who I am.

"So, how can we help?"

"Well, well, amm, could you give me more information?"

"Unfortunately, Mr O'Hanagan would need to come to our office."

I knew it, they want us there but I'll persist, pretending to be distressed. "I'm afraid this has come as a shock, and it's going to be difficult to relay the awful news to Mr O'Hanagan. T'ey were very close, him and his distant cousin. And I have no details of this accident...."

"Oh, sorry, you want information about the accident, not the inheritance. Certainly we can give you *that* information over the phone. Sorry for the misunderstanding. Please wait while I locate the police file and the coroner's report."

It becomes a nice day now, getting brighter as she reads to me. Terry is back with the coffee and there's a beautiful blue sky over Brussels, Belgium Blue, the brightest blue on all of earth. The depression in my life is lifting as she recites, reading the report like it's pure poetry with her exquisite English accent.

The coroner concluded that Scullivan was very drunk but the police could find no witnesses to say where he had been drinking and who he was with. They obviously knew that half the village population was in a pub drinking that night and didn't go home at closing time. Like any other Saturday night, they stayed beyond midnight, drinking illegally. That's the way of things in Ireland; a law in writing and a donkey in practice. Drinking and the craic was better with the lights turned low and the curtains drawn tight. There was fun in scurrying home in the dark. In the morning, not a sinner would admit to being in the pub, and as they hadn't been there it was impossible for anyone to suggest to the constable who he should talk to. However, everyone remembered where they last saw Scullivan, in the middle of the day, in the village. And he was a lovely man, and sure it'll be a great wake.

What a well-spoken woman she is, the solicitor's secretary. And I'm thinking, what a nice afternoon.

"Are you still there, Mr Rabbit?"

"I am, I am. Sure, it would have been a good wake. But read on," and I listen as she tells me about the driver. It was Paddy Funny, and I knew him well. He was the first one down the Boreen High Road on Sunday morning, going to seven o'clock mass. He saw Scullivan asleep on the road, sprawled in a drunken pose. Paddy tried to stop and hooted his horn loud enough to wake the dead but the exhaust pipe cut into poor Scullivan's head. It dragged him by his broken skull, like a fish on a hook, down to the next bend. Like he'd been hit with the blade of a shovel, says the report. A clean cut but it wasn't the driver's fault, concluded the police, not a bit of it. The weather was bad, and this is mentioned several times by the coroner. Go on there, I'm singing in my head, and the solicitor's secretary reads on, a fairy tale. There's a weather report attached to the coroner's comments to confirm what had been stated, that it had been a nice night for a walk, whether a man was drunk or sober, but turned to wet in the morning as a mist came down from the mountain. Rolled down from purple peaks and was getting worse by the minute according to the parish priest. He had to cancel mass to go up and give the last rites and saw the wetness for himself. Nonetheless, the coroner concluded, it's wrong to blame the weather. It was a stupid place for a man to be, on a bend in the road and at the steepest part, wet or dry. The fact that he was lying down was a warning to others who went out drinking illegally. The police were not fooled.

"Very sad, it is. And would t'at be the end of the enquiry?"

"It is, but there are a few personal words directed at the local community, from the parish priest, if you would like me to read on, Mr Rabbit."

"Do, of course."

So she reads the words from the priest who I knew, or at least I had heard give a sermon. It sounds just like him speaking to the otherwise good citizens of Ballybog, to say that they are adults and should know that the police have better things to do than to stand vigil on the Boreen High Road watching for drunks who are unable to get home to their bed.

"And it is true enough," I say. "My mother wrote and told me how a bicycle was stolen in broad daylight the other week."

"Terry, it's a fine day, so it is."

"And is it good news?"

"It tis, Terry, and tell me, would you have spare cash, just enough for some clothes for O'Hanagan. I wouldn't want him to be wearing t'ose rags when he was in for the reading of the will."

"Is he going to be rich?"

"He is, Terry. He owns a farm in Ireland. Not the bog but the finest, greenest fields west of Dublin. He owns it from the boreen up to purple peaks. But, Terry, I wouldn't have enough cash to buy him a suit *and* to get the shopping. I'm sure you know the score yourself with these offshore banks. Tax avoidance is a nuisance but if we dress him up we could get a hefty advance."

"I'm going down the bank now, Squire, if you want to come. But it's just a loan."

"Christ, Terry, I'm a man like yourself, running from the taxman and my cash in hiding. We're speaking the same language here."

It would be a mistake to let O'Hanagan get his big bog hands on the inheritance because he would squander the lot on gifts for strangers, silver cigarette lighters and phone calls to Nicki. If this trail around Europe has taught me anything, it is that O'Hanagan's mother was right. My mother was right. A lot of mothers and others in Ballybog were right about O'Hanagan. He was simple. Too stupid to have money, and for sure, he could not manage a farm. I have no intention of taking him to the solicitor's office in Brussels when I find him. The best place for him is straight back to Ireland, to the local solicitor who knows that he's a simpleton. A bollocks. I'll be credited for bringing him home safely, and I might be in a position to oversee the farm. Ah, sure, Bart, his mother will sing, aren't you the best man to look after the farm, and you are Kevin's friend? You are a saint for bringing him home. And how did you know that he was following you? Wasn't he always like that? And you a man of the world but you were always good to him.

I follow Terry down the stairs and out onto the street.

"You're looking good, Terry. You're looking brilliant. Walking normally. Has your back recovered fully?"

"Told yer, aey? Didn't I tell yer? Fuck all wrong with my back. Just needed that bit of a rest." He strolls towards the bank as easy as he walked down the stairs. Drugs are a wonderful item but all credit to Terry en-route to get me cash.

He'll get enough to buy O'Hanagan's suit but I'll use the money for two tickets to Ireland. I only need enough to get away from Terry, and get the simpleton back to Ballybog. Terry's suspicious though, saw it in his contorted face when I pretended to have my money locked away offshore. He doesn't mind paying for clothes to put on O'Hanagan's back, but he has worked hard all his life and he's no one's fool. Terry won't give it away to scroungers without a guarantee. Nothing sinister in him but I caught him making a note of the solicitor's address.

"And Terry, I just want to say t'anks."

"No problem, Squire, that's what mates are for."

"But t'anks, all the same." Guilt is an awful emotion, especially while I'm plotting to leave without goodbye. I will return the money though. It's the least I should do.

But there might be no need to. He's still destined for an early death. There's something wrong. I see it now, in his eyes rather than his walk, a painful urge to impress me. Yes, his back is better but something else eats deep inside him. Terry doesn't talk but paces himself to prove something to me but I suspect he won't be able to spend his lot.

"Tell me, Terry, what is the other ailment t'at you have?"

"Well, they have to do tests."

"Tests?"

"Yeh, tests, like yer know."

"But didn't t'ey tell you?"

"Well, they don't like to speculate, I suppose. Anyway, what about this bird, Betty? Or Nicki is it? Have yer shagged her yet?"

I'll ask no more about his health because that quiver in his voice tells it all. His vocal cords are as fragile as his limbs, losing fuel with every step. He's living on a monthly recharge. In and out of hospital like a yo-yo for doctors to experiment on while his money earns interest in this bank.

"They're both non-starters, Terry. Yes, women have been bad news. An expense."

"Don't I know it? That Candy cost me…"

"Terry, before you start, lend me your phone. I need to call Nicki. Find out where O'Hanagan is."

He takes it from his pocket, hands it to me, and goes to get the cash.

"Hello, Nicki, tis Bart. Yes, very well t'ank you. Much better today. I just had a crisis the other night but I have survived. Yes, yes, I have money now. And yes of course, I have all my clothes. Yes, clean and all. Yes, Nicki, I'm very clean. You could eat your dinner off me. No, Nicki, I'm much too busy. Not tonight. And not tomorrow. Nicki, can I interrupt you for a moment, just to ask for O'Hanagan? Is he there? Loitering you say? Is t'at across the road in the park? Nicki, please, tell him to wait for me, I'm on my way. With good news."

"Here you are, Squire, that enough?"

"T'anks, Terry, you're a sound man." I shake hands with him, surprising him as I look into his lonely sad eyes. "No truer word said, Terry, I'll pay you back every cent."

"Aey, no problem."

"But I mean it," squeezing his hand.

"I know. For fuck sake."

"But I just want to say t'anks a lot."

"I know."

"But I mean it."

"I know."

"Really. I appreciate it."

"I know. For fuck sake, it's not that yer leaving the country, yer cunt."

39. Now, I've lost O'Hanagan.

Friday night, the weekend, and the Irish pub will be a great place for the craic. Voices are out on the street, workers with a few drinks in them after a hard week. They're like children coming home from school and I'm a free man, able to join them. I can go out to play and work legally on Monday morning. No fear of documentation or questions or speaking my name but here I am, depressed like the weather. I can see the dismal greyness through the window, a blanket of drizzle across the sky.

"Do you want fucking tea or don't you?"

"Yeh." I reply. "Sorry, Terry, but any man would be angry."

"Just drink your tea and wait awhile. Then we'll talk about it rationally."
Terry pours it from the pot. A drop of milk. He sits opposite me, puts his elbows on the table and sinks his skinny face into his hands. "For fuck sake, what happened?"

This morning, after getting the money, I went to find O'Hanagan. It's ironic that I spend so much time searching for the same idiot who I used to hide from. A fruitless exercise around the park and then along endless suburban streets that surround Nicki's apartment. At least I had money. Thanks to Terry I could afford to travel home on the metro.

"My friend," said a beggar. I knew he was one before he said another word. He was too polite and after a few words he asked for money, as I expected.

"Good luck, my friend." I gave him my change and shook hands and I walked out of the station. Then a cup was pressed into my chest, and beseeching eyes peeped out from beneath her hood. So sorry and I tried to explain that despite my clean clothes I was skint of spare change. I had just given my coins away. What I had was needed to get O'Hanagan and myself to Ballybog. I couldn't afford to break into more notes but I did, I had to after peering into her hood to see her long face with oval eyes. She was desperate or clever but I needed absolution. I gave her more than enough to buy a dinner. She took my hand and bestowed a blessing upon me, her bony fingers holding me like she had claws.

"Some gypsy or whatever gave me a blessing this afternoon."

"Didn't work then." Terry looks up at me.

"It didn't, Terry. T'ings were going downhill from the moment that I stepped out from the metro station, after getting my blessing."

As I came in here, I called Terry. It seemed strange at the time because Terry was usually at home in the afternoon, making fried egg sandwiches, even at the height of his recovery. A blister punctured as I climbed the stairs, felt the wetness trickle out. Blisters on my feet, bubbles of them. Air-cushioned soles the size of tractor tyres. I was hoping that he had some tea ready.

Well it's ready now. I really appreciate it after my endurance. I take my tea as I leave the table to walk about, from room to room to dissipate anger. My feet are too sore to go outside but that's where I should walk, in the wet to wash the badness from me. I could kill someone. But not Terry, it wasn't his fault.

"Thanks, Terry. You make a good cup of tea." The flat's clean too. I noticed it when I came home this afternoon. While soaking my sore feet in a basin I let my eyes roam about. It was as clean as Betty's place except my room. I went in there to see my mess. Maybe I was contemplating cleaning it up, feeling guilty for exploiting Terry. Then I saw the note on my door. Big writing so I couldn't miss it. From Terry to tell me that O'Hanagan was around to warn me not to touch his girlfriend. Stay away, it said, stuck to my bedroom door. Just a casual scribble to say O'Hanagan was restless after hearing the good news. He couldn't wait till Monday morning. So Terry took him in the car to the solicitor's office.

I sit down at the table again and reach for a biscuit.

"Terry, you donkey."

"Bart," lifting his head from his hands, "don't fucking start. I'm warning you, don't fucking start. How was I to know he had a wooden brain?"

"Okay, okay." I sip my tea but at the time I could have killed Terry. I was frantic, down the stairs, falling and crashing into the door and limping out to hail a taxi. The Friday afternoon rush was happening and I was like a greyhound wanting to spring from a kennel despite my blistered feet.

"Faster," I shouted at the driver. He turned to see me, to stare at me.

"We are not in a movie, sir. We are in the middle of Brussels, in the middle of rush hour traffic."

"Sorry." He was probably right. I wasn't sure why I panicked because the solicitors were only associates, employed to find us and deliver a message. The traffic was getting heavier and my driver doodling. No problem, I said. He slowed at green lights, in case they turned red. Which they did and he stamped on the brake, the only thing he did in haste. Bollocks, but relax, I said, and something burned inside me. Thorny thoughts like electric elements. Heat poured through my face, red with frustration while waiting for a green light. Relax, I said, and questioned my reasons for rushing.

It was ridiculous; as if the solicitor had the farm rolled up like a carpet in his office, ready to unfold the lush green fields for O'Hanagan's inspection, and livestock in a back room waiting to be brought to market. My behaviour was absurd. Traffic lights turned green; there we are, just a little time. Patience is needed. Heard it said, patience, found seldom in a woman but never in a man. We drove forward while everyone else accelerated into empty spaces. All the time in the world. The driver had a long face down to his lap and studious eyes that gazed upon the road, like he was studying a diagram. Suddenly the reason for my haste came like the shovel through my skull. I was worried by the questions that the solicitor might ask O'Hanagan. Like, were you close friends, and, it must have been a great shock to hear of his death? Oh no, O'Hanagan might answer. We knew all the time that he was dead. We killed him. But Bart thought it was murder so we ran away. That's why you couldn't find us. Murder? the solicitor would ask, what murder? And O'Hanagan would say there was no murder. We just killed him by mistake. Bart said it could have happened to anyone. It was in the dark and Bart would have battered him anyway for emptying an ashtray into his beer. I only hit him with the shovel to put manners on him but he had a big head, so he did. He was always showing off in front of girls, so he was. It would make any man want to wallop him.

The driver wandered into a taxi lane, or bus lane. It was definitely a slow lane cluttered with buses that stopped to fart their fumes and I was fuming. Yes, I had good reason for panicking.

"Faster," I shouted. "Faster."

"This is no time for speeding..."

"When I want your opinion, I'll beat it out of you. Now, faster, you bollocks because t'ere is no tips if I'm late. I'm getting out here and running the rest and then we'll see how fast you'll be. There's enough space t'ere for a fecking bulldozer or what kind of a bollocks of a driver are you?" At last I was speaking his language and he pressed the pedal. A donkey of a driver, into a cluttered junction he went, the dunce. I leaped out like a greyhound before the driver had time to brake, indicate or dip his clutch.

Blisters on my feet popped as I ran. There were glass doors at the top of wide steps, and a porter was waiting to lock them. I was gasping and limping, and O'Hanagan was inside, shaking hands with strangers. Although the windows were tinted, O'Hanagan's beaming face was radiant, a gleaming smile that smashed through the reflection.

"O'Hanagan," I shouted, "O'Hanagan, you big bollocks." He was too busy to hear me, introducing himself to the doorman. It was worse than I thought possible but it got worse. Much worse. I was half way up the steps when O'Hanagan opened the glass door and smiled at me. Then he said it and stunned me.

"Bart, I'm getting married. Me and Miss Nicki is getting married."

It took several seconds for me to respond. I was numb until the moment when I saw Terry coming through the doors, talking. He didn't know that I was ready to bring his death a little closer. It would have been first degree murder, intentional in front of witnesses. He hadn't realised because he was still telling me about O'Hanagan's stupidity.

"...Then yer mate phoned from the solicitor's office to tell that bird, Nicki, that he was rich. Stupid cunt. Said she didn't have to spend a minute longer living in Henry Moore's apartment."

"And you fecking sat t'ere like the big fecking useless AIDS infested bollocks t'at you are?"

"Don't," he warned, with a stiff belligerent face. "Don't fucking start, yer bog man."

"I'll fecking strangle yer skinny neck, so I will...." and I had my hands up to grab his collar but he pushed me back, and almost stumbled down some steps.

"Bart, Bart," interrupted O'Hanagan, "do you want to live on the hill, with me and Miss Nicki?"

I didn't know which one to hit. Terry gave me a push that took all his strength. He retreated, shaky but tense.

"O'Hanagan, yer bollocks, ya, you're living on no fecking hill with that fecking wallet-snapping bitch."

"I am. The solicitor said. And you're jealous."

"Yeh, Terry, that's a nice cup of tea. T'anks."

"Have some more. Pleny in the pot." He reaches for the tea and I'm reflecting on what I called him outside the office. Terry was too ill to argue, went stiff like frost. Even at the best of times he doesn't talk about his withering body. And I've been too selfish to consider his condition or even wonder if it's contagious. I'm actually ignorant and this afternoon I became tactless and vicious. He pours my tea.

"T'anks, Terry. Agh, Christ, we'll probably look back on all this and laugh about it one day." I shut up and sip my tea awhile. "Well, I suppose t'at wallet-snapper can't get it unless she actually marries him."

"Yes she can," replies Terry. "She's getting the working capital." He tops up his own cup.

"What working capital?"

"Working capital, it said. Comes with the farm. The solicitor arranged for it to be transferred electronically. He phoned the Irish embassy, had someone come to check O'Hanagan's ID." Terry carefully places the teapot in the middle of the table and picks up his cup with two hands. "Then yer mate wanted cash for the wedding."

"And you sat there?"

"Look," he snaps, "I didn't know he was going to start all this shit in the office. The solicitor asked me to sit in, be a witness. Asked Hanagan if he wanny money sent to his bank account, if he wanny cash, if he wanny a tax receipt, if he wanny make a will, if he wanny 'av a coffee. Hanagan said yeh to everything and anything. Meanwhile the solicitor is piling on the charges for 'is services. Ten per cent extra for anything from Ireland. Shit, that solicitor was a shark in there, encouraging Hanagan to fill in forms."

"Feck." I stand again to walk about. Slump in the armchair, punctured like my blisters and the energy dribbling from me.

"At least you got yer health."

It was fine land on a green slope and sprayed with an Irish mist. A path cut up the middle to a cottage, his own house, ready for when he found a wife. Although a countryman, Scullivan pursued policies similar to Terry's; worked hard and avoided the taxman. There would be plenty of money in the account, working capital he'd call it so the taxman wouldn't take it.

"What exactly was arranged?" walking back to the table.

"A cheque. A transfer cheque, they said, to move everything to their joint account."

"Joint account? The bitch."

"And papers for the land. That's what I was trying to tell ya, for fuck sake. Your mate had papers for her to sign and a cheque in 'is pocket." Terry sips his tea and looks at me. "I thought that you'd just talk to 'im and take them off him. I mean, he is stupid."

"He is, Terry."

"But do you know where he is now?"

"I do of course."

"So we get to him before he gives her the cheque. Rip up the papers before she signs them. Anything. Come on, let's go."

Terry's coming to life, his withered limbs fighting to be my friend again, comrades going down the stairs, on a mission to his car. It's difficult to keep pace with him when he gets a burst of energy like this. His sudden enthusiasm puts me to shame; Terry the fighter telling me this is what mates are for, to support each other through thick and thin. Healthy or not. I duck to avoid his arms as he punches them through the sleeves of his coat. It's wet out there so I'm struggling with my own coat because we might be searching the streets. There's a penalty ticket on the windscreen that goes the same way as any other demand in Terry's twilight months; a paper ball for the gutter.

Of course, he's right. No one but myself and the crowd back in Ballybog knows the likes of O'Hanagan, a bollocks bred in the bog. The solicitor back in Ireland would know though, so it's still possible that the paperwork will go no further than his desk. The weekend has come and there is nothing I can do until Monday morning but get the cheque. A friend in need is a friend indeed and Terry's Jaguar is weaving through evening traffic en route to Uccles.

We drive past the arch. The same one that I paid a taxi driver to circle three times because Nicki wanted to see it. She was a spoilt child asking for everything she saw and I was madly in love. Infatuated by the lady, more than by any other woman, more than I lusted for the Antwerp therapist who sucked me dry and had me howling and hooting. Nicki was everything; lust and love fusing and igniting. She glanced at me and made me melt like molten metal to her feet. I was mad with a compulsion to be near her. And that's as far as a man could get. For her, it was the chase that counted, the man running and burning while Nicki danced, giggling on swings and flying with birds, reachless but teasing, all the time inviting, a beguiling bitch.

"Bitch."

"What's that?" asks Terry.

"Nothing."

Nicki is in another world. Hers is a fantasyland where money grows on trees and little girls flash their eyelashes to get what they want. She stays in her land of dreams, luring me onto her clouds, treading on tiptoes while drifting away. O'Hanagan would be too heavy, too clumsy to follow; he's already unable to cope with this world. I feel sorry for him, sorry for every big fat clumsy bogman who ever has to tiptoe onto the cotton-wool clouds. Also for muscle-bound jerks who pump iron to impress, or workaholics or studious romantics who labour to the top to earn a fortune to pamper a beauty. There's no place for any of us as players in that world. We're just puppets, providers, there to pay the price. Terry knows what I want to say but I won't mention a word of it for fear of triggering a monologue. I have heard it all before. He has been there and suffered too.

"Sorry, Terry. I flipped."

"Anyone would. He's really stupid."

"Sure, he can't just transfer land as easy as that?"

There's a silence as Terry steers the Jaguar into a lane and down through a tunnel that winds beneath Brussels. The twelve-cylinder engine purrs as we climb out, up to daylight, an evening grey. He replies, as if he had needed the darkness to help him think.

"He had to sign in several places."

"No," I decide aloud, "no way. The solicitor back home will also need to sign it. We'll find out on Monday. The solicitor back in Ballybog will know t'at he is not right in the head."

"They phoned him too, to fax authorisation to Brussels."

"Feck. Technology is a sin when it's t'at efficient."

The wheels of Terry's Jaguar skid into the forecourt. He has a car as good as any of them. Isn't this a bit of style? She'll probably have time for me now, washed and combed as I am and stepping from a Jag. But it doesn't matter, I'm done with her. No negotiation. I'm pressing the doorbell like forcing a drawing pin into a brick. Terry wants to push it too. Maybe he thinks his finger will make a different ring. He's holding it in.

"Does he have much cash?" I ask.

"A bit. Well, quite a lot. The equivalent of a few thousand old Irish pounds." Terry takes his finger off the button. "A bit for the weekend, said the solicitor, until banks opened on Monday morning. That was another charge. Ten per cent extra."

I could strangle him again, wrap hands around his skinny neck and press my fingers through his throat. But it's time to think and order Terry back to the car. He's the chauffeur and lively for a dying man. The drugs have done wonders and please God, don't let him falter until I've found O'Hanagan.

Her local bistro on the corner, of course, a little place for celebration. There he is. I'd recognise that head of his anywhere.

"Stop, stop, t'ere he is."

"Where?"

"The bistro. Just stop and let me out." I'm getting out anyway before poor Terry is able the park his car. Careful because I didn't pay my bill the last time I was in here. Ran out and kicked your man. Can't see a waiter as I peep through windows. There's a woman behind the bar. Groups are gathered around tables between warm yellow walls. It's a cosy place and I push the door slowly, stepping cautiously into the warmth and amongst the laughter.

"Okay," says Terry, coming in behind me.

"A bit livelier than the last time I was here. T'ere they are." O'Hanagan, the lump, is in a new anorak. It's too big and inflated against little Nicki. She's sipping champagne, and dressed as a schoolgirl with her hair in two plaits down to her shoulders.

O'Hanagan has obviously spent some of the cash on the way to here; cigarette lighters litter their table, silver ones. The same shop sold watches, magazines and souvenirs. A spare seat is heaped with the stuff: more silver lighters and some on the floor. There's champagne for everyone, bottles on tables. Youths at the bar have obviously taken advantage of the happy couple's generosity; they're sucking colourful cocktails through spiralled tubes. The bar's lit up with them; alcoholic amber and glaring greens with a slice of shinning orange. Nicki giggles. She's merrily swaying away from O'Hanagan to look at him, laugh at him and hit his chest with a drunken slap.

"Barty baby," she suddenly sings, and her eyes widening with delight. "Jealous baby."

"See, see," roars O'Hanagan, "jealous, told you." He rises from his seat, pointing at me. "See, see, told you, you're jealous."

"But I've come to be your best man." This makes Nicki laugh more. It was already funny that she would marry O'Hanagan, but as I join the circus she collapses into hysterics, her head nodding helplessly towards the table. She looks up and screams at me. Clenching her glass with two hands, Nicki throws back her head to laugh at the ceiling.

"Can he, Miss Nicki, can Bart be best man?"

It causes her to scream her laugh, to the point of pain but O'Hanagan doesn't know it's a joke. His beaming smile is at boiling point.

"Come on, O'Hanagan, have a drink, before you explode. We'll have a toast. I'll buy you a drink."

"But we have champagne. Tis the best in the world, Miss Nicki said."

For Nicki, everything he says is funny; tears in her eyes as he asks again for me to be best man. Can't hear but I can see it in his innocent face, talking nonsense as she rolls forward and shakes with laughter. I bet the youths did not believe their luck. They're sipping their luminous cocktails. I join them at the bar. Terry's here too, drinking whiskey. He has a beer waiting for me but I need a whiskey.

"Make it a big one," I call. "And stick it on their bill." I turn to Terry. "So, what you t'ink?"

"You were right." He finishes his whiskey. "She's a tasty bit of talent."

"Terry, when he gets up, you sit in his chair. Just get in between him and t'at bitch."

"No problem, Squire."

"Kevin," I shout, "the best man must buy you a drink, otherwise it would be bad luck."

"I will then, Bart, I will, I will. And for what will I drink?"

"Something you've always wanted but could never afford."

"T'at sounds a good one, so it does. It does, doesn't it, Miss Nicki, what will I have, do you t'ink?"

Terry throws back more whiskey and goes to get her. He fancies his chances. Terry has handled the likes of Nicki before, lived with one for ten years and has plenty of life left in him to tackle another; one for the road. Go, Terry, go. That's the lad and give her one for me. There's a brazenness in him, kissing her cheek and wishing her luck. O'Hanagan's staring with jealousy but Terry puts him at ease. He has O'Hanagan by the hand, shaking it, telling him he's a lucky man and he has the finest woman in the land.

"A beauty, Mr O'Hanagan. A fine lady. And any friend of Bart is a friend of mine. And this yer girlfriend?" O'Hanagan loves the attention. So does Nicki, to have a stranger come into the party to play her game. "Stand up and take a bow. And Bart," he shouts to me, "best man, have you bought the lucky couple a drink? To wish them luck?"

"O'Hanagan, come here and help with the drinks. One for Miss Nicki and one for yourself, Kevin O'Hanagan from Ballybog."

He's slow to leave Miss Nicki but as soon as he steps from the table, Terry is on his seat.

"Kevin," I'm calling, "come and get the drinks."

"He shouldn't be sitting t'ere, Bart."

"Kevin, my man, a drink for good luck. And tell me, am I to be best man?"

"You are, Bart, why wouldn't you be?" coming reluctantly.

"Well, good luck to you."

"And good luck to you and are you coming to live in Scullivan's house?"

"Kevin, Kevin, I don't have time to t'ink of such things. Being best man is a busy man and I must look after all your affairs. To book the church, the hotel and pay the bills."

"You do, Bart, you do."

"I have to make copies of all your papers, your documents and anyt'ing which you received from the solicitor."

"You do, Bart, you do."

"And do you have all the papers which you received from the solicitor?"

"I do, I do."

"Well let me have all the business and you get back t'ere now with Nicki and enjoy the party. I can take everything and keep t'em safe and have copies ready in the morning."

"You make a fine best man, Bart, you do, a grand job." And he gives me an envelope from his pocket.

"Don't worry about a t'ing," checking the contents. There it is and not as much as a scribble on it. The cheque too. "Don't worry about a t'ing, O'Hanagan. Go back and enjoy the party." Still waiting for her signature, I slip it back into its envelope.

Now I relax, enjoy my drink and think of Ireland. I need to make a careful exit too, because I failed to pay my bill the other night. I'll apologise if the waiter comes in while I wait for Terry. He's sipping champagne from Nicki's glass. Now she sips from his glass. The drunkenness seeps around the bar, loudness as strangers join the party, lifting glasses to give a toast to the happy couple who bought the drinks. The youths are singing.

"And waitress," calls Nicki, "more drink for our friends, these fine singers at the bar."

They love her for it and give her a round of applause.

"Lets drink and be merry," sings Terry, "for tomorrow we die."

"You get out of my chair," says O'Hanagan.

"This is my chair," replies Terry. He's as drunk as Nicki, and she loves his humour. Terry is a comedian with a napkin rolled in a ball and stuck to his chin to make it look like a scab, a wart on a tree trunk. It brings more tears to her face, especially when he imitates O'Hanagan's bog accent. "You get out of my chair."

"You get out of my chair."

"Tis my chair," replies Terry, in the same bog brogue.

"You get out of my chair."

"Tis my chair," saying it louder, exaggerating it.

"You get out of my chair."

"Tis my chair."

Nicki is trying to talk but the laughter overcomes her, choking her as she hangs from Terry's shoulder.

"You get out of my chair." O'Hanagan reaches over heads and bottles, glasses falling and diners moving, dragging chairs to a distance.

"Tis my chair, said mommy bear."

"You get out of my chair."

"Tis my chair, said daddy bear."

"Kevin, fight for your chair," laughs Nicki. "Are you a man or a mouse?" Now she squeaks like a mouse. They fall back, vibrating in hysterics. O'Hanagan wipes away bottles and plates to get at Terry. He can't reach but Terry reaches him with a lanky arm to slap his face. Not hard but a joke to make Nicki laugh. Badness though and I must go to stop a fight.

"Excuse me," says the waiter, grabbing my collar.

"Sorry."

"You will be! Outside." He holds it like he held it the other night, the same waiter, who I kicked between the legs.

"But I must stop this fight…"

"Outside."

"You don't understand."

"Outside."

"Will ye fecking let go?"

"You get out of my chair."

"Tis my chair, said baby bear. And tis is my new girlfriend." Terry puts his arm around Nicki, has her schoolgirl plait in his mouth.

She screams…. "Kill this man," choking in laughter. "Kevin, do you hear me? Kill this impostor."

There's a fire extinguisher above it all. It's swinging through the air with such velocity that it's buried in Terry's skull before Nicki can stall her laughter. In the stunned silence that follows, a moment or two while we catch our breath, O'Hanagan swings it again, a powerfully accurate blow that brings Terry's sick life to an end. And still, the witnesses sit stiff with shock.

Epilogue.

Two matchstick men are walking along a scorched and dusty road, their delicate twig limbs inching near the edge of the path for the shade. They don't have the strength to trample in amongst the bleached trees. It would be too laborious for their thin legs on uneven ground to struggle over lumps and scurry down sandy slopes. Anyway, they would still be cooked because the sun is high now, and the trees are as thin as themselves, with splinters for branches and leaves like singed feathers.

To add to their physical pain, fears of an unknown future labour on their mind. They don't even know where they are, except that it's probably near the equator. It was dark when they jumped overboard. They swam up river, towards the black and against a current that washed energy from their aching bodies. Behind them was a port, an oil depot and a shanty town. The moon illuminated a pipe that snaked along the riverbank, and bits of scrap metal dumped on slopes. Chunks of ships and abandoned cars. The taller man cut his leg as he waded towards land this morning.

At a crossroads, the shorter man notices that there's tarmac under the sand. This is a main road. He tries to explain to his companion by pointing. This is how they communicate, with their hands because neither speaks the other's language. The tall man already knows and has turned left, limping faster, towards a hut. It's white with a thatched roof. As they get close to it, they see that it has a terrace along the front, with tables and chairs. Along the side, there are crates with empty bottles. Despite their desperation, they hesitate, looking at each other, wondering would it be safe to go inside. The short man nods at the sign but the tall man shrugs his shoulder; English isn't his language either. Without words they decide they have no alternative. So they proceed, in through the doorway.

"Hello, there," says a voice to welcome them. "A hot day, tis?"

The sign says, The Inheritance, the liveliest Irish pub between here and there, finest stout imported from Ireland, and Suffolk Ale from England and lager from Holland. Also lodgings and chicken snacks and eggs and omelettes and fried egg sandwiches. Also fresh farm eggs for sale around the back and the fattest chickens on Pipeline Road. Travel information and currency exchange. Cheques cashed at the bar. Postal service, full details inside. Scrambled egg special menu. International tax avoidance service. Ask at the bar. Scrap metal merchants, employment agency, all trades considered especially laggers. Casino. Fast lagging service and pipe repair service. Itch Wool no problem. Laggers wanted. Car hire. Luxury limousine service into town or port. (Jaguar).

Bastard Books

Daring New Literature

Don`t forget.....

More radical literature at:

bastardbooks.com